PENGUIN BOOKS

T0150166

the

H O L L O W

B O N E S

Also by Leah Kaminsky

FICTION
The Waiting Room

NON-FICTION
Cracking the Code
(with Stephen and Sally Damiani)
We're All Going to Die

POETRY
Stitching Things Together

AS EDITOR
*Writer, M.D.: The Best Contemporary Fiction
and Non-Fiction by Doctors*

Praise for *The Hollow Bones*

'An evocative, harrowing story of one man's obsession to preserve nature in a glass jar, *The Hollow Bones* reminds us that creatures of the wild belong there and we destroy their habitat at our peril. Kaminsky has magically woven the dual narratives of past and present through a unique telling of such an important historical tale, which will thrill, enlighten and reward the reader.' – Heather Morris

'In this vibrant, inventive novel, Leah Kaminsky poses knotty questions about the grey zone of collaboration, ambition and political expediency under Nazism.' – Mireille Juchau

'There were so many Germans like Ernst Schäfer, who blew with the wind for the sake of their passions, whether scientific, artistic or musical. This bold novel reveals the perilously thin moral ice they trod, and the human cost for those closest to them.' – Rachel Seiffert

'In this prescient and thoughtful novel, a long-dead animal displayed in the Academy of Natural Sciences in Philadelphia murmurs about the wild places of its lost life, while the story of the scientist who destroyed it exposes the collaboration between totalitarianism, corrupted science and the slaughter of people and animals.' – Brenda Walker

Praise for *The Waiting Room*

'Leah Kaminsky's debut novel, *The Waiting Room*, is nail-biting, but not in a whodunnit way; in the way of an eight-month-pregnant protagonist holding her breath against the dual assault of Israeli terrorism and Holocaust memories. Not for the faint-hearted, but with a surprising surfeit of grace notes.' – Clare Wright, *Sydney Morning Herald*

'An assured debut with a complex, believable and engaging protagonist. Finely observed characters and vignettes give us a human perspective on a culture that is too often portrayed only in political terms. Compelling, moving and memorable, *The Waiting Room* took me to Israel in the way *The Kite Runner* took me to Afghanistan, and shone a light on the generational impact of the Holocaust.' – Graeme Simsion

'Dina, the child of Holocaust survivors, struggles herself to survive the burden of memory and misery that has infused her Melbourne childhood. Far from home, working as a doctor in Haifa and married to a stoic Israeli, she must find a way to quiet her ghosts before their dark voices further dim her own chance at happiness. *The Waiting Room* is both haunted, and haunting.' – Geraldine Brooks

'Leah Kaminsky knows the stress of a doctor's life: she is one. This is why her debut novel about a pregnant Israeli GP has such an authentic flavour. We're right there with her as she rushes about her duties, haunted by her persistently present but dead mother and living on high alert, ever vigilant for the next terrorist attack. *The Waiting Room* convincingly conveys all the intensity of Israeli everyday life.' – Caroline Baum, *Booktopia Buzz the*

HOLLOW BONES

BONES

LEAH KAMINSKY

PENGUIN BOOKS

PENGUIN BOOKS

UK | USA | Canada | Ireland | Australia
India | New Zealand | South Africa | China

Penguin Books is part of the Penguin Random House group of companies whose addresses
can be found at global.penguinrandomhouse.com

Penguin
Random House
Australia

First published by Vintage in 2019
This edition published by Penguin Books in 2020

Copyright © Leah Kaminsky 2019

The moral right of the author has been asserted.

Excerpt of '"Hope" is the thing with feathers' from *The Poems of Emily Dickinson*, edited by
Thomas H. Johnson, Cambridge, Mass.: The Belknap Press of Harvard University Press.
Copyright © 1951, 1955, 1979, 1983 by the President and Fellows of Harvard College.

Cover images: hoopoe © DEA PICTURE LIBRARY/Getty Images;
background © foxie/Shutterstock
Cover design by Alex Ross © Penguin Random House Australia Pty Ltd
Bird illustrations: common whitethroat on page 5 © duncan1890/Getty Images;
mallard duck on page 87 © Hein Nouwens/Shutterstock; bearded vulture
on page 203 © Marzolino/Shutterstock
Typeset in Fairfield LT by Midland Typesetters, Australia

Printed and bound in Australia by Griffin Press, part of Ovato, an accredited
ISO AS/NZS 14001 Environmental Management Systems printer

A catalogue record for this
book is available from the
National Library of Australia

ISBN 978 1 76089 986 8

penguin.com.au

MIX
Paper from
responsible sources
FSC® C009448

For Yohanan, Alon, Ella and Maia Loeffler, with love

Unsteady shapes, who early in the past
Showed in my clouded sight, you approach again.
. . . What I possess looks far away to me,
Things vanished are becoming my reality.
                             – Goethe's *Faust*

'Hope' is the thing with feathers
                             – Emily Dickinson

AUTHOR'S NOTE

While *The Hollow Bones* is a work of fiction, it is inspired by true events. This is an invented narrative, fed by imagination, and I have used artistic licence with historical facts, geographies and character details.

PROLOGUE

21 July 1992
Bavaria

I am searching your face for remnants of the young man, the one who wrote of the cries of the holy Lammergeier as it feeds on the bones of the dead. The brilliant scientist who described the rare Tibetan hunting bird that resembles a flying amulet. Such extraordinary attention to the intricate detail of our world, such careful observation and recording. In your tales you described the faces of Tingri pilgrim women singing for alms, babies tied to their backs. You wrote so beautifully of the ragyapa, *scavengers of the city who collected the horns of sheep and goats to protect the edges of their ragged tents against icy winds. All those fantastical accounts you brought back from distant shores, more magical than any trinket you might have picked up from a village marketplace to carry home to me.*

As you prepare to leave the world you were so hungry to explore, I imagine I can see a tinge of regret in your eyes and I wonder how we both became the people we are. History unfolded in ways we never could have dreamt of when we were children growing up in our pretty town. Who might we have been had we met in a different place, or another time, citizens of a land far away from our own sullied, shadowy one?

As I watch you sleep restlessly, your wrinkled hand against the white sheet, I am conjuring up our impossible reunion, pretending I am standing at the entrance to 30th Street Station in Philadelphia, under the wings of the bronze angel silhouetted against the sunlight as it lifts a dead soldier out of the flames of war. I see your familiar figure walk towards me through the throngs of passengers jostling to board their trains. You carry the leather travelling case embossed with your initials that I gave you on our tenth wedding anniversary. We embrace, and lips meet, our love made inconspicuous as it is swallowed by the crowd.

At our house on the edge of the park, I picture the children awaiting your return. Little Heidi is fluent in three languages and plays the flute, all of my abandoned dreams re-emerging when I see her small fingers positioned above the keys. How long it has been since I held a flute in my hands. Our Brooke is captain of the school archery team. His father's son. You are a professor of ornithology, specialising in rare Tibetan birds, and I sometimes slip into the crowded lecture theatre to watch you standing at the podium, spinning your exotic tales to another crop of enthralled students. You are filled with knowledge about birds: the iridescence of feathers, the wizardry of flight, the vagaries of their migrations. We spend our summers on Campobello Island with the Roosevelt clan and send money home to our families to help them rebuild their lives.

On the bed by the window you stir, and your once strong fist claws at the sheet as you struggle to breathe. Soon we will both disappear forever, our story hidden away in dusty archives. Gone will be those children who followed a slender path to their hideaway in the woods, gone will be the lovers who kissed on that fateful day at the zoo. I want to forget the darkness and remember only the good; illusion is such a temptress. It won't be long before we will both float weight-lessly, unmoored, our bones hollow like the birds'. I remember you once told me about mockingbirds and their special talents for mimicry. They steal the songs from others, you said. I want to ask you this: how were our own songs stolen from us, the notes dispersed, while our faces were turned away?

PART I

PART 1

CHAPTER 1

18 June 1936

'The Reich needs young men like you.' The balding officer seated across the desk peered at Ernst through round spectacles, tiny eyes gleaming like those of a crow that has caught its morning worm.

Ernst wriggled in his seat, smoothing down his froth of sandy-blond hair, uncertain whether a smile was appropriate under the circumstances. The office at Prinz-Albrecht-Strasse 8, the site of a former baroque palace, looked austerely furnished. On the desk were a brass lamp and a neat pile of papers, with fountain pens lined up in a row like soldiers at a drill.

'I am so glad you have returned home, my boy. I shall be very pleased to be your mentor. After all, I am a great patron of the sciences,' he cawed, in a pantomime of exaggerated politeness. 'And I am a collector, too.'

'It is both my duty and a great honour to serve the Fatherland, *Reichsführer* Himmler.' Ernst fidgeted with his collar as he recited the expected response.

His myopic superior grinned.

Ernst scanned the room. It seemed Himmler was indeed an eclectic hobbyist. On a side table sat an antique orrery, a mechanical model of the solar system. Bookshelves sagged under the weight of books on subjects ranging from the Hindu *Bhagavad Gita* to the lost city of Atlantis. Jars of homeopathic remedies, with long Latin names inscribed in ink on their labels, served as bookends. Ernst had heard the man's tastes were rather unusual, but the breadth of his interests proved far more than Ernst had bargained for – from telepathy to the sexual habits of Tibetan tribes, heraldry, reincarnation, astrological signs and ancient runes.

'Do you know why I brought you back?' Himmler brought an unlit pipe to his lips, pretending to puff on it. 'I need you to help me add to my collection.'

'Pardon, Herr Kommandant? I'm not sure I understand.'

'I have been following your recent expeditions to China and Tibet, with that young American adventurer – what was his name?'

'Brooke Dolan, Herr Kommandant.'

'Yes, Dolan – I have been watching with a great deal of interest.'

'Thank you, Herr Kommandant.'

'You were wasted over there in America. I have received correspondence from Fritz Kuhn of the German American

Bund informing me of the mood in the United States. We certainly don't need those Americans for our own expeditions; neither their Jewish vermin nor their money. We can do it all ourselves, and far better.'

Ernst waited cautiously to see if a response was called for.

Himmler watched him. 'I have chosen you, Schäfer, because of your experience in the East.'

Ernst was sweating; the room had no fan, and the day's heat was starting to rise. To get to the meeting on time, he had needed to be on the platform at the Zoo station by 8.30 am to catch the S-Bahn to Potsdamer Platz. Though the city was running like clockwork for the forthcoming Olympics, Ernst had become accustomed to keeping his own schedule, punctuality never his greatest attribute. All those months travelling in the East had dampened his sense of schedule and order. There was no way a porter or his mule could be trained to work to anyone's timetable without being whipped, and he was not stupid enough to abuse those he needed the most. On those misty mornings, camped along the banks of the Yangtze, serenaded by songbirds while yak tea brewed on the campfire, his life had been veiled with a sense of timelessness. Wearing a uniform of dungarees and waterproof jacket, his trusty shotgun by his side, he would sit transfixed, staring out towards the wide, empty horizon.

'It has been my pleasure to read all your books,' Himmler continued. 'Your name does not go unspoken here in Germany – you have a reputation as a great hunter, fearless explorer and respected scientist. You are, after all, the reason the panda, that rarest of beasts, is on show at that museum in Philadelphia.' He lowered his voice and spoke softly, like a priest. 'But I am so disappointed it does not reside in our own fine Natural History Museum, right here in Berlin.'

Ernst pressed his hand to his belly to try to silence its rumbling protests; in all the rush this morning, he'd left without eating breakfast, quickly grabbing an apple from the fruit vendor's cart in front of the station. He was determined to make a serious impression on Himmler. Since being called back to Germany, he wanted to shed the reputation of the famous boy-explorer in order to focus on his studies and finish his doctorate.

'I am not planning to send you on another hunting mission, though. Well, not exactly. Perhaps a different kind of hunt, yes,' he said, smiling at Ernst. 'I have selected you to be the *Untersturmführer* of a prestigious group in search of the glorious ancestry of the *Herrenvolk*, our magnificent Aryan race. You may be wondering what it is I am collecting, Schäfer. In truth, it is our dear Führer's collection really, on behalf of us all.' He banged his fist on the desk and sent the pens flying over the edge. '*Lebensraum!*' he shouted. 'The imperative to reclaim the territory that has been ours from time immemorial.'

Himmler's pallid face turned beet red as he rose from the chair and strolled around to the other side of the desk, where he stood behind Ernst. 'You are to bring back evidence of what we already know is the truth – that our pure German blood comes from an ancient warrior race born in the foothills of the Tibetan Himalayas.'

Ernst had heard of this theory, that the Aryan race emerged triumphant from a great cosmic battle between fire and ice. He understood the importance of having an anthropologist on an expedition of that nature, and he knew Bruno Beger would jump at the chance of joining the team. But he didn't know what Himmler could want from a simple zoologist. How did his own scientific obsession with rare Tibetan birds have anything to do with the tenuous tracing of ancestral links to a mythical super-race? Surely Himmler had checked his credentials thoroughly before calling him back from Philadelphia?

'Welteislehre!' Himmler trumpeted, launching into a forceful monologue that commanded Ernst's drifting attention. 'World Ice Theory is finally receiving the recognition it deserves, overthrowing that madman Einstein and his Jewish pseudoscience. The Führer has at last accepted it as the scientific platform of the Reich. And rightly so. We know the truth now, that ice crystals are the true building blocks of the universe, not those imaginary atoms. You, young man, will travel to Tibet to head into the bowels of the earth where Fire and Ice went to war, and the ancestors of the German *Volk* emerged triumphant as *Sonnenmenschen*. Perfect beings, as radiant as the sun.'

Ernst sat there in silence, listening to the man's diatribe. These theories espoused by those who worked at the *Ahnenerbe*, the new ancestral heritage department of the Reich, were certainly becoming popular.

11

Sponsored by Himmler, the gigantic organisation had already attracted some of the top scholars in Germany. Many in its ranks staunchly believed an icy moon once crashed into the earth, destroying an ancient Nordic tribe whose descendants were thought to have survived in the Himalayas.

Ernst glanced discreetly at his watch; it was already 10.15 am. The meeting was taking far longer than he had anticipated. Herta would be getting worried.

Himmler suddenly placed his hand on Ernst's shoulder. 'Tell me about this lovely *Mädchen* you have been seeing lately.'

'Pardon, Herr Kommandant?'

'Your little girlfriend, Herta Völz.'

Ernst could almost feel the *Reichsführer*'s eyes bore into the back of his head. Could the man read minds?

'You know about her?' He wiped his brow, not daring to turn around.

'My records show you joined the SS in the summer of thirty-three, when you were back in Germany between expeditions. A wise move, my boy.' He patted Ernst on the back. 'As an SS officer, I think of you as my son. And I make it my business to keep informed about my own family. So, do tell me about your young friend.'

Ernst uncrossed his legs. 'She is very beautiful.' He felt himself blushing.

'It's okay. No need to be shy with me. It is of the utmost importance we ensure you are with a girl from a healthy German family, who deserves the great honour of marrying one of our purest and finest.' He returned to his chair.

In spite of himself, Ernst felt like an excited teenager, his words rushing out. 'Her father presided over the prestigious Heidelberg Völz Pädagogium before moving to Waltershausen. He teaches music now, a passion he passed on to Herta. We grew up together, spending time foraging in the woods. She was always a strong, intelligent girl, and I had a soft spot for her even back then. With all my travels, we hadn't seen each other for several years, but soon after I returned from America, a mutual friend and colleague of mine happened to introduce us.' Ernst told Himmler how Herta had moved to Berlin to study flute at the Conservatory. 'She makes me very happy, Herr Kommandant.'

'And before you marry she will be attending our fine Reich Bride School, no doubt?'

There was another awkward pause. Ernst had never heard of such a thing.

'*Natürlich*. Of course, Herr Kommandant.'

'Good. Good. We will have plenty of time to learn more about our Herta later.'

Ernst thought he saw the faintest smile creep onto Himmler's face, but it vanished in an instant.

'First, we must discuss more urgent matters.' He slowly opened a file. 'Our great *Deutsche* Tibet Expedition. Given your experience in Tibet, together with your hunting skills, you are perfectly placed to lead the team. It is you whom the Reich has entrusted with tracing our ancestral heritage.'

Ernst looked once again at the man across the desk. An anxiously tidy person, his thinning hair combed back, Himmler was hardly the picture of Nordic prowess.

As if he'd read Ernst's mind again, Himmler continued, 'Some of us feel that heritage more acutely than others. I only share this secret with those I trust, but I myself am the reincarnation of Heinrich the Fowler, our country's first king. He was a legendary woodsman, of course, so I am particularly impressed with your own aptitude.'

As Ernst waited for the man to elaborate, he felt pinned to the spot. Though his first impulse was to laugh at the absurd remark, he recognised in the depths of Himmler's eyes the stealth, patience and determination of a hunter waiting to pounce. This is how prey must feel, Ernst thought, lined up through the sight of a gun, unknowingly waiting for the swift moment of their death.

'Yes, I would like to send you to Tibet once more. This time, though, you will travel all the way to Lhasa.'

Ernst cleared his throat, realising this was not an invitation. It was an order. Not that it wasn't his dream to go back to Tibet, especially if he might trek to the foothills of the Himalayas this time. He thought about how Brooky would have laughed his head off at Himmler's esoteric plan, refusing point blank to have anything to do with it, but things were different in America.

'I will personally make sure that only the finest of our scientists will be joining you.' Himmler's voice was calm and reassuring now. 'They will be from every branch of science possible, each one a dedicated SS man, like your good self. I want the famed archaeologist Edmund Kiss to be part of the team. I have just finished reading his excellent book about the true origins of Atlantis.' His voice dropped to a whisper again. 'Tell me, my son, about your previous trips into Tibet. I am curious to know what the people there are like.'

Ernst cracked his knuckles. Himmler had not yet mentioned anything at all about Ernst's scientific qualifications; even so, he could feel himself warming to the idea of another expedition. 'I found them very accommodating, Herr Kommandant.'

'Yes,' he said with a smirk. 'I've heard some stories about how friendly their women are.'

'Oh! My apologies. I wasn't actually referring to the women, although they do have a certain exotic beauty about them. I meant that, on the whole, Tibetans are hospitable and kind. But they are superstitious and strongly believe in magic, which, of course, as a man of science I find quite ludicrous.' His words flew out of his mouth like a flock of startled birds.

Himmler seemed not to have noticed the unintended slight. 'Did you come across any natives with blond hair?'

'No, Herr Kommandant. The peoples of Tibet are of a much darker complexion.'

The *Reichsführer* got up from his chair and paced up and down the room, rubbing the back of his neck. He moved over to the window and looked up at the sky. 'You have a lot to learn, young man.' He turned to face Ernst, who had beads of sweat forming on his upper lip.

'But I will take it upon myself to help you understand. Meanwhile, you will meet a group of us for lunch each month to discuss preparations for the expedition. I want you to leave as soon as practicable, which means we have much organising ahead of us. You shall receive further instructions shortly. That is all.'

The meeting ended abruptly, with Himmler raising his right hand in salute: 'Heil Hitler!'

Ernst rose quickly from his chair. 'Heil Hitler!'

The sentries guarding the door led him back along the corridor, which was lined with the marble busts of generations of prominent German men. He glanced up at the vaulted ceiling, sunlight pouring in through huge arched windows. Ernst was escorted down a gilt staircase towards the front of the former art school turned Gestapo headquarters. The sentries saluted and waited for him to leave.

Ernst walked back out onto the street and faltered for a moment, deciding which direction to take. Then he strode off, swinging his arms like a toy soldier.

CHAPTER 2

All the outdoor tables at Café Kranzler were crammed full at this hour. Cars vied with horse-drawn carriages spilling customers out onto the busy footpath. The waitress swept by and shook out a white linen napkin with a flourish, draping it over Herta's lap. Around them, people jostled each other; men in suits and ties stood next to women who wore the latest summer frocks, with hats that matched their elegant gloves and leather clutches. They all waited in line to be seated. Above them an Olympic flag hung from the corner of the ornate building, fluttering in the warm breeze, in unison with another emblazoned with a swastika. The whole city was busy preening itself for the forthcoming Olympics; new trees lined the length of Unter den Linden boulevard, and flyers that until recently had screamed *Jews not allowed* were nowhere to be seen. Some estimated that more than forty million Reichsmark had already been lavished on construction.

Herta twirled the corner of the tablecloth around her fingers. She watched the waitress bring over a tray laden with coffee and slices of Linzertorte, a blob of jam smeared on the pocket of her white apron. She mused that to an onlooker she would appear so separate from the busy, laughing crowd that was engulfing her. A slim young woman in a blue dress, her fair hair falling loosely around her face, there was a gravity to Herta's expression uncommon for her age. She moved her flute case onto the chair beside her, saving a place for Ernst. He was over an hour late already; his meeting must have stretched on. A good sign perhaps, she thought.

The lunchtime swarm pressed in on Herta, the owner of the café circling as though he might give her table to someone else if she so much as shifted in her seat. A raven cackled overhead, gaunt and ragged for a city-dweller. Herta tried to look busy, flipping through the sheet music for Wagner's 'Bridal Chorus' from *Lohengrin*, the piece the new director, Herr Kittel, insisted she play for the summer concert. She missed the familiar sweet sounds of Mendelssohn and Mahler that her father taught her as a young girl, the music her new teachers at the Conservatory of the Reich Capital now referred to as a discordant pattern of perverted squeaks.

Herta sipped her coffee and dug her fork into the cake, slicing off a tiny piece. Ernst would be pleased to see her eating; she had grown so thin since moving to Berlin. Their peaceful little town, Waltershausen, seemed a world away, an enchanted place she sometimes thought she must have evoked out of sheer longing. She dreamt of the endless skies of their childhood, filled with a riot of birds that changed with each season: swallows, skylarks, lapwings, plovers, hen harriers. Ernst used to observe them when he was a boy, as they grew restless in the lead-up to the Zugunruhe, the mysterious call of their migration. Late one autumn, Ernst had caught a tiny common whitethroat and kept it in a cage in his bedroom, carefully observing its behaviour, recording everything in the back of his algebra book. The bewildered bird fluttered and hopped about, tilting its head as if checking some inner compass, listening for a silent starter pistol that signalled the beginning of a thousand-mile race to its wintering grounds.

Back then, Herta wondered how the bird knew in its heart when it was time to leave. What hidden message did it sense, what ghostly call to other lands? Was it the same force that drove Ernst to stray from home the moment he could walk? Twilight seemed to be when the bird was at the height of its distress. Young Ernst would place the caged whitethroat on the windowsill so it could see its fellow travellers soar across the darkening sky, Orion rising on the horizon. Perhaps they possessed some sixth sense that allowed them to follow the magnetic lines of the earth? Even as a child, Herta knew that one day her friend would become a great scientist who would try to find the answers to all these questions. Meanwhile, Ernst kept observing the creatures, collecting as much data as he could, writing down everything in meticulous detail. Herta would watch the pitiful whitethroat, which warbled as it darted from one side of its tiny cage to the other. She felt jealous of the birds that seemed to know instinctively when to migrate.

Ernst was always coming and going, struck with wanderlust. He never wanted to be a businessman like his father. From an early age he was set on becoming a naturalist, a huge disappointment to Albert Schäfer. Now, in his mid-twenties, his son was already a revered veteran of two successful American–German expeditions to China and Tibet. Ernst was living and studying in Berlin, following a long line of great scientists who put Germany on the map, men who invented everything from the wire rope to the gramophone, geniuses who pioneered exciting new ideas such as synthetic materials and quantum mechanics. But Ernst's wanderings had always seemed like mere folly to Schäfer Senior.

Herta's father hadn't wanted her to leave either, agreeing only reluctantly to allow her to travel to Berlin when she was accepted to the famous Stern Conservatory in 1934. In those first lonely weeks in the city, Herta feared Vati was right: that it had all been a big mistake. She arrived during a winter fiercer than any she had ever known in Waltershausen. The streets seemed perilous and menacing, the ice slippery, everyone huddled into themselves. Nature was in abeyance. Herta could never have imagined such desolation, such relentless chill. The tiny room she rented in Frau Lila's apartment was draughty and damp, its small window looking out over a metallic wintry sky that hung above gloomy rooftops. She could see the mist of her own breath in the frigid air.

Herta shared the room with Hildegard, the only friend she had made. The two girls would curl up under the covers of the iron-framed bed, cuddling Klaus, an abandoned kitten they had rescued. They whispered their dreams to each other. Hildegard was enrolled at the Berlin Drama School, hoping to become a famous actress and travel the world, performing on the stages of Broadway and the West End. Some nights she would recite her lines as they lay in bed and Herta would drift off to sleep, her mind filled with the doomed women of drama, Ophelia and Hedda Gabler, both abandoned to their particular fates. Each morning of that first long winter, the two girls sat together drinking bitter coffee and eating stale bread, before Herta left for her lessons at the Conservatory on Bernburger Strasse.

After the deep snows melted, crocuses and forget-me-nots burst forth in celebration. Warm weather arrived on the wings of a pair of doves nesting in a linden tree outside the window. By the time winter finally ended, she found herself alone with Frau Lila. Like a doe-eyed protagonist in a cheap Hollywood movie, Herta's young actress friend had been swept off her feet by a man she met at one of her theatre performances.

Herta didn't care much for Hildegard's new husband. Bruno Beger was tall and handsome in a brutish kind of way. Along with his long, sharp nose and neatly parted straight blond hair, he cut the perfect image of a Nordic man. But the tone in which he spoke to his wife betrayed who he really was. He claimed that it was love at first sight when he saw the poised and luminous Hildegard standing in a pool of light on the stage. But Herta could see straightaway that Bruno was intent on being the only star in the relationship, and not long after the courtship began Hildegard gave up any notions of becoming an actress. They married at the end of spring and moved in to a cramped apartment on Marburger Strasse, not far from the zoo. Morning and night, the hyenas laughed at their penury. Bruno's moods grew darker. The memory of his well-to-do childhood as the son of a family who had owned huge tanneries around Heidelberg plagued his restless nights. He was still a student, trying to scrape together enough money to support himself and his new wife.

Returning to her own spartan room after classes, Herta would sit on the bed and look out of the small window. Often Klaus hobbled into her lap, licking his bad leg as he purred contentedly. When she used to dream of Berlin she never imagined such a forlorn existence. Since the Nuremberg laws had been enacted, Waltershausen seemed caught in cobwebs of silence. It was easier to turn a blind eye to small incidents there. Now though, living in the city, Herta's eyes were open to an army of haters spinning their sticky threads among the populace. Every day, the newspapers were filled with tales of the ranks of pale, steadfast citizens performing their civic duty, proudly denouncing neighbours and friends. Stormtroopers ensured their shoes were polished before kicking Jewish shopkeepers to the ground.

But then she found Ernst again. More than a year after Herta arrived in Berlin, they met unexpectedly at the Begers' home one Sunday in May. Hildegard, who was already seven months pregnant by then, invited Herta to escape from Frau Lila's dingy apartment and join them on a picnic in the woods with Bruno's new friend. When she walked into the parlour and saw Ernst seated in an armchair beside the empty fireplace, she felt as if she was coming up for air after having held her breath for half a lifetime. Ernst looked up, barely able to speak when he saw that it was Herta standing there. She laughed nervously as he jumped up and took her hand in his.

'Herta! I can't believe it's you. My, how you have grown into such a fine woman – *eine schöne, blonde, grosse, erwachsene Frau.*' He turned to Bruno. 'Where on earth have you been hiding this beautiful specimen from me?'

In Waltershausen, their childhood friendship had turned into a fledgling love that sometimes overwhelmed Herta with its intensity. As children, they would make their way to a secret hide-out in the woods every day after school: a threshold of wonder, the portal to a world in which they were merely creatures among other creatures. Bees hovered over wildflowers as young Ernst and Herta walked across fields where horses flicked their tails at flies and farmers called to their dogs. Jumping from rock to rock across the stream in which fish were swimming like beads of quartz in porphyry, the children followed a slender path

23

up a steep rise, walking hand in hand. A golden oriole sang to them, accompanied by the distant lowing of cows and the chiming of church bells. Herta would sit cross-legged in the small clearing among a copse of pines, threading berries onto a twig. Her favourite tree was a scarred old oak, grown tall in its solitude. It was the perfect listener, giving everything and asking nothing in return.

Sometimes Herta's sister, Margarete, joined them in the woods. As they sat together in the sun, Herta plaited the younger girl's hair, which was sleek and blonde and reached down to her waist. Her features were so fine that Herta wondered if poor Margarete had been blessed with an abundance of beauty to make up for all she lacked. When Margarete was six months old, they realised she was deaf. Her paroxysms began around her fifth birthday. Her face would contort, her writhing little body bent backwards, arms reaching up like a ballet dancer. Finally, she would slump to the floor in a wet heap, lying motionless beside her wheelchair.

Most days in their magical shelter, Herta would open Ernst's school satchel and take out his books, helping him finish his homework. Even though she was two years younger, she wanted to save him from Herr Vogel's fearsome strap. If she could get it done quickly, she might still enjoy what was left of the afternoon. Ernst usually ran off into the forest the moment they arrived. She knew, though, that he would return in time for them to get Margarete home without arousing any suspicion. Herta would set to work in Ernst's exercise book, her pencil forming neat columns of figures as she answered the problems on Herr Vogel's arithmetic worksheet:

1) *The construction of a lunatic asylum costs three million Reichsmark. How many houses, at 9000 Reichsmark each, could have been built for that amount?*
   Answer: ....

2) *To keep a mentally ill person in an asylum costs approximately two Reichsmark per day and there are 300,000 mentally ill in care.*
   a) How much do these people cost to keep per year?
   Answer: ....
   b) How many marriage loans, at 500 Reichsmark each, could be granted from this money?
   Answer: ....

When Ernst turned fourteen, he left abruptly for boarding school. Each July he would return to Waltershausen, where he and Herta escaped to the woods together again, spending whole afternoons lying on the grass and watching the clouds move across the high summer sky. Their relationship began anew every year. Once school was over, though, and he passed his Abitur, Ernst finally stepped out into the world, first to attend the University of Göttingen. He eventually chose to leave their small town for good, travelling further afield to the East with a young American adventurer, Brooke Dolan. That first expedition in 1931 was when Ernst felt truly lost to Herta. She tucked his letters under her pillow, but after a while all he would send was a postcard filled with scribbled banalities.

When the cards eventually stopped arriving, Herta marked Ernst's absence by retreating from the natural world. The woods, stippled with sunlight, were as deserted as a silent graveyard without him, despite all the chirping, rustling and baying hidden in their greenish folds. She rarely ventured out into the forest again, preferring the bright notes of Vivaldi to wild birdsong. What nature had been for Ernst, music was for Herta. It became her life's breath, animating the tedium of the years spent caring for her ailing sister. Herta played sweet notes for a girl who could not hear, and for a boy who was far away.

Occasionally, a reminder of those forays into nascent love with Ernst came creeping back when she saw a flicker of his image bejewelled in the wings of dragonflies, or a hint of his strong body sailing high among a gyrating flock of starlings. When Ernst had first left, Herta clung to the memory of their friendship, even though his life was somewhere else. Their secret forest hide-out, where she had flown in the air on the makeshift swing he fashioned for her out of vines, still held the fine dust of his being. But in time, her feelings for him began to calcify.

On that Sunday afternoon in Berlin so many years later, reunited once again thanks to the Begers, they picnicked together in the Tiergarten. Ernst and Herta talked for hours, about the perils and wonders of his trips, and his work at the museum in Philadelphia. She told him how Waltershausen hadn't changed much in all the years he'd been away. Hans the shoemaker still fought with Herr Hauptmann, the postman, who was always leaving letters on top of his mailbox instead of inside it, complaining that it was far too small and that Hans needed to build a larger one. The Felstyner family on Bremerstrasse found themselves evicted from their home the previous year, but no one seemed to bat an eyelid about their sudden disappearance. People simply plodded forward in time. Meanwhile, Herta saw that Ernst had become an exotic creature with a secret call. He asked her what she had been doing before she left for Berlin.

'Vati found me a job at König and Wernicke, the old doll factory,' she said. 'But business dwindled, and they were forced to close down.' She couldn't bring herself to explain how she ended up spending most of her free time caring for her sister, and how much it broke her heart to leave Margarete behind. 'You know I've always dreamt of following my passion and becoming a professional musician.'

With the panicky impatience of a caged bird, she had begged her father for permission to apply to music school in Berlin. And, to her surprise, Vati agreed.

What she didn't tell Ernst was that the night before they were to reunite, not twelve hours earlier, when everyone was tucked into their beds and the streets were emptied of life, Herta walked alone past the dome of the Reichstag, all the way to Königsplatz. She stepped into the Victory Column that strained skywards, climbing the spiral staircase to the very top. A faint scent of malt wafted across from the breweries. Sheltering from the wind beneath Victoria, a goddess-turned-angel, Herta clutched the rail. Below her, in the distance, the Tiergarten was enveloped in darkness, save for lone lamps winking, luring her towards them. One leap into the granite sky and she would fly, falling through the night air. Skeletons weighed humans down with the hardness of mortality, honeycomb layers crammed full with the marrow of life. Herta was jealous of the angels who flew boldly through the air, that liminal space between man and God. She wished she could escape all this madness; sometimes she felt there was nothing left to tie her to this world.

She stood there, teetering on the edge of earth and sky. Victoria held in her wings the magic of flight that mere mortals could only dream of. Herta was so far from all those she loved. Vati, shrunken to a mere shadow of himself, now spent his evenings in the embrace of his armchair, reading sheet music by candlelight, the notes of Mozart and Bach playing in his head. Margarete, so far away, unable to answer the letters that Herta wrote each week. Her mother, pale and sorrowful now her elder daughter was gone.

Herta had long ago lost the ballast that tied her body to solid ground. It was such an ordinary heartbreak and they had been so young, but Ernst was the one who had filled the long hours of her youth with the wonders of nature. Since then, she had wrapped herself in music, a comfort that shielded her from the convulsions of the outside world. But even this no longer seemed a solace, her practice hindered by a tethered tongue, jarring, airy notes conquering the soul of her flute with their wild howls.

A hard gust of wind slapped her across the face, ramming her against Victoria's golden body. Herta looked up and imagined herself ensnared in those wings, hauling her away from the edge of darkness, back towards the urgency of life. It was in that moment that she saw a tiny, fleeting shape as it darted across the gibbous moon, sounding the call of a forest, distant in time but so close in memory. The owl beckoned her to return to this world of beauty, reminding her of the place where tall trees reached up to the stars and where pine needles and cones became a cosy bed. She could never have imagined, after all this time apart, that Ernst would reappear in her life so unexpectedly.

CHAPTER 3

'Will that be all, *Fräulein*?'

The waitress hovered nearby, waiting for Herta to finish the last morsel of cake so she could clear the table.

'No!' a voice called from behind them, in a deep baritone. 'I'm starving. Bring me a ham sandwich.' Ernst's stocky frame appeared before her; he had always been strong, his muscularity making up for his lack of height. He kissed Herta's cheek and lifted her flute case from the chair. 'And two more helpings of that Linzertorte, with plenty of cream.' He sat down beside her, smiling triumphantly. 'And we'll have two glasses of your best champagne.'

Ernst leaned across the table, speaking quietly now. 'He wants to send a team of German scientists on a special mission to Tibet.'

Herta drank the remains of her coffee.

'And you'll never guess what,' he said.

Placing her cup back on its saucer, she looked up.

'He asked me to lead the expedition.'

His words might as well have been a volley of shots fired from a pistol. Herta felt a sharp pain in her throat.

'But what about your doctoral studies? You said that was going to be your first priority this year.' Her voice was shrill. What she really wanted to say was that now they had found each other after so long, she didn't want him to leave again.

Ernst was so preoccupied by the morning's meeting with Himmler that even her comment about his never-ending studies, usually a sore spot, seemed to wash over him entirely. People who didn't know Ernst would have seen a cheerful man casually chatting to his attractive girlfriend. They would have smiled at this charming romance, a couple filled with the desire of youth – intimacies whispered over a café table. But no one except Herta could have noticed a trace of wariness in his eyes. She listened, without another word, to what Ernst had to say. He was already musing about whom he might invite to join the expedition team.

Ernst's previous trips, under the auspices of the Academy of Natural Sciences in Philadelphia, placed him in the orbit of a host of influential people. His friend Brooky, a wild boy who travelled all the way to Germany to recruit him for their first trip to China back in 1931, came from a wealthy and well-connected family. Brooky's grandfather was known as the man who 'electrified' Philadelphia.

Dinner parties with the Dolans and the Roosevelts were regular events for Ernst. But this flamboyant social life, as well as the subsequent expedition to Tibet in 1934, came at the expense of his academic career, forcing him to interrupt his studies twice. Ernst's thesis on migratory birds had become a giant gnat biting at his ear. He would have loved to taste the sweetness of completion instead of feeling pressure on his back day and night.

Herta knew Himmler's flattery that morning had been fuel to Ernst's fire; the plan to return to Tibet, pushing deeper across the plains into the mountainous regions of the Himalayas, would be more than enticing. He had always dreamt of leading an all-German expedition into Southern Tibet. But he also told her that Himmler had suggested something beyond his wildest dreams – to enter the holy city of Lhasa. With Himmler's support, alongside the sponsorship of the *Ahnenerbe*, he would be able to put together the finest team possible. They would be young and fearless men, the best in each of their fields, scientists willing to forgo the comforts of Europe for the harsh terrain of Tibet.

'I think I'll ask Bruno,' he said, taking a huge bite out of the sandwich the waitress had placed in front of him. He spoke with his mouth full, a piece of ham falling out onto his plate. 'He studied under Günther, that famous racial scientist, so Himmler will adore him. Some of the theories he writes about in his dissertation are a bit harsh, but he's a solid friend. I'm sure he and Hildegard could use the money, too, especially now with a baby on the way.'

He noticed Herta blushing and quickly changed the subject.

'I couldn't quite believe my ears, but towards the end of our meeting, Himmler mentioned he is the reincarnation of a tenth-century Saxon king.' Ernst laughed when he saw Herta's jaw drop. 'It's true! I've heard he visits the crypt in Quedlinburg every year, to lay a wreath. Herta, I know it all sounds strange, but he and the folk at the *Ahnenerbe* are utterly convinced about this World Ice Theory business.'

'Ernst,' she said, dabbing at the white tablecloth, 'you are a real scientist.' She collected wayward crumbs with her forefinger, placing them back onto her plate.

Ernst looked at Herta, her wavy long hair swept behind her ears, eyes so sober. She worried far too much.

'No need to fret, my *Liebchen*. I know exactly what I'm doing.' He reached out and stroked her hand.

Was it a dream that she was back in his life after all these years? He had thought of her often since leaving Waltershausen, and now that she was here with him in Berlin he felt a fierce desire to keep her close. When they were growing up, they had lived two streets apart. They often played marbles and jumped rope together, but whenever they could they snuck off into the woods. Although she was younger than Ernst, Herta had always been tall for her age. Even as a child, she harboured a sliver of diffidence tucked away under her fierce sense of pride.

'I am, after all, an expert in animal behaviour,' he said. 'Like the beasts of the wild, one has to rely on adaptation, changing one's coat to suit the season. It's the law of nature.'

Trying to shift the direction of their conversation, he asked about her flute lessons. Herta complained that the new director was too strict at the Stern Conservatory, where she had first studied under the guidance of Siegfried Eberhardt. But all the Jewish teachers and students had been forced to move across to a separate school on Sybelstrasse not long ago.

'They've all been replaced by musicians who are good party members, even though they hardly know how to play a simple nursery rhyme. Did you hear Jews have also been banned from our Olympic team?'

Ernst noticed the couple seated at the next table had stopped drinking their tea, their eyes and ears focused on Herta, taking in every word. He glared back at them and they quickly looked away. When he had stepped off the boat from New York, back onto German soil, his father came to meet him on the dock in Hamburg. 'Be cunning like a snake,' Albert Schäfer whispered, sounding like a cryptic oracle. 'The danger has already started.' Since being back in Berlin after two years in the wilderness and his time in America, Ernst was starting to unravel what the old man might have meant.

He gave Herta a peck on the cheek, to silence her in front of the prying strangers. Never having been the patient type, unless he was out in the wild stalking an animal, homing in on the kill, Ernst pulled out a small jewellery box from his pocket and placed it in front of the woman he had loved since childhood.

'For you,' he said.

She reached across, gingerly fingering the blue velvet casing. After she prised open the lid, Ernst took the fine gold necklace from the box and fastened it around her neck, not giving her a chance to say a word. He wondered how Herta might have reacted if he had actually been able to pluck up the courage to buy a ring instead.

The waitress approached, asking them if they needed anything else. Yes, he thought, I want this woman seated next to me to say *yes*, right now, *yes, I will be your wife*. He imagined how she might throw herself into his arms with delight and make a scene in public as a show of her love.

'No, thank you,' he said. 'That will be all.'

The waitress moved on to the next table.

'It's exquisite, darling.' Herta leaned across and kissed him. 'I'm so lucky to have found you again.'

He knew then they would make a home for themselves together here in Germany, in the not-too-distant future. Right now, he didn't want to think about what would be required of her in order to marry an SS man.

'Come. Let's go,' he said, throwing a few coins onto the table. 'I have work to do.' He pulled her chair out and placed his hand around her waist.

'Oh, Ernst,' she said. 'It's such a beautiful day. Can't your specimens wait a couple of hours? After all, they're not going anywhere. Let's visit the zoo this afternoon and see some live animals for a change. Hildegard told me about the new baby at the Elephant House. I'm dying to see it. Its photo has been in all the papers.' Even though she didn't think it was right for wild animals to live in such confined spaces, she still felt a thrill each time she saw them up close.

Ernst agreed, reluctantly. It was hard for him to say no to Herta. They were, after all, making up for lost time. And it was an opportunity to pop in to his laboratory, which was housed on the zoo grounds, and catch up on a few things.

They held hands on the short tram ride, only letting go when the conductor, who wore a crisp blue uniform, asked to check their tickets. Walking through the stone entryway to the Zoological Garden on Budapester Strasse, they strolled along a pathway through the shady garden to the elephant enclosure, past children building sandcastles in the playground. A large pond was throbbing with frog music that filtered through a heavy cloak of waterlilies.

Built in the 1800s as a replica of an ornate Indian palace, complete with a mosaic dragon on the doors, the Elephant House was an imposing display. The giant creatures paced around the sandy forecourt, picking up dirt with their trunks to spray over their wrinkled hides. Herta and Ernst stood behind a metal railing next to a group of schoolchildren who were stepping up onto the iron bars to get a closer look. Beyond the thin strip of grass and the concrete moat that divided the enclosure from visitors, an adult female elephant was reaching her trunk forward to the small crowd. A sign placed in front of her warned visitors: *Vorsicht! Sehr böse*, although she didn't look angry. Herta had read the pachyderm was called Jenny II, and was shocked to see a chain tied around her leg, anchoring the huge animal to a column. She shuddered to think what became of Jenny I. The elephant stood behind seven rows of sharp metal spikes nailed into the ground, preventing her from getting too close to the edge of her enclosure. Beside her, Indra, the now famous infant of two months, was busy playing with a grey ball.

A teacher scolded the children, ordering them to climb down from the railing at once and line up in pairs. Ernst turned to watch the red-faced woman do a headcount. She herded them off along the path in the direction of the children's corner, telling them to behave as she prowled close behind.

While Ernst wasn't looking, Herta rummaged through her bag and found a red apple, which she held out for Jenny II. The elephant took a step towards the edge of the moat, carefully placing her huge feet between the spikes as she stretched her trunk out towards Herta's hand. She didn't seem at all vexed. On the contrary, Herta felt the animal's gesture was one of curiosity, or even friendship. She threw the apple across the moat and it landed in the dirt between Jenny II's hind legs. Ernst turned around to see Herta's hand outstretched, a guilty smile on her face. His gaze fell on the apple.

'Can't you read the signs posted everywhere? *Don't feed the animals.*'

Her smile was replaced by a defiant glare as she fingered the necklace he had given her not an hour before. 'I feel so sorry for her. She looks like some stage actor placed there simply to show off this farcical backdrop. The poor thing was ripped out of the wild for our own selfish pleasure.'

Ernst, realising he had spoken too harshly, stroked Herta's cheek. 'Don't be upset, darling. You are too kind-hearted. An animal doesn't really care much about where it lives as long as it's fed well. I'm sure it's happy, otherwise it wouldn't be breeding.'

Jenny II retreated. She found the fruit and caressed it with the end of her trunk, lifting it towards her mouth. Little Indra sheltered under her belly, searching for a teat to suckle on.

'Come, Herta. I must get to work now.' Ernst took her by the arm and led her away.

Herta clutched the Berlin Zoo guidebook in her hand, scrunching up the picture of a chimpanzee on the cover. They walked quickly, past the camels in their mosque and the ostriches strutting around in their Egyptian temple, both the brainchild of the zoo's director, Lutz Heck, a colleague of Ernst's.

Women were such a puzzle to Ernst. Understanding animal behaviour was indeed challenging, but compared to the vagaries and perils of female human beings it was child's play. Even if he were to study Herta for a lifetime, he would never be able to predict her curious ways. Yet, during his meeting this morning with Himmler, he had been made to understand how important it would be to at least try. A beautiful woman like Herta could be a wonderful asset to his career and wellbeing.

*

As they walked back out towards the zoo's grand entrance, Herta was distracted. In a strange way, the trapped elephant reminded her a little of Margarete, so sweet-natured and delicate, but locked away from others. Mutti and Vati prayed for years that they might bring Herta a little brother or sister, and just as their hair began to turn grey and they had given up all hope, she came along. God's little miracle. She was born during a particularly harsh winter, Mutti fighting a bout of influenza as she laboured. But poor Margarete's soul never did cross fully into the world.

Father Gerhard suggested they hide her away. He thought Margarete might place the family in danger. Strange things had already started happening to those who were seen to have problems; the villagers were a superstitious lot, fearful the child was marked by the Devil. Mutti and Vati were so scared of losing her that they went along with the priest's idea to record Margarete in the church ledger as having died of pneumonia. He even helped them fashion a false grave with her name inscribed on it, and held a small funeral service, in case anyone might ask questions.

When she was of an age parents usually prepared their children for school, Margarete simply vanished from life outside the family home. Vati and Mutti painted her tiny room at the rear of the house in pastel blue, decorating the walls with folded paper cuts of gulls and swans, boats and lighthouses. There little Margarete lived on an imaginary island, watching her mother's lips move as she sang lullabies speckled with sadness, songs the child would never hear. When Herta and Ernst took Margarete on outings to the woods, they could never stay away for long. They needed to get back before anyone in the village might see her.

All of a sudden, Ernst stopped in his tracks and turned to face Herta, bringing her back to the growling and baying of the zoo. He spoke in a loud, confident voice.

'Marry me.'

It sounded as if he was giving her an order. Herta was used to Ernst's direct and blunt manner; even his name held within its meaning his very nature – *serious*. He wasn't the greatest romantic, of that she was sure. But this time he'd caught her completely off guard. She didn't move. After a moment, he smiled, holding his arms out slowly, inviting her into his embrace, the safety of his body, the certainty of his life. She hesitated before stepping forward. He was an SS man, embodying many qualities she disliked about the Reich – the unyielding rigidity, the categorisation of life itself. But somewhere inside, she still found the real Ernst Schäfer, the kind boy she had known since she was a young girl. He would be the one to protect her and keep her family safe.

'Yes,' she found herself saying just before they kissed. *Yes, yes, yes!* A parrot shrieked, hidden somewhere in the branches of an oak.

Behind them lay the zebra enclosure, a slice of fake grassy savannah. She looked over Ernst's shoulder as he held her close, catching a glimpse of a group of skinny African children standing around in front of straw huts.

Posters displayed along the iron fence advertised Sunday's forthcoming *Völkerschau*, a human zoo, where these captured people would be put on public display, caged in alongside the animals.

CHAPTER 4

21 July 1936

'I want my men to enter a marriage in which they can find a *rassisch wertvolle gesunde deutsche Familie*,' Himmler told Ernst during their second meeting. 'A healthy family, deserving of the honour of German heritage. You will need to go through the process of the *Verlobungs- und Heiratsbefehl.*'

Ernst stared at him blankly.

Himmler drummed his fingers on the desk. 'It is a collection of rules concerning the choosing of a fiancée and marriage partner worthy of an SS officer, my boy. It's all very straightforward. You will supply both of your family trees, going back as far as 1800.'

Ernst scratched his chin, a habit born of the long months in the East surrounded by snow, where his beard grew wild. Herta often told him how handsome he was – good teeth, a full head of hair and an impish smile – though it still bothered him that many of his colleagues in the SS towered above him, strapping examples of Aryan perfection. That said, he could outrun anyone through the harshest terrain, bounding up ragged slopes like a mountain goat.

'I want you to marry soon,' Himmler said. 'You have had a restless, demanding life and it is crucial for you to have the stability of a wife always waiting for you at home. My own Marga is my biggest support. Even though the pressure of my work keeps me away from her much of the time, we write every day and when I do see her, she makes me so proud. A beautiful, pure home is where you can keep the filth of the outside world at bay.'

Himmler crossed something off a list on his desk. 'I will have to insist this girlfriend of yours attends a short *Mütterschulungskurs*. I will see to it personally that my dear friend, Frau Scholtz-Klink, enrols her in the next available place at her renowned bride school right here in Berlin. There is a long waiting list, you know. It is considered the very best in Germany.'

'That is very kind of you, Herr Kommandant.' Ernst wasn't sure if he should tell him he recently proposed to Herta. SS officers were supposed to seek Himmler's approval beforehand and he didn't want to risk angering his superior.

Himmler pulled out a photo from a file that lay open on his desk and held it up for closer scrutiny. 'Although Fräulein Völz is certainly a beauty, she will also be required to undertake the *Reichssportabzeichen* as a test of her physical strength and endurance.'

He paused and turned the photograph of Herta towards Ernst. How much more might the man know?

'I must ask you one more thing, though.' He lowered his voice. 'You've never suffered from any problems, my boy?'

Ernst cleared his throat. 'I'm not sure I understand, Herr Kommandant.'

There was an awkward silence.

'It's okay. You can tell me, man to man. I'm not recording any of this on your file. It stays confidential; just between you and me. You haven't been playing around with those whores in Philadelphia, perhaps? You've been away from our glorious Fatherland for a long time and we all know what loose morals they have over there.'

'No, Herr Kommandant.'

'Or perhaps there was a little exotic delicacy on the side, to warm those cold winter nights in the wilds of Tibet? A man can get very lonely out there in the wilderness.'

'I would never do such a thing. You have my word.'

'Don't get me wrong,' Himmler said. He looked over at the door and leaned in closer, his voice an oily whisper now. 'A little tipple on the side is quite natural for a man, take it from me. But just make sure you keep it home-grown and restrained.'

Ernst pulled at a loose thread on the seam of his trousers.

'I'll have my dear colleague Herr Doktor Schwartz organise a thorough gynaecological examination for your little friend soon. One can never be too careful, you know.

After all, we want to make absolutely sure this girl's pelvis is of the right dimensions to bear you a large brood of healthy German children. I'd hate you to be wasting your time on unfertile soil, as it were. Understood?'

'Yes, Herr Kommandant.'

He picked up a book and handed it to Ernst. 'Here, a gift. Written by the late Professor Max von Gruber, who was a brilliant professor at Munich University in his day.'

Ernst glanced at the title: *Hygiene des Geschlechtslebens*. He opened it to the contents page and saw a list of chapters dealing with every aspect of how to have a healthy sex life.

'You will find some fascinating and practical information here, such as how often it is advisable to have intimate relations. His research concludes that any more than twice a week puts too much strain on the body. And there are some crucial facts on onanism, with helpful tips on how to distract yourself from the urge to spend your seed outside a woman's vagina.'

Ernst sat motionless.

'Don't be embarrassed, young man. Healthy body, healthy mind, I always say. I take very good care of all my officers, but you are a high priority for me right now. You will help bring this country the glory it so richly deserves.'

What Ernst assumed would be a simple process was going to take several months to complete. Himmler told him he needed to provide testimonials from the mayor of Waltershausen, as well as the dean of the University of Göttingen. Photographs were required of both Herta and Ernst standing beside a measuring stick to prove their correct height, along with albums of their extended families on both sides. Ernst was to fill out lengthy questionnaires about their health and endure intimate medical examinations. The whole idea behind the screening, Himmler explained, was to weed out partners who were ill or infertile, or who harboured a genetic flaw.

With another abrupt '*Heil Hitler*', Ernst's meeting with the *Reichsführer* concluded. Ernst thought of how humiliating the application process would be. Besides, it was such a pointless waste of time and resources. He couldn't understand why they needed to endure the whole process, both coming from good, honest German families. No one would ever find out about Margarete.

CHAPTER 5

Ernst's laboratory at the zoo was a refuge, his private slice of the wild. Here, he surrounded himself with creatures brought back from all his travels. Their rigid bodies sometimes dissolved into the grey mists of his memory, in which he imagined their feathers quivering or their ribs inhaling small breaths. Those stirrings made him feel strangely at home.

Ernst sipped his morning coffee, scanning the pages of the *Völkischer Beobachter* he bought daily so he could keep up with the latest party news and views. The newspaper's headlines boasted about the Olympics. Much to Ernst's surprise, Himmler, who had taken such a shine to his young protégé, invited him to the opening ceremony, held the day before. Ernst had found himself sitting on the podium with Herta overlooking a throng of 100,000 spectators. The newspaper reported almost a million people lining the Via Trumpalis, between the Lustgarten and the stadium, to watch the Führer's motorcade procession. They threw flowers, saluted and fervently shouted *Heil Hitler* and *Sieg Heil* as he passed. When the torchbearer arrived early that morning, he was welcomed by loud whistles from all the new industrial plants surrounding Berlin. The ruckus of celebration lasted well into the night.

Ernst would have far preferred to keep working on his specimens than take part in this circus. He scoffed at all the pomp and pageantry inside the shiny stadium. A three-thousand-strong choir, all dressed in white, performed the new Olympic Hymn. Herta was excited to see the elderly composer Richard Strauss conducting a military orchestra. They gawked at the Hindenburg, a bloated giant floating above as it trailed an Olympic flag under the threat of grey, heavy skies. A cloud of 25,000 pigeons was released into the air just a minute before a round of cannon-fire. Ernst was glad he and Herta kept their hats on, stifling his laughter as bird droppings showered down on the crowd. But the spectacle could never compare to a beautiful sunrise over a faraway lake, or the thrill of chasing a bear across rocky terrain.

The newspaper reprinted the opening speech of Dr Theodor Lewald, the head of the German Olympic Committee. Gossip had spread that the Reich covered up the fact he was a *Mischling*, part-Jewish, on his father's side, to avoid international embarrassment. Herta and Ernst whispered to each other, while Lewald spoke, that it would only be a matter of time before the Nazis jettisoned him from his honorary post. Ernst almost fell asleep in his seat listening to the stuffy, bald man drone on about the huge black cauldron that stood at the top of a set of concrete steps.

'In a few minutes the torchbearer will appear to light the Olympic fire on this tripod, when it will rise, flaming to heaven, for the weeks of the festival,' he announced. 'It creates a real and spiritual bond of fire between our German Fatherland and the sacred places of Greece founded nearly 4000 years ago by Nordic immigrants.'

All this talk of Nordic ancestors. It seemed to be the only thing that interested anyone nowadays, especially the people at the *Ahnenerbe*. You could hardly get a project off the ground if it didn't show some kind of link to the investigation of Nordic heritage. Ernst needed to play the game if he wanted the *Ahnenerbe* to fund his expedition, but he would still seek additional backing to cover any shortfall. He was far from naïve; he knew the importance of making contacts. Although a fundamental principle of science was that only the experiment and results mattered, in reality it helped if the scientist who presented his findings had the support and backing of influential people. That was why Ernst had made sure to attend an event the night before the opening ceremony, in which the renowned Swedish explorer Sven Hedin delivered a formal address. In a 'Call to the Youth of the World', he urged young people to strive for what they didn't even think they were capable of – to aim for the unattainable.

Ernst had strategically manoeuvred his way across to his childhood hero, taking advantage of the opportunity to chat with him after his speech. He asked Hedin, now in his seventies, if he might consider contributing to sponsorship of the expedition. A confirmed bachelor, famous for mapping huge swathes of hitherto undiscovered regions of the Himalayas, Hedin confided that although he had been in love many times, Central Asia was his true bride.

'She has held me captive in her cold embrace, and I have been faithful to her, that is certain,' he told Ernst. He explained that he too held a firm belief that Tibet was the cradle of the Aryan race.

'My friend Himmler has told me about your great mission. I'm sure the science of *Welteislehre* will lead you to extraordinary discoveries there.'

Ernst bit his tongue. Was the whole scientific world going mad?

'Thank you,' he forced himself to reply, finding himself playing along with the old man. 'Of course. Just because something is unobservable doesn't mean it is totally anathema to physics, or to science as a whole. But surely, the more truth becomes elusive, the more it needs to be examined scientifically.'

'Precisely, my boy. According to the Theory of Relativity, postulated by that Jewish scientist Einstein thirty years ago, a thimble can hold a quintillion atoms. That is something very hard to imagine. Current-day equipment might just not be up to the task of detecting the unseen.' Hedin smiled and scratched his grey moustache. His eyes darted about the room searching for someone more important to talk to, and he excused himself from the conversation as soon as he saw Himmler enter the room.

How could Ernst have held this fawning old man up as a hero all these years? Intuition could not be accepted as proof of a thing's existence. Ernst's work, in its own way, aimed at invoking the undetectable, but finding creatures unknown by scientists was not only important, it was good for mankind. Generations later they would still be writing of the great Ernst Schäfer's achievements, with or without the help of Sven Hedin.

As Ernst sat at his desk finishing his coffee, he thought about how it was Herta who believed in him more than anyone else. She knew there was always a blurry line between what was observable and what lay hidden or imperceptible. Ernst liked the way she challenged him, kept him sharp, but she held an angel's feathery view of the world. Although she had led such a sheltered life, she was still able to penetrate his innermost feelings. He was glad she had agreed to be his bride.

Ernst tossed aside the newspaper and went back to inspecting the skin of the *Tetraogallus tibetanus*, a Tibetan snowcock.

Over the next two weeks, his lovely fiancée tucked under his arm, Ernst did the rounds of all the grand parties and receptions, where guests were plied with expensive champagne. Visitors from around the world strolled along

Unter den Linden, the new trees sporting Olympic banners, and loudspeakers booming *Achtung!* to draw their attention to the radio broadcast of the latest results. Whenever a German team won, the speakers would blast out the full rendition of the 'Horst-Wessel-Lied'.

One evening, an elaborate party was thrown by the self-appointed *Reichsjägermeister*, Hermann Göring, and his wife, the actress Emmy Sonnemann, at their city palazzo. Opulent decorations included lights that were mounted on neighbours' roofs, suspended from trees or submerged in a swimming pool where swans floated gracefully. Guests were greeted by the 'master of the hunt' himself, who lounged with his wife on a divan in front of a tea pavilion. Ernst and Herta strolled through a replica eighteenth-century French village, stopping at the re-created post office, inn and bakery. The State Opera's corps de ballet performed during a lavish dinner; Herta observed that Göring possessed the limitless appetite of a parvenu. Afterwards, there was a huge festive carnival with a merry-go-round and peasant folk-dancers doing traditional knee-slapping. Ernst felt most comfortable milling around several shooting galleries that were flanked by performing bears, their muzzles bound with leather straps. Trainers held them tightly leashed as the huge creatures paraded around on hind legs. Herta sat quietly on a couch beside him, staring at her lap.

Seemingly not wanting to be outdone, a week later the Minister for Propaganda, Joseph Goebbels, threw a lavish affair on the Pfaueninsel. The small island was decorated to resemble a giant movie set, complete with trees clipped in the shape of animals, elaborate bandstands, torch-bearing half-naked young actresses and a stunning firework display after dinner. Ernst and Herta sat by themselves again, drinking beer and watching the parading peacocks of the human and animal kind. It was all such a spectacular bore. Ernst would have given anything to escape, be somewhere out in the forest, his trusty shotgun slung over his shoulder.

His first kill in the wild had been an accident of play. In early spring, when afternoon stretched out like a lazy cat, Ernst would flee the confines of his home in Waltershausen and seek out solitude in the Thuringian Forest, scrambling through the dense, tangled undergrowth between luxuriant pines and tall birch trees. He would circle the roosting places of the pied avocet, in search of its speckled eggs – a delicacy also sought after by squirrels – ignoring the desperate antics of the parent bird on guard, who would fake a broken wing to try to distract the intruder's attention away from the nest. On one particular day a flash of reddish fur ran up a nearby oak, giving Ernst a fright. Forgetting about the eggs, he took out the worn slingshot, a present from his father for his fifth birthday, and aimed. The squirrel fell on top of a bed of pine needles, an acorn spurting out from its mouth, the furious rise and fall of its tiny breast slowing to a halt. He watched the creature shrink into stillness. With the realisation that killing was such a simple act, a strange feeling of exultation mixed with awe crept up on young Ernst.

He carted the dead squirrel back home and hid it under his bed for a week, until the maid complained to his parents about the stench coming from their son's room. As punishment, his father, an accomplished horseman, stopped taking him out on rides. He also banned him from Sunday walks with the family, depriving him of paddle-boat rides on the lake. But young Ernst's escapades only widened in scope and daring as he set off across distant fields and forests. He would leave as soon as the school day ended, returning home at dusk muddy and scratched. He grew stronger, his chest and shoulders broadening as spring passed into summer, then autumn. The bondage of winter curtailed his adventures, the cold winds from the north bringing snow and ice. His need to be outdoors felt even more urgent and uncontrollable during those months, so he made do by turning his room into a mini-ature woodland, hibernating there until spring.

Sometimes he heard his mother tiptoe softly across the floorboards upstairs. Ernst knew she was listen-ing on the other side of his door to the strange sounds coming from within – the scratching whimpers of mice, the operatic trills of birdsong. From the corridor, the melo-dious warbling of his common whitethroat might have sounded like a breathless plea: a sad, fretting call, begging for release.

The evening of Ernst's first kill in the wild, as Frau Schäfer sat darning her young son's socks, there would have been no mistaking Ernst's cries for any bird's shriek-ing. Her husband's incoherent grunts caught her breath as she tried not to think about what cruel form of punishment was taking place behind the study door. It was no use trying to cage her son; she could see she would lose him soon enough. He had changed from a gaunt and ragged waif into a fiercely independent and headstrong youth. His mother understood that Ernst was a boy who would never be tamed.

CHAPTER 6

2019
Academy of Natural Sciences, Philadelphia

My veins are filled with polyurethane, winding their way up my limbs towards the heart-shaped hole in my chest. Beside me lie rocks, ghostly bamboo forests and a pool into which they have me gaze sometimes, though no reflection looks back. I prefer the days they move me closer to Glass, towards the left side, behind Guard.

My mother would tell me stories when I was a cub of when our ancestors, white as snow, lived high up in the mountains. Long ago, a gentle shepherd girl from the valley below would take her flock to graze up there. Sometimes a young white panda would join her, perhaps mistaking the sheep for its own kind. One day, while the panda was happily playing with the flock, a leopard jumped down from a tree and began to savage the helpless cub. The brave girl picked up a stick and tried to beat the leopard. The panda ran off, but the leopard turned on its attacker, killing her instantly. When the other pandas learnt of the tragedy, they all came to the girl's funeral to pay their respects. They covered their arms with ash, as was the tradition. They wiped their eyes to dry their tears and hugged each other, sobbing so loudly they had to cover their ears with their paws. To this day, the black stains from the ash remain as markings on their white fur. Overcome with grief, the girl's three sisters threw themselves into her grave, the earth shaking violently with their sadness. Siguniang, a huge mountain range, swallowed all of them and continues to protect the pandas to this day, nestling them in the ridges between the peaks formed from the bodies of each sister.

'Wunderlichs, wunderlichs,' were the last words I heard the sturdy shape whisper as it approached me, before the sudden thunder and the sky turning grey. I stopped chewing when I saw Him, clenching a bamboo shoot in my paw. He stood there, waiting. No telltale signs that He was up to something. My inaction might have been almost comical if it wasn't such high tragedy, me lounging on my perch up a tree, Him pointing a stick at me. All we shared together while I was alive was that swollen moment, a tiny liaison where my eyes bulged as His narrowed.

Afterwards, He dug into a hessian sack and sprinkled coarse salt onto my skin, which lay spread out on a rock like a pile of linen bleaching in the sun. When I was all dry, He cradled me under his arm. The crunching of footsteps, His shouts to the local guides to prepare the mules for travel, invaded the silence that had settled on our scene. They called Him Bara-Sahib, while others called Him Schäfer, which means Shepherd here in the Glasslands. My heart drained as I became wrapped in myself. He stroked me gently with His bloodied hand, and made scratches on some bark I would later learn was His notebook. The tag He tied to me taught me that my home was in the mountains of Washu, in the bamboo forests of Kham, on the border of Tibet. And that fateful day we met was marked on His calendar as 5/13/31. The others, His travelling companions, Brooky and Weigold, lagged behind on the pathway like foul odours. Weigold was the first of Shepherd's type to see a live one of us in the wild. He told us he had bought a Small just like me years before, but it didn't live very long.

When they opened me up I stepped out of myself, sinew and bone divided, scraps thrown to the dur bya, those sacred birds of death. They stabbed at my eyeballs, which would soon be replaced in their sockets by ground glass.

Guard is my constant companion now, his face a reflection of past and future boredom. Sometimes I hear him curse. On quiet days, he dances a little, high-stepping it to Gloria Gaynor's 'I Will Survive'. Most days it's just him and me, and the joyous Galaxy he holds in his hand. It is his treasure, for inside he has captured rays of sunshine.

Some days are quite dull, I must admit. Even Bamboo Replacement Day has lost its thrill after so many years. Frankly, Guard's daily tuna-and-lettuce sandwich looks far more appetising. Other days are happy ones; a new level on Clash of Clans might have been unlocked, or Guard thinks he knows the answer to Final Jeopardy. Moments like these are when I truly regret the rigidity of my form. From the corner of my eye I've seen his finger hover over the wrong answer. An understandable mistake, under that kind of pressure. But I've learnt to keep my cool and take my time.

Some days my mind wanders back to Wild, to the mists of the forest with its gnarled, moss-covered tree roots abandoned among the grasses, like skulls of Torosaurus from Dinosaur Hall. And that's the hardest, remembering the smell of freshly cut bamboo, the shrieks of the vultures circling in the blue above and the singing of distant villagers who knew well enough to leave us alone. When I was a cub, I used to gaze across treetops that were shrouded in fog, wondering what was out there beyond Wild, but I never imagined I would end up here beside Exit.

The happiest days for Guard and me are the ones when they bring in Smalls: tiny specimens that jostle and push each other out of the way so they can get a closer look at me. They splay their palms against Glass, their fish-like lips trying to suck me towards them. I have been chosen to teach them Nature, a job that weighs heavily on me. But I wear it as a badge of pride; besides, it's better than being stuck in Basement, draped over some coathanger like poor old Hsing Hsing.

Girl comes every Saturday afternoon. She sets up a small folding chair and pulls out a sketchbook and charcoal pencil from her leopard-print backpack. I've caught a glimpse of some of her drawings, delighted to be her model for Super Panda, Kung Fu Panda and Ninja Panda. She calls me her BFF. Best Friend Forever. But Forever is such a long time.

She has several red striped markings above her paws, which seem to be fresh wounds. I hope no one is trying to prepare her for Glass. Perhaps I should warn her?

I wish I could visit the woolly Takin, which inhabit the Glasslands over the other side of Exit. He brought them here from Home, not long after I arrived. I have an ache inside to share my story and hear other tales that have given birth to this New Life we all share. Shepherd used to say that each one of us He brought across the waves was 'an object of remembrance from an impoverished past', in which we were merely 'temporary and evanescent'.

'Now you have the power of immortality,' He would whisper in my ear while we were in Basement, stroking my head with His strong hand. 'No room for wistful memories of a distant joy; your collective past will exist forever in the present. You have risen above the personal apocalypse we mere mortals suffer.'

I am so grateful to Him. His desire to make sense of our world and His fellow man's place within it was so admirable. And He was as devoted to me as a father. Sometimes, in the middle of the night, the lights would come on. I heard those familiar footsteps approaching along the corridor. He would forget to sleep, go for long stretches without food or drink. There was only me, and He would worship my every bone, even the Phalanges of my toes, which He kept in a special drawer. He was trying to find the right potion that would bring me back to Life. He wanted me ready for that moment, in my best pose to re-enter the world, my Glass Mother beside me, as if I'd never died.

CHAPTER 7

April 1937

During her first week at bride school, Herta slipped up one evening while rehearsing how to keep up conversations at cocktail parties. These were the most difficult classes, social niceties not being her forte. The Directress was pretending to be a high-ranking SS officer, trying to engage the girls in a conversation about how German women were desperately needed by the Reich as sustainers of the race. The absent look on Herta's face was an invitation for the formidable Gertrud Scholtz-Klink to mount a stealthy attack.

'We live in exciting times, Fräulein Völz, don't you think?'

'Yes, Frau Scholtz-Klink.' Herta was trying hard to calm herself, concentrating on filling her lungs.

Frau Scholtz-Klink, her two long braids woven neatly around her forehead, spoke to the group. 'You are the spiritual caregivers, called upon by fate for this special task!' she recited in a syrupy tone. '*Deutschblütig*. Aryan women are participants in the resurrection of the sacred German bloodline. You will be the secret queens of our people.'

The girls tittered.

'May I remind you this is no laughing matter.' Her face turned to marble. 'Our Führer relies upon you, and your duty to him must be your priority. He should be your role model for health and wellbeing – I know him personally and can tell you that he abhors smoking, doesn't drink and eats an almost vegetarian diet. He has the highest respect for the role of the German woman in making this country great again. He denies the Liberal-Jew-Bolshevik theory of "women's equality" because it dishonours us. He said in his famous speech, *"A woman, if she understands her mission rightly, will tell a man: You preserve our people from danger and I shall give you children."* The Führer shall forever remain your first love.'

She looked back at Herta. 'Now, step forward, young lady! Imagine I am *Reichsmarschall* Hermann Göring, and you have just been introduced to me at an official function by your husband.' She puffed her chest out and took on the corpulent man's manner. 'Good evening, Fräulein,' she bellowed. 'I am pleased to make your acquaintance, and happy to see you have embraced one of the Nine Commandments for the Workers' Struggle – *"Take hold*

of the frying pan, dustpan and broom, and marry a man!"
I'm very proud to have made that one up myself. Do you
like it?' The Directress, staying in character, let out a
deep guffaw.

The hall echoed with her laughter before turning silent.
Everyone looked at Herta, waiting for a response. She
stood there wishing a chasm might open up between them
to swallow her deep into the folds of the earth, as far away
as possible from this place, this country, this time. The
words came out slowly, heavier than stone.

'Women must speak the truth.' Herta paused, realising
she must have missed something, judging from the tiny
gasps that echoed around the hall. 'Sir!' she added.

'No, no, *Mädchen*! No opinions. No jokes. And no
poetry. Starting from right now, you must learn to be
politely talkative.' She paced back and forth in front of
the line of young women, hands clasped behind her back.
Whispers spread across the group like waves licking the
shore, ceasing the instant she shouted, 'I'm speaking to
all of you!' The Directress kept talking as she prowled
around Herta. 'In your application form, you said you
are hoping to marry your sweetheart this summer, am
I correct?'

Herta tried to hold back her tears, but it was too late.
The older woman had already picked up the scent of fear
in her prey.

'Getting all weepy is rather pathetic, girls. Don't you
think?' She turned towards the group, who tried hard to
stifle their giggles this time.

'You are going to need me to sign your certificate if you want the prestige of being the wife of an SS officer.' The Directress moved up close to Herta. 'Tell us. Who is this fortunate man of yours?' The sarcasm oozed out of her like molten lead.

Herta spoke quietly. She almost choked on her words, but managed to cough out, 'Ernst Schäfer, Frau Scholtz-Klink.'

There was a collective breath of surprise among the brides-to-be.

The woman's eyes widened. 'The explorer?'

The pack seemed to draw closer, twenty girls waiting excitedly for the imminent attack.

The Directress circled her victim, and Herta felt the stout woman's hot breath on her face. It reeked of garlic.

'Really? What would a man of his standing be thinking, marrying a mouse like you?'

Herta looked down at the tiled floor. On that day last June when Ernst proposed, she had felt so light and happy, as if they had both come full circle back to where it all started, their hideaway in the forest. She remembered how confident he seemed about their future together. A solitary bird sang. And with raw-voiced love she had chosen to join its refrain: *Yes. Yes. Yes!*

'You'd better pay attention and work hard here, young lady.' Frau Scholtz-Klink took a step back, still glaring at Herta. 'Believe me, if you do not pass your exams, *Untersturmführer* Ernst Schäfer is not going to forsake his brilliant career for a lowly fiancée like you. Now, recite for us the Ten Commandments for Choosing a Spouse.'

Herta was blushing. She felt as though she might throw up. The others craned forward to see her.

'Immediately!'

'*Kinder, Küche, Kirche!* Children, kitchen, church!' she blurted out, now breathing as quickly as if she'd been asked to drop and do fifty push-ups.

'*Keep your body pure.*'

Her mouth felt dry as she tried to regurgitate the morning's very first lesson. Clearing her throat, she started over again.

'*Remember that you are a German.*

'*If you are genetically healthy you should not remain unmarried.*'

'That's enough for now. See me in my office immediately after lunch tomorrow, Fräulein Völz.'

Herta's lips started tingling. Surely the woman didn't suspect anything? She always tried to keep a straight face whenever there was any mention of genetic illness in the blood. Nobody knew about Margarete outside of the immediate family. No one except Ernst or Father Gerhard, that is.

Thankfully, Frau Scholtz-Klink moved on to quiz her next target. 'You!' She pointed to a freckly, red-haired girl. 'Continue!'

Her new victim proudly obliged, reciting the rest of the Commandments.

'*Keep your mind and spirit pure.*

'*As a German, choose only a spouse of the same or Nordic blood.*

'*In choosing a spouse, ask about his ancestors.*'

'All of you! *Schnell!* Join in.'
'*Health is also a precondition for physical beauty.*'
'*Don't look for a playmate but for a companion for marriage.*'
'*You should want to have as many children as possible.*'
'*Marry only for love.*'

At dawn the next day Herta lay on her bed, drifting in and out of sleep, dreaming about Wannsee, the most romantic place in all Germany. A slice of nature right in the heart of Berlin. Herta was surprised to find herself loving this place after having felt such dread when she first arrived there, the weeks lying endlessly ahead of her. But she imagined how much Ernst would enjoy it here – majestic swans gliding on the Wannsee lake, and the crescendo of birdcall at dusk echoing across from the Grunewald forest. Herta could picture his cheeky smile as together they raced from the majestic villa across the finely manicured lawns, down towards the shore. He would dive straight into the blue, splashing about like a little boy, while she sat on the banks, sunning herself. Sometimes she fantasised that a few years from now this stately mansion might become their own home, little Heidi tottering along the path, pushing her dolly around in a pram, young Brooke bouncing a ball against the back wall, scolded by the groundsman for leaving dirty marks on the perfectly whitewashed bricks. And they would hold such wonderful parties for their friends, where together she and Vati would play the 'Flower Duet' from Delibes' opera *Lakmé*, the invitations sent out on embossed cards, handwritten in her elegant cursive script:

$$Herr \text{ & } Frau \text{ } Ernst \text{ } und \text{ } Herta \text{ } Schäfer$$

Cordially invite you to a musical soirée,

at their residence

Inselstrasse 28

Schwanenwerder Island

Sunday 7 September 1941

7 pm sharp

By then, Ernst would have long ago returned triumphant from his third Tibetan expedition, the darling of everyone they knew. Having published several more books, he would be in huge demand as both a speaker and an internationally renowned scientist. The Schäfer family would be rich and mix in the most influential circles. No longer would she have to scrimp and save. These six weeks at the *Reichsbräuteschule*, the most sought-after school for brides in Germany, would have all been worth it.

When Ernst first told her about the school she was horrified, but since he had become so important in the SS there was no choice really, and certainly no room for protest. If she wanted to marry the man she loved, she would have to go along with what was expected of the future wife of an SS officer. When Ernst explained to her it was a non-negotiable condition for their marrying, he also made it very clear that his career depended on it. *Reichsführer* Himmler treated his men as one big *Sippe*, an extended family, and, like any caring father, enforced strict rules concerning their choice of partner and plans for having children. Now that they were engaged, she was expected to become the best bride possible for a man of Ernst's standing. At first she didn't give the notion much thought, focusing instead on her studies in between relishing the heady joy of romance. It was only after she had read the application form a few months later that she felt a creeping sense of trepidation. The Reich promised to take each girl in turn and reassemble her as an ideal National Socialist woman, 'truly worthy of an SS officer's love'.

Her reveries were cut short by the morning wake-up call. Later today she was to present herself at Frau Scholtz-Klink's office. Herta jumped out of bed, carefully running her hands over the wrinkles in the sheets, then rushed outside for rollcall, immediately followed by gymnastics. With daylight just peeking over the horizon, she stood in line with all the other girls beside the driveway, wearing the standard white T-shirt and black shorts. They ran around the perimeter of the grounds then stood in a circle performing lunges and squats, led by an enthusiastic and well-built instructor. Herta certainly fitted in on a superficial level. Most of the girls were strong and slim, with blue eyes, sharp aquiline noses and blondish hair. Aside from hiking in the woods with Ernst as a child, she was never one to enjoy exercise, always preferring to read a book or play flute, but the Reich placed a huge emphasis on maintaining a fit and healthy body.

After an open-air bath, followed by a hearty breakfast, they would attend classes on cooking and nutrition, interior decorating, sewing and household budgeting. Herta's favourite lesson was childcare, in which they were each given a baby doll and taught how to bathe and dress it. The plastic stare of the doll's mechanically blinking blue eyes mesmerised her, calling her towards motherhood. She found the classes on how to fatten geese or make perfect floral arrangements rather boring, but there were other skills she would never have envisaged herself learning, such as how to starch and iron SS dress uniforms, or polish Ernst's SS dagger and gun. At times it all seemed comical, but the busy routine kept her from feeling homesick.

Lessons continued. The women danced in the garden, swaying as they stretched their arms above their heads. They made sure to try their best at all times, always on guard, as it was rumoured that the *Reichsführer* himself would on occasion pay a secret visit to watch the girls from behind a hedge. Their classes on *Volksgemeinschaft*, or community spirit, focused on the importance of genetics and race. They learnt how the national stock was weakened by those who carry defective genes, especially Jews and the mentally ill. Everything in their lives centred around country and sacrifice.

While the other girls sewed or sang together during their free time, Herta preferred to spend evenings alone on her bunk, quietly practising her flute. Sometimes an owl nesting in the tree outside joined in. It reminded her of when she was a young girl and her grandmother, an old woman with a belly like a pumpkin, would tell her about the owl that hooted the day Herta was born.

'I'm afraid it means you are destined for an unhappy life, my child,' she made sure to warn her young grand-daughter, over and over again.

Ernst would try to sweeten the old lady's superstitions about evil owls by telling Herta stories of the bird's reputation for wisdom. He showed her a specimen of bone from a tawny owl he kept hidden inside a wooden music box, lifting it out carefully to place on Herta's outstretched palm.

'Birds' bones are filled with air. Well, mainly the ones that can fly, that is.' He carefully chose another laid out in the box.

'Hold out your hands.' He placed the other bone in her free hand. 'Which is heavier?'

Like the weighing pans of a scale, she moved her palms up and down.

'The one on the right?'

'Correct,' he said, grinning. 'But do you know why?'

She shook her head.

'The one on the right belonged to a grebe and is heavier. This helps it dive underwater. Since the other comes from an owl, it's hollow. Birds that fly need lighter bones.'

'And what about this?' She pointed to a pale green egg that had caught her eye.

'That's from a mallard duck. The female is the main one who sits on the nest and cares for her chicks once they've hatched. She is far more heavily camouflaged than the male so that if a predator approaches, she doesn't need to leave her young. Blending in with the nest surroundings helps protect both her and her offspring.'

At noon, Herta sat on the leather couch outside Frau Scholtz-Klink's door, flipping through a well-worn Reich-sponsored magazine, *NS-Frauen-Warte*. Women Waiting. She scanned the pages, glancing at recipes for how to fillet a fish and patterns for *sommerliche, leichte Kleider*, summery frocks designed, it seemed, for lifeless mannequins. Herta felt curiously calm. Right under an advertisement for Nivea sunscreen, she saw it; knew straightaway this was what she'd been looking for. It would be the perfect wedding gift for Ernst, something that would bring such joy to the lonely hours that awaited him in the wilderness of Tibet. The advertisement promised, *A beautiful sound from an exceedingly light instrument – Hohner Mundharmonika. A beloved friend, inside and out.* A harmonica. She knew Ernst would love it.

She looked around the room. The secretary's desk was unattended. Everyone was still at lunch, but Herta had left the dining room early, her appetite not whetted by pork roast and mashed potatoes with gravy. She jumped up from her chair, grabbed a pair of scissors and hurriedly cut out the advertisement. By the time the secretary returned,

Herta was seated again, straight-backed and smiling, the magazine stealthily placed at the bottom of the pile. Frau Scholtz-Klink walked past the desk and, without looking up, called her in. Herta followed the dreary woman into her equally drab office, fingering the clipping in the pocket of her skirt.

'Sit down, my dear,' she said, smiling. 'I just wanted to have a chat with you.'

Herta sat and folded her hands in her lap.

The Directress lowered herself into the chair behind her large desk. 'I feel perhaps you have been struggling a bit to adjust to our little bride school. It is such a long time to be away from your beloved.' She cocked her head, studying Herta's face.

Herta tried to relax a little. Perhaps she had misjudged the harshness of the woman.

'Are you feeling homesick?'

'A little.' Herta blushed.

'In less than three months from now you will take your formal vows, Fräulein Völz. It is time to step up. I must warn you, we do not tolerate weakness here, of any kind.' The woman embarked on a belligerent tirade – country, duty, sacrifice, no make-up, no gossip, no books, no smoking, no alcohol, no hesitation, no impurity, no work outside the home. '*Ein Volk, ein Reich, ein Führer.* Have I made myself clear?'

'Yes, Frau Scholtz-Klink.'

'Good. Because this is my first and final warning to you.' The smile was still fixed on her face, only now she began to resemble a wooden marionette. 'You will have to give up this silly flute-playing of yours, too. We do not tolerate such selfish pursuits in our girls. Do you understand?'

'Yes, Frau Scholtz-Klink.' There was no way Herta was going to surrender her music for anyone. She had left her beloved sister behind in order to pursue her passion for music in Berlin. After such an agonising decision, it was unthinkable not to complete her studies. Besides, her final examination was coming up soon.

As if the Directress was reading her mind, she tapped her finger rhythmically on the desk.

'Your only focus from now on should be pleasing the Führer by making a wholesome German home.'

CHAPTER 8

14 July 1937
Waltershausen

Swallows dived between wisps of cloud, swooping above the fountain in the town square, celebrating the glorious summer afternoon. Inside the church, guests gathered to watch the ceremony. Vati was wearing his best suit. He sat stiffly in the front pew, a still life surrounded by a sea of men in black uniforms who filled the three levels of curved balconies. Mutti had promised she wouldn't cry, but of course she did.

Herta held the bouquet of blue cornflowers tightly as she peeked through her veil at Ernst, his face blurred in the dim light. The warm air enveloped them like translucent skin. It would only be a matter of moments before this man she had known her whole life became her husband. Soon she would taste every part of him. Their stories were now intertwined, tangled together with years of history.

She glanced up at the ceiling fresco, the white dove of the Holy Spirit flying before the sun. Angels were perched atop the giant organ, statues boasting golden wings and trumpets. She felt as if she was falling, before being jolted back into the moment by a blast of music.

Herta had graduated with merit from her course at bride school. Frau Scholtz-Klink issued her with a certificate of accomplishment, stamped with the Germanic tree of life. In spite of the Directress's strong advice to give up her music, Herta had also excelled in her flute examinations. Herr Kittel called her his star pupil. He had even invited her to be a flautist in the orchestra for a forthcoming performance of Handel's opera *Hercules* at the Waldbühne amphitheatre, celebrating the 700th anniversary of the founding of Berlin. Ernst had been working night and day to finish his dissertation, as well as writing several articles about his previous adventures, and was busy with preparations for the Tibet expedition. He would be leaving in a matter of months. Their lives had been so chaotic in the lead-up to the wedding that they had barely seen each other over the previous weeks. There would be no time for a honeymoon.

Just before the wedding, Herta had managed to squeeze in a couple of days with Mutti and Vati. Mutti had been busy organising floral arrangements; Herta refused to be involved with them, as they brought back memories of bride school, but she did help her mother finalise catering for the reception, to be held at the beautiful Hotel Ratsherberge, just off Hauptstrasse.

Herta brought her wedding dress along to show her parents, and stood on a stool in the middle of the parlour as her mother pinned the hem. Hildegard had helped with the sewing, insisting on an intricately beaded long train and delicate white veil.

'Who have you invited to be your bridesmaids?' Mutti asked, reaching for the pincushion.

'Just Hildegard.'

She stopped what she was doing and looked up at Herta. 'But surely you need more than one?'

Herta's voice turned to steel as their eyes met. 'Then perhaps I should ask Margarete?'

Mutti's face turned white. She was kneeling on the floor, head bent like a sinner in silent prayer. Vati, who had been playing a Chopin nocturne in the background, slammed the piano lid down and left the room.

'What's up with him lately? I'm finally with the man I have loved my whole life and you'd think I was marrying some kind of monster.'

'Calm down, Herta. He is very fond of Ernst's family. You know he and Albert Schäfer hold similar values.'

'Mutti, I understand more than anyone Vati's attitude to the Reich, but I'm begging you, please ask him to keep his views to himself while the guests are here.'

Mutti cleared her throat and returned to pinning the hem of Herta's gown. A silence hung between them for several seconds.

'And why won't you tell me the truth?' Herta asked, her voice sounding shaky. 'Where is Margarete?'

Mutti jabbed herself with the needle, and the clatter and crash of pins falling on the floor filled the room. She grasped the gold cross hanging from her necklace, glancing over towards the doorway then up at her daughter. Tears welled in her eyes.

'Herta, we simply couldn't manage her anymore after you left. She became so difficult, lashing out and biting us whenever we tried to wash or dress her.'

Herta leaned forward, clutching her mother's hand. She pulled out a handkerchief tucked inside her brassiere and wrapped it around the tiny puncture wound.

'But you promised you would look after her. You know I would never have gone to Berlin otherwise.'

'When you left, Father Gerhard offered to take care of Margarete, under the wing of the Church. He told authorities she had been found in a wheelchair on his doorstep one night, and was taken in by the nuns, with no identification papers.' Her mother lowered her voice. 'Father Gerhard has been good to us. And we didn't want there to be repercussions for anyone. Especially now, with you marrying Ernst.' Her voice was unsteady.

Herta began breathing rapidly, a tightness rising in her chest. Her mother went on to tell her that one day, around six weeks earlier, two police officers had come and taken Margarete from Father Gerhard. They bundled her into a car without taking any of her belongings with them and drove off. At first, Mutti and Vati thought it might be the authorities wanting to make sure she could never have children, following the law passed a few years ago. They assumed she would be brought back after an operation. One evening a couple of weeks later, when Margarete still hadn't returned, they decided to go to the cinema, to help take their mind off things. There, they saw a movie trailer, *Das Erbe*. It described a proposed new law, for 'the Prevention of Hereditarily Diseased Offspring'. *Gnadentod*, it was called: merciful death. After that, Vati had become nervous and went to Father Gerhard, begging him to intervene, but he said it was simply God's will, and nothing could be done. In the weeks since, they had begun to hear rumours around the village, of young people who were not quite right at birth, or those who suffered terrible seizures like Margarete, being designated *Lebensunwertes Leben* – life unworthy of life. Herta's father was too scared to make any further enquiries, which would risk placing Father Gerhard in an even more precarious position.

Herta felt the room spinning.

Her mother's voice sounded more and more muffled. 'I don't think we will ever find out what really happened to your dear sister. All I know is she is gone.'

The words trailed off into the air. Herta felt like screaming, but fear gripped her throat. What would Ernst say about all of this?

She ran out into the hallway to escape her mother's sobs. Vati stood there, waiting. She tried to rush past him, avoiding his eyes.

'Herta, stop!'

Slowly and reluctantly she looked up, but felt herself staring right through him as though he were a ghost. Herta hadn't spoken much to her father since moving to Berlin; lately, any conversation between them seemed so dour and guarded. She imagined it was because he didn't approve of Ernst or, rather, whom her childhood sweetheart had become. A father trod such a precarious line between protector and peacemaker, and now he had to relinquish his daughter.

Leaning forward, Vati whispered, 'I taught you how to take your first steps, and now you are walking away from me, straight into that nest of hornets.'

'You're wrong about Ernst, Vati. A man's love is far greater than his politics,' she said, her voice still tremulous.

He grabbed her hand. His fob watch fell out of his pocket, dangling on its chain. It was a family heirloom, passed down to him from his father. Herta froze. She watched Vati's knuckles turn white until suddenly he let go, a look of horror on his face. This was the first time he had ever hurt her. Maybe he hoped the pain would somehow bring back the Herta he once knew. She lowered her gaze and ran from him. Disappearing into the shadows at the top of the staircase, she felt part angel, part phantom, the chiffon trail of her dress flying behind her. She glanced back momentarily, wondering if he would follow her, only to see her father turn and walk straight out the front door.

Why had Vati become so narrow-minded? Why could he not trust her, hold out his arms and embrace her and Ernst as one? Maybe if she could convince Ernst to use his influence to find out where Margarete was, Vati would change his mind. Yes, she would speak to Ernst about it after the wedding.

Herta closed the door behind her before changing out of her bridal gown. Her bedroom was like a diorama of her childhood. A row of dolls, their glass eyes open wide, a box holding her treasured feather collection and a worn chess set sat on the shelf beside her bed. In the corner, her old music stand was tucked away. Beside it, resting on a wicker chair, was the first instrument her father ever gave her. Still trembling, Herta stroked the red velvet lining of the familiar case as she lifted out the tarnished flute. Unfolding the brass wings of the music stand, she propped up some sheet music she found in a drawer and held the instrument to her lips.

Vati had taught her to play when she turned eight. During their first lesson, he showed her how to curl her fingers over the keys and rest her lower lip on the outer rim of the silver mouthpiece. She had blown tentative, tiny breaths into the hole, but wasn't able to sound a note.

'Stand straight.' He placed his hand against the small of her back. 'Now breathe in deeply, as if it were summertime again and you were about to dive into the lake like a swan. Remember, though, the instrument will swallow only half the air you blow out, so you need to take the biggest breath you can.'

She tried again. This time a feeble sound spluttered out, which Herr Völz seemed to think was an improvement.

'Bravo, *mein Kind*!' He reached for some paper on the desk and tore a piece off, crumpling it into a tiny ball, which he rested on his outstretched palm.

'Now, blow!'

She pursed her lips and fired tiny breaths.

'No, no. Relax! You're not cooling down hot soup.'

Herta held her breath, fighting back the tears.

'Think of the songbird in the linden. His serenades had to start somewhere, too. He practises and practises until he finds just the right note.'

She tried again. This time, her efforts sounded more like a snort of disgust.

'Pretend you are trying to make a hummingbird's feather fly up into the air.'

She was determined to make Vati proud of her. Closing her eyes, she blew gently on the mouthpiece. As if by magic, a sound she would never forget emerged from the flute. Love at first breath. A note as pure and sweet as birdsong.

The wedding ceremony was perfunctory and brief, conducted by a military chaplain. Father Gerhard sat alone, watching from the back of the church. The *Reichskonkordat* treaty between the Church and the German

Reich, signed four years earlier, stated that 'Catholic army officers, personnel and men, as well as their families, do not belong to the local parish communities and are not to contribute to their maintenance.' But an exception was made in the Schäfers' case, possibly due to Ernst's rank in the SS. The young couple were allowed to marry inside their local church, on the condition it was run as a civil service. When they were pronounced husband and wife, Ernst lifted Herta's veil and they kissed.

Afterwards, at the reception, Bruno and Hildegard came up to greet the married couple. Bruno slapped Ernst on the shoulder, congratulating him.

'This is all thanks to you, Bruno,' Ernst said, holding his hand out.

Bruno, already tipsy after having downed several beers, placed his hand on his wife's shoulder instead. 'Well, it wasn't really my intention for you two to fall in love.' Ernst's friend chuckled. 'You have my wife, your lovely bridesmaid, to thank for that. Personally, I didn't think Herta was your type. I would have chosen someone slightly more salubrious for a man of your standing.'

Ernst tightened his hold around Herta's waist. Hildegard took a big sip from her glass, her cheeks burning red. Her curls were coming unpinned, and she teetered slightly as she drank.

Bruno turned to Herta. 'Must be quite an overwhelming experience for you, being at the centre of everyone's attention all at once, especially the crème de la crème of the SS.'

Herta's smile disappeared. As much as she disliked him, he was right. Standing there in front of all these well-heeled guests, Herta felt like a simple country girl. It wasn't so long ago she and Ernst had been children, throwing mud cakes at each other behind the barn. Yet here they were, sipping champagne from crystal glasses brought to them on silver trays by elegant waiters.

A group of good-looking men came up to greet them, saving Herta from Bruno's inane banter. Hildegard pulled her husband aside, making way for the bridal couple to be engulfed by Ernst's SS friends, all dressed in immaculate uniforms. After a few minutes, the chatter stopped abruptly. The men parted like a black sea, from the depths of which emerged a short, balding man.

'Quite delectable.' Ernst's Kommandant stepped forward. He took Herta's hand in his and stroked her arm with his stubby fingers. 'Adorable, in fact.'

She tried not to flinch.

'And what a smile. A shining specimen of Aryan perfection.' He grinned, then looked sternly at Ernst. 'A good counterbalance for a stocky bastard like you.'

Ernst scratched his sideburn. There was an awkward pause before the words sprang out from somewhere inside Herta, just as she had practised reciting them over and over at bride school.

'Our children will be blue-eyed and blond, Herr Kommandant. The hope of the Fatherland lies in the next generation.'

There. It could not be unsaid. Laughter spread like a wave of relief through the crowd.

Across the other side of the room, Vati raised his glass and called for the attention of the crowd. 'A toast to the bride and groom. May they live out their lives in happiness and peace. *Prost!*'

Himmler held up his own glass. *'Heil Hitler!'*

Everyone followed suit, clinking glasses and shouting, *'Heil Hitler!'* Everyone except Vati. Out of the corner of her eye Herta saw Mutti glaring at him, silently urging him not to make a scene. Vati mumbled something and brought the champagne to his lips, finishing the glass in one shot. She watched as he sidled up to a table for a refill, gulping that one down too. In between smiles and small talk, Herta kept an eye on him. Despite the alcohol rising to her head, she could see through the hairline crack that appeared in her father's mask, revealing a raging fury coiled inside. He looked up and caught her staring at him, her eyes begging him to behave.

Herta left Ernst with Herr Stresemann, his supervisor, to discuss the latest techniques in ornithological specimen preparation. She joined Vati, who was seated on a stool in the corner, brooding and silent. An unruly strand of grey hair fell across his forehead. He stood abruptly.

'I have something for you,' he whispered, and made his way over to the back of the hall, slipping through a small doorway. She followed him, all her senses heightened like an animal desperately trying to find a way out of a trap it has fallen into. She found herself wedged in a narrow corridor with her father, whose face appeared strangely animated. A bubble of saliva formed at the edge of his mouth as he spoke.

'First and foremost,' he whispered, 'you must promise me that you won't breathe a word of this to Mutti.'

She nodded, unable to fathom what he wanted to hide from the woman he had always worshipped.

'Many years ago when you were still a child, I was out in the garden taking photographs of some early blossom. You ran past, on your way to one of your jaunts into the forest.' His forehead became a knot of veins. 'I had always wondered where you disappeared to after school, so that day I decided to follow.' He rummaged for something inside his jacket. 'You stopped at a clearing and, to my delight, as I watched through the branches of a giant oak, I saw Ernst seated on the ground beside little Margarete. She was surrounded by a storm of wildflowers, her wheelchair nowhere to be seen. I knew he must have carried her there himself and was waiting for you to join them. And soon enough, you came running through the trees.'

Herta felt her life, which was just beginning to open, instantly fold back on itself.

'I'd never seen you so happy, huddled there on the ground, the sun pouring through a filigree of lacy leaves, shining down on the three of you. I just couldn't let myself lose that moment of pure innocence.'

His hand shook as he fished a small photo out from the left pocket of his jacket. It was faded, the edges torn. He handed it over as if he were serving up his heart for her to devour.

'This is my real wedding gift to you both.'

She reached out to take it. A fleeting moment of wonder caught her before she looked up. Vati was staring at her.

Without a word, Herta stuffed the photo into the bodice of her wedding dress and rushed back inside the reception hall, leaning against the wall to gather her thoughts. As she watched the crush of guests chatting loudly while they ate and drank, she saw Vati make his way to the entrance. He looked so pale. A young man in black uniform was leaning against the doorjamb, and Herta could see a cold smile creep across his face. She edged her way over to them, close enough to overhear what the officer was saying.

'You must be very proud your beautiful daughter has now become the wife of an SS man, Herr Völz? She is the image of perfection.'

Vati did not answer. He stood there, daring the officer to look into his eyes and all that they held. Instead, the youth shrugged and offered him a cigarette. Vati took one and lit up, breathing in a deep lungful of smoke before stepping outside.

PART II

CHAPTER 9

Basement held the world for me in those early days, when He first brought me here. I had no need to travel. A huge arm had swept across the mountains and the shores, trawling the depths of forests and oceans, bringing narwhals, armadillos, zebras and hummingbirds to surround me. Some were bloated from the journey, others shrunken and wretched, but they all watched me with unseeing eyes.

Shepherd's role was to restore us from these repulsive caricatures of ourselves, so we might reflect the true poetry of Wild. He was an artist, paying as much attention to His model as Michelangelo did to his David. (Guard got that one right on Jeopardy *last month.) He stretched our skins, moulded noses and muzzles, preserving the elegance of life with a steady, dissecting hand. His gentle breath held the essence of love; His touch turned a stiffened, wiry carcass into a work of beauty. His skills went far beyond just counting teeth or* measuring limbs; it was His carnal knowledge of Wild that Shepherd brought to our lumps of skin and bone. No, He was not crude. He prepared us for the theatre of Glass with a deep understanding of character – orchestrating the sluggish indolence of sloth (Folivora), with its strange three claws, or helping choreograph the static combat of savage lion (Panthera leo) and docile antelope (Hippotragus equinus).

He cast his spell on us all, crafting an eternal mood on display for the world. We continue His legacy, showing our Truth through this staged spectacle. I see the reaction every day in the eyes of Visitors, my very presence a magnet for their imagination. Each brings their own story to me, trusting my silent listening. They spill out their chaotic, confused lives before the altar of Glass. Some linger, absorbing this counterfeit wilderness lovingly, connecting with the simulacrum of creaturely life. Others rush past as quickly as they can, squeamish over death on display.

For months, I lingered in Basement, in the land of Temporary Storage, gathering dust, until they dragged me out to live in my new Home. I never chose to be Immortal, laid bare to strangers staring at me with awe, revulsion or voyeuristic fascination. They impose all manner of narratives on me. But none seem to know about Him. I wonder where He is now, my young Shepherd. With the passing of the years our Story has been lost, and with its disappearance I have changed. Once I was Storyteller of His verve, His insatiable lust for adventure; now I am mere Decoration. I have become a kind of tombstone whose inscription has worn away with the passing sands.

I no longer belong to Him. I am Guard's and Smalls' and Girl's and Cleaner's and Jerkoff's. How to explain myself to Visitors, from inside this suspended time? Of the past, but not belonging there anymore. In Glass, we cast no shadows; freed from our inner flesh, we are masters of our own world. No predators, no cages. All our life, we struggle against this final silence and yet, when we cross beyond the mortal agony, we are left breathless.

Our eternity is based on a strict timetable:

10 am – 4.30 pm, Monday to Friday
10 am – 5 pm, Weekends and Holidays

When Museum is Closed and Guard gets to rest, we are forgotten. I live on First Floor. Directly across Street, beyond Window, is a strange Glass that holds grey squares, behind one of which sits Woman. Woman's timetable is different from ours. She is on display there from 9 am – 5 pm, Monday to Friday. Guard looks at her a lot, but she doesn't seem to notice him. I am jealous she can still move her limbs, although most of the time she sits facing out, staring up at the clouds as she sharpens her talons, or rubs blood on her lips.

I wonder if the Woman whom Shepherd spoke about sometimes had similar markings. I would have liked to have met her one day. Her name was Herta, scientific name H. Völz. I am curious to know if she was as beautiful as He described – pale fur, blue eyes and a lithe and graspable waist. Even though they hadn't seen each other since they were almost-grown pups, He said He would always love her. Love is

a foreign language they speak of to me – Visitors and Guard.
Over the years I have tried to understand its sounds, the yawps,
howls and growls they have displayed. I imagine it might be
like the rains returning after weeks of dry.

His Past emerged in snippets and I tried to piece His Story
together over time, waiting patiently for Him to unfurl the
map of Life He held rolled up in His heart. But He made it
difficult, determined to follow His instincts of Order, in which
everything had its Proper Place. His species are such deter-
mined taxonomists. I think by now H. Völz must have been
placed in Permanent Storage a while ago. From what He told
me, she sounded as if she might have been one Specimen that
He could not catch. I suppose He was frustrated He would
never catalogue Her in His Book, the one in which He wrote
our names beside our numbers and descriptions. I peeked at
my entry once when we were still down in Temporary Storage:

Ailuropoda melanoleuca
Bamboo forest of Kham, Eastern Tibet [May 13th, 1931]

One male juvenile. The entire underpart badly abraded.
Shoulder height 35 cm, round head, stocky body, and
short tail. Distinctive markings – limbs, eyes, ears, and
shoulders are all black and rest of the body is white. An
enlarged shoulder and neck region, along with a smaller
back end, produces an ambling gait. A *baculum* (bony
rod in soft tissue of penis) is present. In other bears it is
straight and forwardly directed, while in giant pandas it
is S-shaped and backwardly directed. Skull has a large

sagittal crest, wider and deeper than other bears, resulting in powerful jaws. The molars and premolars are wider and flatter too, with extensive ridges and cusps for grinding tough bamboo. A notable feature is an extra opposable thumb-like digit on the hand.

I'm sure He caught me looking, because He quickly placed the Book facedown, its pages still open like the wings of a dead bird whose feathers ruffled in the throes of its dying.

Mother says one day we will all go Home. Of course, she is not my real mother, although she cares for me here in Glass as well as can be expected. She promised that before we leave, she will teach me to walk again. The clay that He replaced my metatarsal bones with is so stiff. On that day, when we line up to board the same boat that brought us here, the dur bya *from other Glass countries will rise up and fly homewards, although I pray they will not fall from the sky on their stiffened wings.*

Behind me is Horizon. I watched while they created the Heavens and the Earth under His guidance. Shepherd wasn't the one to paint the World, but He directed the Creation and saw that it was good. Some days I will my clay feet to turn around so that I might face the Purple Mountains, my glassy eyes aching to see the sky over Wild. But they will not budge, and I am forced to gaze at Exit. Day and night take turns chasing each other on an endless Merry-go-Round. A Small once brought one of those in to show me, with gaily painted ponies, tigers and giraffes racing each other in a circle as the music played.

CHAPTER 10

September 1937

Afternoon turned to evening as Herta waited for Ernst to appear in the doorway of their first-floor apartment at Hohenzollerndamm 36. Her husband – it felt so strange to call him that – was still at the laboratory. Klaus, who had been with her since the day she found him mewling outside Frau Lila's apartment, kept her company as she played the flute. The cat was her greatest comfort of late, and her most trusted confidant. There were things she could say to Klaus that she would never tell any human being. Who in their right mind could ever believe there was no soul behind feline eyes?

Herta had been made to understand, by those in Ernst's orbit, that as the wife of an SS officer she could not become a professional flautist. In the end, all that time at the Conservatory, studying for and excelling in her exams, had been for nothing. Even so, she was determined to keep up her practice as her own small act of rebellion. She had been playing Debussy's *Syrinx* this week, returning to the piece her father taught her as a child. As she sounded the final note of the solo, Ernst arrived home. He threw his bags on the floor and gave her a peck on the cheek, glancing over her shoulder at the sheet music spread out on the stand.

'That's funny. A syrinx is the anatomical term for the voicebox of a bird. It's their lower larynx.' He sank into his armchair. 'Who is Debussy?'

'He was the most wonderful French composer who ever lived, but they've banned his music now. Some say the real reason it is regarded as "degenerate" is because he was married to a Jew.'

Ernst kept talking as if he hadn't heard her answer. 'It's quite fascinating, you know. Songbirds have the largest and most developed syrinx of all creatures. It has a very different structure from ours, so they can produce several sounds at once.' He took some tobacco from a tin and placed it in his palm, rolling his pipe in a spiral over the top. 'Actually, I have an excellent specimen of an American mockingbird at the laboratory. Brooky gave it to me as a gift. He told me it used to be Thomas Jefferson's pet, and called it Dicky – such a silly name for a bird. But I never believed a word that Brooky uttered, the old soak.'

Ernst checked the draw for blockage, then lit a match and teased the top gently. He tamped the tobacco down and relit the pipe, puffing on it distractedly. A waft of smoke made its way across to Herta.

'Anyway,' he said, 'mockingbirds are brilliant at mimicry, stealing songs from others. Remind me to bring old Dicky home to show you one day.'

'Of course, darling. That would be wonderful.' Stifling a cough, she forced herself to smile.

Her husband and his unlovely specimens. What she didn't tell him was that the true inspiration for Debussy's piece was the incessant drive in men to collect what was well beyond their grasp. Vati had told her the story as a child: how the lustful god Pan fell in love with the beautiful virgin nymph Syrinx and wanted her all for himself. But his love went unrequited. In order to avoid Pan's amorous pursuits, she ran away and turned herself into hollow reeds. Determined to keep her honour, she hid from him in the marshes. When his frustrated breath blew across the reeds, though, he was enchanted by the sound of the sweet, liquid song that seemed to answer him. He cut down the reeds to make pan pipes. When he discovered that Syrinx had been among them, he was deeply saddened, but comforted knowing he would have her next to him for eternity. Some days Herta wished she could be like Syrinx, hide away from all men, shake herself loose from this city.

She placed the flute carefully back in its case. The harmonica she had saved up to buy Ernst as a wedding present lay on the shelf, untouched. What possessed her to think he might play it? He'd never shown the slightest interest in music. Even when they were children he would pick up a book while Herta practised flute. Karl May's adventure stories had been far more interesting to Ernst than Mozart's *Eine Kleine Nachtmusik*.

'I'm hungry as a wolf,' he said.

Herta went to the kitchen and turned on the stove. 'Dinner's almost ready.'

She tucked some loose strands of hair into her headband and tied her apron around her waist. As she uncovered a plate of drumsticks, Klaus rubbed his side against her legs.

'Mmm, those look good.' Ernst came up behind her, kneading her buttocks with his strong hands. He untied the strings of her apron, kicking Klaus aside as he whispered in her ear. 'You'd better be careful, my wife. You look so delicious tonight, I might eat you up instead.'

'Go wash up!' She wriggled away from him.

While he was in the bathroom, she started frying the chicken, throwing a small scrap into a bowl for the cat. When Ernst returned, he sat down in his usual chair at the table, placed an embroidered napkin on his lap and waited to be served. He lit a cigarette and took a quick puff, resting it on the pewter Liberty Bell ashtray brought back as a souvenir from Philadelphia. He had promised to take Herta on a visit to America one day, said she would love it there, with department stores as fancy as Hertie, only much bigger. And he would show her around Philadelphia's attractions: the Academy of Natural Sciences, the beautiful zoo and the grand main hall of 30th Street Station.

After a few minutes, during which Klaus nibbled at chicken scraps, Herta placed a drumstick, some sauerkraut and a slice of Limburger cheese on rye onto Ernst's plate. She went to serve herself, but by the time she returned to the table with her own meal, he had almost finished eating. One thing was certain: there were never any niceties at dinnertime with Ernst. Food was something that had to be devoured. She spooned out some more chicken for him and he stripped the flesh from another drumstick, chewing loudly on the gristle before spitting out the remains. He bit into the slender thighbone and sucked out the soft marrow, crunching on the ends until only a mound of white splinters remained on his plate. As she watched him, Herta pushed her food from one side of the plate to the other with her fork.

Ernst held up a wishbone between them. She tugged on one end of the scant bone and broke off the larger piece, then closed her eyes and made a wish.

Ernst got up from the table. 'As if the fused collarbone of a bird can magically bring us what we want.'

His napkin dropped to the floor and Herta bent to pick it up. If only she was brave enough to tell him what she had wished for.

After clearing the table, she washed the dishes and boiled the kettle. She joined Ernst, who was already seated in the parlour, and placed a cup of strong black coffee on the small table beside him. She added a dollop of milk and stirred in some sugar. Reaching across to the shelf, she chose a record to play, hoping to lift the mood. The wonderful Hans Albers warbled the song that had been so popular back in '33: 'Mein Gorilla hat 'ne Villa im Zoo'.

Ernst sat in his armchair, shielding himself from the music with his newspaper as the record squealed its tinny tune:

> My gorilla's villa's in the zoo
> My gorilla lives a happy life, it's true
> If anybody bugs him he gets angry and he spits
> He's joyful he knows nothing about politics
> His wife keeps silent if he wants to kiss her
> And if he wants it, be sure gorilla will-a.

He peeked over the front page of the newspaper, which reported that Japanese warplanes had bombed Canton.

'This world is becoming unbearable,' he said. 'This is sure to add complications to our expedition. By the way, there's an article here about the *Entarte Kunst*, that degenerate art exhibition in Munich you were telling me about. You know they're getting over 20,000 visitors a day?'

Herta was ignoring him by now, her good cheer restored by the music. 'Will you put down that Nazi rag and come dance with your bride!' she trilled, shimmying around his chair, trying to lure him away from the day's news.

Ernst had never been an enthusiastic dancer. Back in Waltershausen, dance school was where they had both learnt to waltz and glide together, although some of their compatriots never got beyond stepping on toes. It all seemed so simple to Herta, the rules and proceedings laid out for them in advance by the instructors. Even so, she remembered how she felt her insides crumble the first night at dance school as she and her friends had stood huddled together against the wall, waiting for a boy to invite each of them onto the dance floor.

'Here comes Freddy,' Gretchen had said, giggling. The others moved aside, leaving Herta directly in the line of fire of a pimply youth.

Herta stood like a statue as Freddy waited before her. The ensuing silence was broken by Gretchen, who whispered instructions to Herta to hold out her hand. She reached out reluctantly, and the boy hesitated as he placed his fingers under her palm, which rested there like a dead fish. In his haste to kiss her, in the way they had been taught to do when asking a girl to dance, he accidentally slobbered over her wrist. She withdrew quickly, as if she had been bitten, wiping her hand on the linen pocket of her pinafore. Her friends, carefully watching Freddy's every move, drove the poor boy across to the other side of the room with their laughter alone. He was swallowed back into the folds of his fraternity, who rallied around him to hide his mortal suffering.

These lessons of etiquette read like hieroglyphics to young Ernst Schäfer, he had later confessed to her. Feeble versions of Sturm und Drang. Having witnessed Freddy's melodramatic retreat in a cloud of abject humiliation, Ernst took the opportunity to conquer his nervous unrest and leapt over to where Herta was. She was surprised to see him standing before her, and her girlfriends tittered, covering their mouths to exchange gossipy squeals. He looked as light as air, but Herta's feet seemed chained to the earth. He bowed slightly. One must be a gentleman, or at least make a show of it, the dance instructor had told the boys. She held out her hand in return and felt the rest of her life unfold with the touch of his fingertips.

'Would you care to dance, Fräulein Völz?' he asked, smiling at her.

Without answering, she followed him. As the band struck up, they both performed the steps of the waltz they had learnt as a group only an hour earlier.

He spoke softly. 'We are one in the other, Herta. Always have been.'

An invisible flame hovered over them. She sensed the urgency in his voice, this boy she had always known.

'Why are you telling me this now, Ernst?'

'All shall be clear soon. Birds of prey do not sing.'

She found out the reason for his confession later that week. Her family was invited over to the Schäfer home for an afternoon tea of strudel and lebkuchen, as part of a small farewell for Ernst. He was being sent away to boarding school. After the announcement, Herta was seated on a sofa in the parlour, pretending to read a book so no one would suspect how upset she was that Ernst was leaving, when she overheard Herr Schäfer chatting to her father in the hallway.

'There's no taming him.'

'Albert, have patience,' Vati said.

'He's just turned fourteen and still behaves like a petulant child. Sending him to Heidelberg is the right thing to do, for him, as well as for us. The boy needs strict discipline. I only wish he had a head for numbers; at least that way I could have guided him. I expected Ernst to take over the factory when he was older. I'm so bitterly disappointed. I've built that business from scratch, and once I am gone it will all go to ruin.'

'Your business is nothing to sneeze at, my friend. And Ernst is young, and may still surprise you.'

Herta looked up from her book to find Ernst standing in front of her.

'Now do you understand?' he whispered.

'What's to understand?'

'They don't want me back in Waltershausen, Herta. They say I will only be at the school for a year, but I know what my trajectory is from there. They will force me to stay till I get my Abitur, and then who knows where I'll end up.'

He sat down beside her and placed his hand on hers. She tried to cover up the book in her lap.

'What's this?'

'Nothing,' she said, sliding it to the other side of the sofa.

'Show me!' He laughed, reaching to snatch it away from her.

'No! Ernst, it's private.'

Even all these years later, Herta could still remember her embarrassment as he opened the cover and saw the heading decorated with sketches of flowers and birds: *Mädchen tagebuch*, her girlhood journal. He turned the page to find a life-size drawing of the feather of a rare skylark they had found together three summers earlier. The next few pages held her sketches of Ernst's zoology collection: tadpoles, the intricate lacework inside a bird's bone. The journal was filled with these testaments to the love they shared for nature. Just as he was about to close it, he turned to a picture of himself, drawn so lifelike on the last page. Beside it, she had written, *I will always love him*. He looked up and placed his lips to hers, a fluttery kiss lighter than angel's wings.

They heard their fathers entering the room. Herta jumped up quickly, grabbing her book from his hands.

'*Auf wiedersehen*, Ernst,' she said, curtsying. 'And good luck in Heidelberg.' She turned and walked away.

Shuffling around on the carpet now, in a quick waltz to please his rosy-cheeked bride, Ernst light-heartedly asked Herta what she had wished for over dinner. Klaus spun around beside them, chasing his own tail.

'No! Don't tell me. Let me guess.' The music was making him feel joyful again. 'You have a birthday coming up soon and you would like a string of pearls.'

She didn't answer. Her chest was pounding, filled with a mixture of yearning and dread.

'Wrong?' He smiled at her. 'A fox stole, perhaps?'

Herta stopped dancing and walked over to the gramophone, scratching the record as she lifted the steel needle off it. She turned to face him. 'I wished that you might help me find Margarete.'

CHAPTER 11

September 1937

It was hard to kill perfectly.

Feathers shone under the morning sun that poured in from the window. Ernst sat in his study surrounded by piles of papers and books, cupping his aching head in his hand, the skins of twenty species of bird spread across his desk. He'd been up all night cataloguing the tiny corpses, unpacking them one by one from wooden crates he'd brought from the laboratory, cradling each specimen like a newborn. The collection was huge, but he needed to get through it quickly in order to finish up his thesis by November, so he could focus entirely on preparations for the trip. They were hoping to leave early in the new year.

Since that first meeting with Himmler more than a year before, Ernst's willingness to be associated with the

Ahnenerbe had abated as he watched his colleagues at Berlin University refuse to take him seriously. The ludicrous conspiracies doing the rounds, that he was at the behest of the lunatics running the *Ahnenerbe,* were slurs on his professional integrity and reputation. He made it clear from the outset that he would not compromise the rigour of his science for anyone. Perhaps the others were simply jealous; scientists were, by necessity as well as nature, competitive.

Leaving the specimens on his desk, Ernst went to get ready for the day ahead. He was dressed and had finished breakfast well before Herta woke up. Ernst had spent most of their two months of married life studying or planning for Tibet. Herta kept herself busy, though, filling her days adding a woman's touch to the apartment, sewing new lace curtains and trying out recipes from the leather-bound book Mutti had given her, passed down through three generations.

The fiery eroticism of their first month was already waning. Marriage seemed to reverse a woman's desire so rapidly. He couldn't understand why she held back, telling him it was too painful or that she was tired or, worst of all, simply grimacing when he rolled on top of her in bed, as if his hairy leg against her thigh belonged to a tarantula. Admittedly, he'd been so preoccupied with his thesis lately that there wasn't much time left for romance. His heart wasn't in academia anymore; the qualification was something he needed to get out of the way. He much preferred channelling his energies into preparing detailed maps for the expedition. He knew how to navigate the route through China into Eastern Tibet far better than he could make his way through the streets of Berlin.

Tibet was a land that had always held a strange fascination for Westerners as a mystical utopia, Shambhala, Agartha, as far back as the Rosicrucians in the seventeenth century. Madame Blavatsky, with her strange theosophical ideas of a hidden master race in the mountains, claimed she had lived there for seven years. It was all lies. Most of those who purported to understand Tibetan society, privy to the so-called secrets of its ancient spiritual knowledge, held one thing in common – unlike Ernst, they had never been there.

Seated at his desk, he pushed his pen across the page in a frenzy, filling his notebook with illegible spidery scrawl. When he referred to 'uncharted territory', he meant *terra nullius* in every sense of the word, from the geography and biology of the land to the ethnographic characteristics of the people. His plan was almost ready to present to the *Deutsche Forschungsgemeinschaft*, the German Research Foundation, for some additional funding. He still didn't want to rely solely on the *Ahnenerbe*. He had put together a team of the finest young scientists: Edmund Geer, a botanist and hunter with a keen talent for logistics; Karl Wienert, an expert geophysicist and geologist; and Ernst Krause, an entomologist with a passion for wasps, who could double up as the expedition's photographer and filmmaker. At thirty-eight, Krause would be the old man of the team. And, of course, there was Bruno.

*

That evening, Bruno sat on the sofa at Ernst's apartment, long legs stretched out as he puffed on his pipe; at a height of six feet and two inches, Bruno Beger towered over most people he met. Klaus rubbed against him, purring for attention.

A news bulletin on the radio hummed in the background, reporting that Hermann Göring had just given a speech in Stuttgart. He was calling for Jews in Germany to pay for any damages incurred as a result of a threatened boycott against the Fatherland.

Ernst looked up from his papers and maps of Tibet. Herta brought in a tray laden with cakes and biscuits and started pouring the tea when Bruno lashed out and kicked Klaus, trying to get him out from under his feet. She hurriedly placed the teapot down, knocking over the cup she had just filled, while the terrified cat raced across to the window ledge and clambered up the lace curtains, his bad leg dangling like a second tail.

Herta mopped up the steaming liquid as the men continued their heated discussion.

'Why do you care what anyone thinks?' Bruno said. 'As long as we get some of the funding for the expedition, let them believe whatever nonsense they want.'

Ernst's colleague was the exemplary son of a well-respected Heidelberg family that staunchly avoided racial mixing. No mongrel blood had ever been sown into the Beger clan. Nordic prowess and strength shone from each of their tall, wiry, golden-haired specimens. At university, Bruno had often gone to listen to the eminent visiting scholar Hans Günther speak about racial ethnology. Even now, when he spoke of Günther's lectures to Ernst, his eyes lit up. Bruno had decided he wanted to pursue a degree in anthropology and moved to Berlin to further his studies in the field. He set about acquiring the intricate and exacting research skills of anthropological measurement, together with mathematical expertise, to analyse his findings, and aimed to develop a taxonomy of human types and to highlight the perils of miscegenation.

'It's our reputation at stake, Bruno. No one will ever take us seriously again if we are seen to throw our lot in with these cranks. And turning a blind eye to the *Ahnenerbe*'s wishful untruths, or laughing them off as a crazy fringe, means risking that they will eventually become accepted into the mainstream of modern science.'

As he spoke, Herta tidied up the tray and quickly served them.

'Thank you, darling,' Ernst said. He took a sip of tea.

Bruno leaned in closer. 'You're exaggerating, my friend; you're just getting cold feet. Don't get so hysterical. It's a passing phase. Besides, Hörbiger was a true genius. We should learn some lessons from him on how to curry favour with the public.'

'What on earth are you talking about?'

Across the room, Herta stepped up on a stool and reached for Klaus. 'Here, kitty,' she called, trying to coax him down before he shredded the curtains.

'Get that pathetic creature out of here, Herta,' Bruno growled. 'We have important matters to discuss.'

Herta swore under her breath and stepped down.

'Ha!' Bruno slapped his hand on his thigh. 'Let me guess. Was that directed at me or your defective cat? Why don't you put the pathetic creature out of its misery?'

'Shut up, Bruno. Don't speak to her like that.' Ernst felt it his duty to shield Herta from his friend's ugly taunts. He climbed onto the stool and grabbed Klaus by the scruff of his neck, handing him to Herta like a piece of dirty laundry. Hugging the cat, she retreated into the bedroom.

'I love it!' Bruno bellowed. 'The great hunter can't control either his animals or his wife.'

Ernst, refusing to rise to the bait, sat down again.

Bruno continued their discussion, unfazed.

'Listen, Ernst. Hörbiger wasn't bothered with trying to convince the academic establishment of the veracity of World Ice Theory, *Glazial-Kosmogonie*, call it whatever you want. He simply targeted the masses. It's a brilliant model, and true scientists like you and me should use it more to publicise our own theories.'

Ernst listened, appalled. He knew his friend was ambitious; Bruno had joined the SS in 1934 as a promising *Rassenkunde*, or racial anthropology expert, and being invited to join the Tibet expedition was perhaps the most exciting moment of Bruno's life – probably even more so than the birth of his daughter. It was a windfall for the twenty-six-year-old; there could be no better way of establishing himself as a pre-eminent racial scientist than cultivating relationships with mentors the likes of Himmler.

'Hörbiger used scientific terminology to embellish what was essentially a fairytale,' Bruno said. 'He wasn't the first to propagate an entire theory on a vision that came to him. Who wouldn't be captivated by the notion? "Eureka" is as old as the hills. Look at Archimedes and Galileo.'

'You've gone mad, Bruno. You, a respected man of science. I bent over backwards to get you on board for this trip.'

Ernst hadn't told Bruno how at first Himmler insisted Edmund Kiss from the *Ahnenerbe* join the expedition. Ernst refused to have the lunatic novelist and pseudo-archaeologist on his team, and stuck his neck out for his friend. In his book *The Sun Gate of Tiwanaku*, Kiss wrote about an ancient city in the Andes. He was convinced it was built by Nordic ancestors and collapsed during a cataclysm that was set off by a falling icy moon.

'What you are telling me, then, is that you are willing to accept the doctrines of a man who has a dream about a cosmic "truth" in which the moon is made of ice?' Ernst said. 'And the basic building block of the universe, the atom, has been replaced by the venerated ice crystal? *Scheisse!* The moon might as well be made of cheese, and we should all bow down to the god of Camembert. Himmler and his cronies from the *Ahnenerbe* read no books other than those of Blavatsky, or this Hörbiger-themed trash.'

'Thank you for the fascinating lecture, Ernst, but I'm telling you, Himmler did us all a huge favour.' Bruno smirked.

'How so?'

'He helped get rid of Jewish science. Cleaned the corridors and lecture halls of vermin like Einstein and his stinking Theory of Relativity. For too long they have been held up as remarkable scientists. Jews even jumped on top of brilliant German academics such as Schrödinger and Heisenberg, twisting their creative genius about quantum mechanics into absolute drivel.'

'It's one thing to hate Jews, but this is a separate issue. How can we turn a blind eye to the idea that the entire universe is made up of ice?' Ernst stood up and took a book down from the shelf, handing it to his friend. 'Have you read this?'

Bruno looked at the cover, flipping through the first few pages. '*Wirbelstürme, Wetterstürze, Hagelkatastrophen und Marskanal-Verdoppelungen*. Hurricanes, weather crashes, hail catastrophes and Mars canals.'

'He sure couldn't have found a catchier title, could he?' Ernst snorted.

'You can laugh as much as you want, Ernst, but I believe it sold very well. Hörbiger's public lectures were always packed out. And he wrote a novel that was made into a movie. The man was a master of publicity and self-promotion.'

'Do you know Hörbiger was a steam-engine designer, not a scientist?'

Bruno laughed and threw the book back at his friend. 'Some would argue that you are a hunter, dear Ernst, and not a zoologist.'

'How dare you compare me to such a shyster? Ice moons, ice planets, global ice ether. And that insane theory of an ancient war between fire and ice.'

'Hitler doesn't seem to think so poorly of Hörbiger and his theories. I remember reading somewhere that he believes the reason academic scientists hesitated to accept World Ice Theory was because, and I quote, "Men do not wish to know."'

'I don't care! I think it's all got completely out of hand.'

Bruno lowered his voice. 'You'd better be careful who you say that to, Ernst. I am your dearest friend, but others cannot be trusted when it comes to passing on, shall we say, delicate information. It's not worth the risk nowadays.'

Maybe Bruno was right. What did it matter if the official aim of their expedition was to search for the descendants of Aryan forebears? If the public believed in World Ice Theory, well, good for them. But no matter what Ernst thought privately of all this nonsense, if it meant in the end that the government was going to subsidise his expedition, he should not jeopardise this once-in-a-lifetime opportunity to map and photograph a new landscape.

Bruno yawned and rose from his chair. 'I'd better be getting home to Hildegard. Hopefully the baby's asleep by now and she's tidied up the infernal mess at home. I wish she could have spent some time at that excellent bride school Herta attended. You can really feel the difference when a woman isn't focused on her man.'

Ernst handed Bruno his hat and coat, which had fallen on the floor during the fracas with the cat. He could have

112

sworn there was a whiff of cat pee on his friend as he walked out onto the landing.

Ernst fumbled with the rusty deadbolt and locked the door. Herta came out of the bedroom and made her way to the kitchen.

'Is Klaus all right?' he asked, his voice a little shaky.

A pot of soup was bubbling away on the stove, the air fuggy with the earthy smell. He watched as she sat down, ribbons of potato peel strewn across the wooden chopping board in front of her.

Hadn't he shown Herta how deep his feelings for her ran? Asking him to use his connections to try to find the whereabouts of Margarete was like placing a live grenade in his hands. Yet Herta had held out such hope. He envied her unwavering faith in people. What she didn't seem to understand was that if he dared do what he promised, to start asking about an invalid relative, they would all soon be tossed into the void of history. Every few weeks he heard about another SS colleague vanishing, and shiny new recruits taking their place, no questions asked. Sacrificing himself and his family for the sake of finding out what happened to Margarete was unthinkable, but telling that to Herta might cost him his marriage. No, he would continue to deflect her questions by pretending he was covertly making enquiries.

Ernst pulled up a chair. 'Let's talk about your sister.'

CHAPTER 12

October 1937

Klaus was almost dead. If only there were some way to bring him back from the brink; the poor cat had been ailing for weeks, off his food and sleeping most of the day, his breathing punctuated by tiny whimpers. Herta stroked his matted fur, sitting vigil on the rug where he lay so still, curled up on himself. She sang lullabies and offered up tiny morsels of minced-up chicken Ernst would have gladly eaten instead.

Herta watched the creature slowly fade away. She imagined Ernst would have already wrung the poor cat's neck if she had allowed it. He'd say that was the mercy of a hunter's heart, unable to understand how his kind and caring wife could be so cruel to an animal, prolong its suffering for her own selfish inability to lose its love. This business of dying was lengthy.

What Herta didn't know was that Ernst was plotting to sneak the wretched creature out, pretend it had wandered off and become lost during its final efforts to return to nature, dying peacefully under a bush. But he soon realised that was no solution. Herta would be inconsolable and distraught. She'd probably end up searching the neighbourhood day and night, calling the mangy beast. It would be better to wait it out until both cat and its mistress were ready to let go of each other. Ernst sometimes wished his young bride might show as much devotion to him as she did to her beloved, moth-eaten creature, lavishing attention on it with every flicker of movement it made.

Eventually, by the end of the week, when Herta had fallen into a deep sleep after the day's vigil, it happened – the cat, too tired to purr or meow anymore, took its final gasp. It was late at night. Ernst carefully wrapped the limp creature inside a coat and snuck out through the back stairs, so as not to wake his exhausted wife. The air was chilly. He headed towards the zoo on foot, a half-hour's walk.

Once he reached the laboratory, he worked quickly, placing the body onto a steel dissection table, where Klaus looked peaceful for the first time in weeks. Ernst picked up a scalpel and made a midline incision from the throat down along the belly, careful not to puncture the turgid intestines, a messy and odious business he would rather not have to deal with at this hour. The body was still warm, which made it harder to work on than the usual frozen carcasses, but there was no time to lose.

Herta's birthday was in a fortnight, and the hide needed to be salted for at least five days before being sent off to the tanner. He could already imagine her face when he presented her with the surprise gift: her beloved Klaus, preserved as an eternal pet. Meanwhile, he would build a false kitty grave in the rose garden downstairs, where Herta would be sure to want to hold a small memorial service.

Ernst worked painstakingly on the cat all night. How to invoke the appearance of life in a lifeless body? Taxidermy was the closest he would ever get to performing magic; his job was to animate the inanimate. He needed to ensure the features and pose were just right for Herta to forget that Klaus was no longer in this world. Ernst had witnessed cruel oddities among specimens in museums around the world. Like the two raccoons placed in a mating position, on display at the Royal Geographic Society when Ernst gave a lecture there in 1934. It had been hard for him to keep a straight face standing at the podium.

The salt stung the cuts on his fingers. A series of wax models stood on a shelf above his desk, a gift from the artist Friedrich Ziegler, who supplied the major universities with teaching tools for the study of embryology. He had sent them from his Freiberg studio just before he died. The captions were inscribed in Ziegler's own handwriting: *The Development of the Chick Embryo*. The first was labelled *Primitive Streak Stage – 16 hours*, and it reminded Ernst of a shallow flesh wound, as if someone had taken a stick and scraped it along the surface of a tiny lake. The next model showed the *Headfold Stage – 20 hours*, and Ernst couldn't help but think how much it looked like the secret haven tucked away between Herta's thighs. He ran his finger down the groove in the wax model, leaving traces of salt along its fold.

He remembered the time after his first expedition with Dolan in 1931, when he was back in Philadelphia for a while, working down in the basement of the Academy of Natural Sciences. The juvenile panda's head rested on the table as it stared at him from eyeless sockets. Ernst was so behind in his work, with thousands of specimens from the trip still waiting to be labelled. Thirty-three cases, which might end up destroyed due to mould, were still waiting to be checked. Hopefully he would be able to salvage something from that shipment. These Americans and their fickle ways; he would never understand them.

Stepping away from his desk, Ernst had strolled down an aisle that was lined on either side by yellow filing cabinets. He pulled open a wide metal drawer, reached in and gently unfolded some crumpled tissue paper. Ernst uncapped his pen and held the lid between his teeth as he wrote the words *Bat Foetus* onto a label. He tied it to one of the wings, thinking how much the developing creature looked like a tiny, fragile angel. They were such exquisite specimens, works of art in their own right. A strange beauty lay in death. In the next drawer, resting on a bed of cotton wool, were the tiny bones of the baby panda's feet, yellow as an old man's teeth.

Back at the table, Ernst had rummaged in a bowl filled with what looked like lentils, only he felt these orbs staring back at him. He chose two glass eyes and set them down. These were the most important part of a specimen. With their perpetual gaze, the eyes transformed what was otherwise just a carcass into a thing of wonder. He fixed them into the panda's sockets and, almost immediately, felt as if the creature had come back to life. He found himself sharing secrets with the dead animal as it watched him.

Ernst's head had started throbbing at that point, a wave of nausea rising up. Fatigue blunted his brain, or maybe it was the formaldehyde fumes; the ventilation in the basement wasn't as good as back home. He needed some fresh air. Ernst pushed his chair back and rushed towards the door, almost tripping over the thylacine specimen the curator had been working on. It was to go on display in time for Roosevelt's visit to the museum. The thylacine laughed at him with a fixed grin as he steadied it, patting its wiry fur, which was still a little wet with arsenic.

Thankfully, the fumes in his Berlin Zoo laboratory weren't as pungent. Ernst began to skin Klaus, hoping to remove the hide in one piece, in the same way he had taught the natives on those trips with Brooky to the East. It was important to scrape away all traces of flesh and tissue. As he gently pulled Klaus' penis backwards out of its sheath, it popped out, a long pink member Ernst wouldn't have credited with belonging to an old tomcat. When the skin was finally removed from the bloody carcass, he sprinkled it with more salt to remove all moisture and oil.

It was almost dawn when Ernst headed home to get some sleep. He was woken several hours later by the plaintive sounds of Herta calling Klaus. Before he even had a chance to pull on his slippers, she came racing into the bedroom.

'I can't find him anywhere, Ernst!' Her face was pale, her hair flying wild. 'I left him on the blanket by the heater last night. I've searched everywhere, but he's disappeared. How can he have just wandered away?' She looked like a helpless doll.

Ernst sat on the edge of the bed and pulled his young wife towards him, urging her to sit down. He squeezed her hand and kissed her cheek. He had already carefully thought through what he was going to tell her. 'Darling, I know this will be very hard for you to hear, but Klaus passed away overnight.'

Her eyes were wide with disbelief.

'I didn't have the heart to wake you. You were so exhausted, *mein Liebling*. I got up to check on him in the middle of the night and he'd already left this world.'

A tear rolled down her cheek as she searched his eyes for solace. 'Where is he?'

'I buried him down in the garden early this morning. I didn't want you to see him like that. Better you remember Klaus as he was when he was alive.'

She was silent for a moment before throwing her arms around him. 'Oh, Ernst!' She sobbed, her body crumpling with grief.

Ernst was relieved she bought the story. 'I'll work from home today. Maybe we could hold a small funeral for him later?'

'Yes,' she said, wiping the tears with the hem of her silk nightgown. 'Thank you. I would like that.'

After breakfast they dressed and went downstairs to the small courtyard garden. Whispering her sad farewell to Klaus, Herta placed the last of the marigolds on top of a tiny mound of dirt wedged between two rosebushes. She stood very still, holding Ernst's hand as he gave a brief eulogy.

That afternoon, Herta sat on the sofa, idly flipping through the book Himmler gave them as a wedding present. On the title page of his bestseller, the Führer himself had inscribed: *To the newlyweds, with best wishes for a happy and blessed marriage. Munich, 1937.* She needed something to distract her from the anguish of losing Klaus, as well as take her mind off Margarete, a subject she and Ernst had skirted around ever since he assured her he would look into it. Ernst sat nearby, busily sorting through the results of his previous expedition with Brooky as part of his thesis research. Herta could recite by heart the notes she helped type up:

UPUPIDAE

Upupa epops saturata

Citation: Lönneberg

Common name: Hoopoe bird

Five males: two, Jyekundo, 1 April 1935; two, Jyekundo, 9 April 1935; one, Yalung (Camp 79), 18 April 1935. One female: Tunggnolo, 11 September 1934.

Though the differences between Upupa epops epops *and* U. e. saturata *are very slight, I finally decided to refer my specimens to the latter race. The Tibetan hoopoe does not occur in the Hsifan mountains but is commonly found in Kham and Chinghai, Tibet. It frequents the nomad country and the agricultural districts north of the timberline. It has semi-migratory habits, descending in winter into the erosion-canyons of the river gorges, where I found a few specimens wintering near Batang at an altitude of 2700 metres above sea level.*

'All this meticulous categorisation, Ernst. I just don't understand it.' She slammed the Führer's opus on a side table. 'And when it comes to humans – their eye colour, family background, disability – surely that labelling only serves the party's bureaucratic needs?'

'You're right, *mein Liebchen*.' He wanted to avoid an argument, today of all days. 'The Führer sees the Jews as a grotesque pestilence that feed off the *Volk*. I know it sounds ludicrous, but who would the radiant Nordic German be without a swarthy antagonist?'

She threw the book into the bin. 'Glory needs its devil to define it.'

Two weeks later, Herta celebrated her twenty-fifth birthday. She spent the morning sitting on a corner of the sofa beside her overflowing darning basket, stabbing her needle into Ernst's socks, carefully mending holes made by his big toes. What a year this had been. She finally felt like a grown woman, even though today she was as excited as a little girl. Ernst had gone to work, promising her a big surprise when he got home from the laboratory. She wondered what it might be: perhaps some nylon stockings, or a box of chocolates? The radio hummed softly in the background, playing Puccini's opera, *Gianni Schicchi*. Ernst's colleagues had banded together to give them a *Volksempfänger*, or 'people's receiver', as a wedding gift. This saved them seventy-six marks, but it still cost two marks a month for the broadcasting fee. The radio was a simple box made of brown Bakelite, embellished with a screeching eagle below the dial, the emblem of the Reich Broadcasting Corporation. Herta loved listening to performances of some of Germany's most famous musicians, although more and more programs were punctuated with news broadcasts or staccato blasts of the Führer's speeches. Today, the radio interrupted the opera every so often with news of pro-German riots in the Sudetenland. She reached across during those little interruptions and fiddled with the knob to turn down the volume.

Late that afternoon, Ernst returned home with a parcel tucked under his arm. He rested it on the floor beside his briefcase. Flinging his jacket on the back of a chair, he came over to give Herta a hug, peeling her shawl off her shoulders.

'We are going to celebrate your birthday in style. We'll be having dinner with Bruno and Hildegard this evening. We're meeting them at Hotel Kaiserhof on Wilhelmplatz at seven o'clock.'

'*Mein Gott*, Ernst! It's so expensive there. That's where all the party officials go.'

'Only the best for my darling wife. We will simply ignore them all as we raise our glasses to your health. Now, *Schnell*! Hurry up and go put on your finest gown.'

Herta smiled and headed to the bedroom, trying to decide if she should wear a floral frock or a tailored suit.

'Wait!' Ernst called after her. 'Just a minute, *mein Liebchen*. Before you get changed.'

She stopped in the doorway and turned to look back at Ernst, who was shifting from one foot to the other.

'I almost forgot to give you your present.' He reached down to pick up the package he brought home, placing it on the table.

Smiling, she came back and ran her hands over the brown butcher paper, trying to discern from the shape what the gift might be. It was uneven yet firm. It couldn't be a new sewing machine? Ernst wouldn't have spent two months' salary on such an indulgence. The old Singer her parents had given them was rickety, but it still worked perfectly.

She unpeeled one side of the wrapping to reveal a flash of brown fur. A sewing machine was one thing, but a fur stole? She thought he'd been joking; they couldn't afford that kind of luxury.

'Ernst!' she squealed. 'I don't believe it.'

'Do you like it?'

She threw her arms around him. 'I love it. But it's way beyond our means. You shouldn't have done it.'

He laughed as he placed his hands on her waist. 'Don't worry, darling. It didn't cost a thing.'

'How's that?' She planted a kiss on his cheek. 'Did you steal it from the zoo?'

He seemed puzzled. 'No, Herta. I did it all myself.'

She turned her attention back to the package and ripped off the rest of the paper. What stood before her was so unimaginably macabre that she held her breath in disbelief.

'Surprise!' Ernst was grinning.

She felt her lips go numb. 'How could you?'

Ernst took a step back. 'What's the problem? You just told me you loved it.'

'I thought it was a fur.' She forced the words out between sobs.

'A what?'

'A fur stole!' Her whole body was trembling now. 'I never imagined it would be my poor little Klaus.'

*

As she lay in bed alone, having consigned Ernst to sleep the night in his study, surrounded by his maps and specimens, she remembered the day of Margarete's eighteenth birthday. Herta sat beside her sister's single bed, and the silence was broken by an icy wind creeping in through the cracks in the window frame. Sad daisies drooped their heads over the edge of a white vase on the washstand. Margarete's fingers clawed at the metal frame of the bed.

Back then, Herta thought of leaving Waltershausen all the time. She knew she would miss home, the reliable smell of Mutti's cooking at noon, the scratchy sounds of Stravinsky playing defiantly on Vati's gramophone each evening. But she could not stay in this small town anymore, fashioning unseeing eyes for dolls by day and singing to her unhearing sister by night. Berlin was where she could dedicate herself to music. It was where she belonged.

Margarete breathed quietly, jolted awake every few minutes by the violent shuddering of her withered legs. Caught somewhere between anguish and slumber, she rolled her head back and glanced at Herta. But her eyes soon flicked away as she retreated into sleep again. Herta looked around the room, its pastel-blue walls yellowed by time, paper gulls with crumpled wings held aloft by frayed string. A spoon lay abandoned in a wooden bowl resting on a placemat, embroidered chicks half-covered in blobs of mashed pumpkin. The air tasted of disinfectant, Mutti's attempt to keep illness at bay.

Outside, the light had started to fade. Herta would be gone before sunrise. How to say goodbye? Her fingers laced with Margarete's, who gripped them tightly as if she might never let go.

CHAPTER 13

Late October 1937

Ernst was back in his patron's office, this time surrounded by the team of fine scientists he had put together. The *Reichsführer* removed his gloves before shaking each man's hand in turn, presenting them with angora-wool pullovers.

'We don't want you catching colds in Tibet!' Himmler said with a laugh.

Ernst's colleagues stood there like a flock of pigeons waiting to be thrown some scraps by their auspicious feeder.

After a few formalities, Himmler abruptly cut the meeting short.

'My apologies, gentlemen. I must rush to see the Duke and Duchess of Windsor, who are arriving today. But I am very much looking forward to officially presenting you all to the public at this year's winter solstice celebrations.' He turned to Ernst and grinned. 'And you, my dear Schäfer, on this occasion will be awarded the rank of *Hauptsturmführer*.' With a perfunctory '*Heil Hitler!*', Himmler dismissed the men.

The rank of captain was more than an honour; it meant a decent increase in salary. The last time Ernst received such a promotion was at the end of his last summer in Philadelphia, as he celebrated his birthday at Seven Oaks, the Dolan family's property.

The closer his departure date for the new expedition loomed, the more often Ernst found himself thinking about Brooky. A tender madness had coursed through Brooky's alcohol-soaked veins, a streak carefully covered over by his family's wealth and influence. While it wasn't that unusual that Brooky had commenced his studies in zoology at no less than Princeton, it was also no surprise he soon became bored with academia and dropped out. Meanwhile, he busied himself hatching a plan. Always one to seek out adventure, Brooky started organising an expedition to China and Tibet, and so Ernst's career as an explorer began.

Ernst also found himself thinking more of the day, five years down the track, when he was summoned back to Berlin and his ties with the Reich were fixed in place. On 26 April 1936, after two expeditions with Brooky, Ernst's time in Philadelphia working at the academy was cut short by an unexpected telegram.

'Sign here, please.'

Ernst had scribbled his name hurriedly. The delivery boy handed him the envelope, addressed to SS-*Untersturm-führer* Ernst Schäfer. There must have been some mistake. That wasn't his rank; he was only a sergeant major, not a second lieutenant. A bicycle rested against the railing on the stoop and the youth shuffled awkwardly. It took Ernst a few moments to realise what the kid was waiting for. He dug into his pocket for some pennies, which he deposited onto an outstretched palm. Doffing his hat, the messenger turned, mounted his bike and was gone.

Ernst went inside and sat down on the bottom stair. He tore open the envelope. Under the heading, *Deutsche Reichspost Telegramm*, four words blazed across the slip of paper: *RETURN TO GERMANY REQUESTED*.

The next line was equally unexpected.

You have been awarded a commission as an honorary SS-Untersturmführer.

Signed: Reichsführer *Heinrich Himmler.*

Ernst replied immediately:

I am so proud and happy that I cannot express it. I hope I will be able to show my gratitude through my actions. The greatest honour for me is to have been promoted.

Ernst felt no hesitation in leaving Philadelphia. Though he was a shrewd and clever operator, the academy had refused to guarantee further funding of his research. Himmler's attention was tantalising for a young scientist like Ernst, so it didn't take him long to pack up his things and book a berth on the SS *Bremen* back to Hamburg.

Albert Schäfer, delighted to have his son home again, knew as a businessman that flexibility was an important quality to cultivate. Although he prided himself on being a liberal thinker, he saw that times were rapidly changing. That was why, back in 1933, when his son had come home for a brief visit after his first joint German–American expedition, he took the opportunity to convince the mayor of Göttingen, a good friend with a solid background, to encourage young Ernst to join the SS. Albert Schäfer knew better than most that one could never be too careful when it came to matters of career, having used his networks to build a fine company of which he was proud. The convoluted SS application process hadn't been easy at the time – they had to dig up all the family records from the previous ten generations – but their ancestry proved to be entirely clean. Ernst received his *Ahnenpass*, a genealogical passport, which would ensure he could rise up the ranks in his career, unimpeded.

Herta stood by the window, her back to her husband. It had started raining outside, the drops slowly chasing each other down the glass. Two pigeons huddled together on a nearby branch, their grey feathers ruffling in the wind. As the meeting with his men at Himmler's office ended much sooner than expected, Ernst had rushed home to check on Herta, who he thought was looking a little pale of late. He filled the kettle, placing it on the gas burner to boil, and busied himself preparing her a late breakfast. As he reached up to take the tea canister down from the shelf above the stove, he knocked over the candelabra they received as a wedding gift from Herta's parents.

Herta was still in her nightdress, even though it was mid-morning. She hadn't slept well. Ernst heard her whispering prayers into the night as she wrestled with her pillow. He felt as though he tried so hard to please her, but it never seemed enough. Lately, her eyes followed his every move, watching closely, accusing, as if he were somehow betraying her. The radiator hissed and clanged.

'Are you hungry, *mein Liebling*?' He spooned some mulberry jam into a dish and set it on the table.

She didn't answer, staring blankly ahead as she moved across the room, lowering herself onto a chair. Ernst put a plate of rye bread in front of his young wife but she refused to eat. The kettle shrieked on the stove, steam shooting out violently. He poured water into the teapot and brewed some tea. The cup rattled in the saucer as he carried it over to her.

He told her about the meeting with Himmler, and the winter solstice celebration.

'This whole business is a disgrace,' she said. 'Remember how last year we were told to put a swastika on the top of the tree instead of a star?'

Herta was disgusted that a Christmas tree was no longer to be referred to as a *Christbaum* anymore; now it was called a *Julbaum*, a Yule tree. Even poor old Saint Nikolas had turned into Odin, with a grey beard and slouch hat, riding around on his white charger. Mary and Jesus' dark features were suddenly transformed into blue eyes and fair hair, and the manger was overrun by toy deer and rabbits instead of wise men.

She leaned forward, reaching for a department-store catalogue lying on the table.

'And just look what they've done since they took over beautiful Wertheim last year.' She flipped through its pages. 'Chocolate SS soldiers and toy machine guns for the children. What has this world come to when we are told that even Jesus has been replaced by a new saviour – our beloved Führer himself!'

'Shh! Herta, darling. Lower your voice. We don't want the neighbours hearing.'

'I don't care what anyone thinks. What is the meaning of Christmas without Christ?'

She started crying. Ernst stood behind her and stroked her hair.

'Calm down, my sweet.' He spoke quietly, as if he were trying to lure a wild animal into a trap.

She turned around, her eyes unyielding. 'And this stupid Yule lantern Himmler gave us. No doubt made by those miserable wretches in Dachau.' She lifted the clay ornament from the table. 'What am I supposed to do with this thing? Conjure up dead spirits, expect a visitation from Madame Blavatsky's ghost? Your friends over at the *Ahnenerbe* are busy rebranding Christmas as a propaganda tool for their occult drivel. I, for one, refuse to go to this absurd winter solstice of theirs. They are destroying everything we hold dear.' She slumped back in her chair, exhausted.

Ernst saw there was no point telling her about his promotion right now.

Little Heinz chirped in his cage, his clipped wings flapping. He chattered wildly, as if to fill the void of the sudden silence in the room. Ernst had brought the bird home yesterday as a gift for Herta, to make up for stuffing Klaus. He still could not understand why she hadn't been delighted when she unwrapped her beloved cat, forever dead but not gone. Although he'd seen so many species of sadness in Herta over time – homesickness, loneliness, guilt over abandoning her sister – she had never seemed to grieve so deeply. Couldn't she understand how much time he had spent perfecting Klaus? He'd even straightened out the cat's bad leg so that the beauty it lacked in life would become apparent in death.

He watched Herta scrape her chair back and walk over to the metal cage. The bird fluttered excitedly as she approached. She refilled his seed bowl. 'Pretty Heinz. Good boy,' she said, poking her finger through the shiny bars to stroke his blue-green feathers.

Ernst fumbled in his bag and pulled out a book: *Abrichten und Sprechenlernen des Wellensittichs*. Training the bird to talk would be a lovely project for them. They had spent so little time alone since the wedding, what with him being so overwrought with his thesis and preparations for the expedition. She was obviously feeling lonely, and it might help her forget about Klaus.

Ernst wanted to teach the bird to say *I love you* before leaving for Tibet, so a small part of him could still be there with Herta while he was away.

He stood beside her and opened the book at Lesson One.

'Hello, Heinz!' he said.

The bird chirped in response.

'Good bird. Hello, Heinz!' Herta said, a smile gradually appearing on her face.

'The book says to repeat it over and over.'

The bird squawked, cracking some seeds in its beak.

'Hello, Heinz. Pretty birdy.'

Right on cue, as if to prove Ernst's motives could never quite land in the way he intended, the bird started to chirp: *'Heil Hitler!'*

Herta turned pale. 'What did he say?'

The feathery patriot repeated himself, screeching the same words over and over: *'Heil Hitler! Heil Hitler! Heil Hitler!'*

'Get rid of it!' she yelled.

'Herta! Calm down, please.'

Heinz, becoming more and more flustered by Herta's shouting, launched into another frenzied display of his limited vocal talents: *'Heil Hitler! Heil Hitler! Heil Hitler!'*

Herta stepped back, horrified. 'Take it back right now.' She threw the cover over the cage.

The budgerigar's squawking, now muffled, continued.

'We can't have this creature living under our roof.'

'Relax. We'll teach it to say other things.'

'No, you have to return it immediately! I don't want it in our apartment another minute. Where did you get such a horrid little thing?'

'It doesn't understand what it's saying. I repeat *Heil Hitler* like a parrot, too, a hundred times a day. That doesn't make me a certified Nazi.'

'You were a sweet young thing too once, and look at what happened to you with just a little training.'

'Does that mean you want me gone as well?'

Herta sighed. 'Do what you want.'

Ernst grabbed the birdcage and stormed out, slamming the door behind him.

Herta had a vivid memory of when she was a little girl, sitting on her bed, looking out onto the back garden at the blossom pushing its way out from the branches of a plum tree. An orange beetle crawled across the lace curtain, its feelers searching for a pathway that might lead outdoors. The thrum of early cicadas harmonised with the birds, sounding like a chorus of tiny angels. Even though Herta practised her flute two hours every day, she knew she could never be a match for the starling perched on a branch of the old oak, singing its melancholy tune. The bird made it look so easy. How could such a perfectly formed melody spill out from a creature with no lips and a throat the size of the button on her collar?

She wished she were an animal, born to make music, like Schutzi. Her dear budgerigar, sitting up there in his cage beside her bed, spontaneously burst into song, taking tiny breaths between his vocal gymnastics. He would wake her every morning with this pandemonium of gossip, joining the rapid-fire dawn badinage with the feathered choir outside. Some songs were wild and urgent, others petulant and whiny. She loved Schutzi, not only because of his rambunctious chatter and exquisite song, but also because he listened. Even with those minuscule holes for ears, he was a better listener than any human.

When Vati first brought him home, the bird was only twelve weeks old. He would sit on his perch abjectly, refusing to sing. Every morning she would find a new pile of feathers in the bottom of his cage, until his pink skin was almost entirely exposed. She asked Ernst to come over and examine him after school one day.

'He is moulting,' he announced confidently.

'Maybe we should take him outside, so he can have some fresh air?'

'No, no! You mustn't do that. It could kill him. He will be very sensitive at this time. Leave him where he is. Moving him around would be far too stressful. He won't sing for you now, but believe me, he is listening. Be patient.'

The days passed, and a fine layer of fluff pushed its way through Schutzi's skin. Then one day, at the start of autumn, after an entire summer spent trying to get him to say *hello*, he finally replied. At first all he could manage was a raspy squawk, but in a short while she had taught him a love song, a tune he would faithfully sing for the rest of his small life.

CHAPTER 14

After He left to go home, they stored me in Basement for a while, right beside Thylacinus cynocephalus, *the Tasmanian tiger. Such strangeness and eloquence in her form; those odd stripes on her slender back made her look like the lovechild of a tiger and a dog. And a smile so charismatic, yet elusive. Her ears erect, she listened intently to everything around us. She was never the talkative type, old Thyla, although once I plucked up the courage to ask her what she carried around in her pouch. I'm sure I saw a tear form in her eye as she told me about the baby they stole from her. I tried comforting her, telling her I was sure her child was still alive somewhere, enjoying the freedom of Wild. That made her even more glum. Her aura grew fainter as they moved her further in towards Permanent Storage, almost hidden away behind elk antlers and armadillos.*

'I come from a Wild called Tasmania. I have heard that my clan are gone from there forever,' she said, and never spoke again.

They have said that about me, too, that I am headed to a place called Extinction. Also, there have been rumours in the past that I am a mixed breed. Experts have visited from around the world, standing before me, engaging in heated debates over whether I'm a bear or the relative of a type of raccoon. I am a living fossil, apparently. They say my scientific name means black-and-white cat-footed animal. The Chinese call me pinyin, a big bear-cat; in fact, a man called Professor came from there several years back to talk to Smalls about me. He told them over time I have had many names – zhuxiong (竹熊), bamboo bear; huaxiong (华雄), spotted bear. He said people thought for years that I was a missing link. But in 2009, his friend, Scientist, wrote a story in a book called Nature, trying to explain how my body is built to eat bamboo.

'The panda holds a unique place in evolution,' Professor said, 'with continuing controversy about its phylogenetic position.'

Smalls wiggled their sticks immediately over their tree bark when he said that. One lifted his arm up, as if reaching for the most tender bamboo shoot that was just out of reach.

'Sir!' he asked. 'What does "phylogenetic" mean?'

Professor looked shocked that a Small would not know a Fact of such importance, but then explained, 'It's how animals with similar genetic make-up have evolved over time.'

But the look on Small's face showed I wasn't the only one who didn't understand a word of what he was saying.

'Do you mean they are all family?'

Professor scratched his ear as if he was trying to flick off a biting flea.

'Sort of. Yes.'

Then he told them I didn't have umami. I was worried at first, because I didn't know what that was either, and was starting to feel like some kind of freak. But when he explained there are five types of taste – sweetness, saltiness, sourness, bitterness and umami – and that pandas don't have the last one, I felt a little better.

'Umami is the meaty taste picked up by receptors,' he said.

Why would I need that? Disgusting to eat another being when there is such an abundance of bamboo in the world. Professor told them my people are 'vulnerable', although I do not know why he singled us out – isn't everything, both inside Diorama and beyond Exit, vulnerable?

I miss Shepherd with an ache deep inside the hollow of my chest. The longing has made itself felt so many years later – the same kind of pain as the day we first met, when blind love fired its arrow into my heart and I knew I was His forever. It was at its worst the day He came to tell me He was going back to the Land of his Father. He told me He would come back one day and that meeting me was the proudest moment of His life. The waiting for His return, the hope I will see Him again, is anguish. I wish someone would tell everyone beyond Exit about our Great Love, but some stories are fated to be lost.

CHAPTER 15

2 November 1937

Funkturm Berlin, the tall radio tower, cast a shadow across a cordon of soldiers lined up to greet the dignitaries as they arrived. Visitors had come from all over the world to attend the *Internationale Jagdausstellung,* a huge exhibition with everything related to hunting that one could ever dream of. Purple rhododendrons decorated the base of the tall podium, which was adorned with the ubiquitous red flag emblazoned with the swastika.

As Ernst and Herta walked towards the entrance, Göring himself greeted them, flanked by soldiers standing at attention. A tuft of wild-boar hair poked out from the rim of his hunting cap, which partially covered his thinning hair. He shook Ernst's hand eagerly.

'I am so pleased you agreed to come. I am so lucky to get to see the intrepid explorer himself yet again.'

They hugged like long-lost brothers, slapping each other on the shoulder.

'No, no! The honour is all mine, *Reichsjägermeister* Göring.' He turned to Herta. 'And you must remember my dear wife.'

The portly man bowed down to kiss her hand. 'My dearest, I insist you and your fine husband come visit us next week at our summer house. I'm sure Emmy would love the chance to get to know you better.'

'Thank you so much.' Herta blushed, not knowing what else to say.

Just then, two men wearing white fur coats and mink hats trotted up on horseback in front of the group, falcons perched on their gloved arms, thin leather straps tied to the birds' legs. They had travelled all the way from Iceland. An entourage of Frenchmen dressed in red jackets blew their trumpets and a pack of beagles responded by wagging their tails eagerly, as if they were off on a hunt.

Göring led the way inside the hall, and the men commenced the tour of the exhibition. Surely Herta was doing her duty today as the wife of an SS man; she had offered her body up to her husband in the morning, made a hot breakfast for him, tidied the house. And this afternoon, she forced herself to make polite conversation with all manner of men, held out her hand to be kissed as they whispered lewd comments in her ear, which, thankfully, Ernst did not hear. How wearisome to stand

141

by politely, looking ornamental and picture-perfect. She tried not to yawn as Göring chatted to her husband about the dwindling numbers of bison and wild boar to be found this season. For a man who bragged about spending so much time in the great outdoors, Göring's skin looked the colour of eggshell. And his rotund belly made her think he spent more time chasing beers than bears. She watched his stubby fingers, which tapped insistently on the ornate dagger strapped to his belt. Göring seemed thrilled to finally have the opportunity of crowing to Ernst about his hunting prowess.

Herta took her leave while both men were still engrossed in conversation and snuck away under the pretence of needing to freshen up in the powder room. She stood on the ornate balcony, gazing down onto the strange scene, clutching the program to her chest. Herta had flicked through the pages earlier, looking at dinner-party recipes for how to prepare wild game. She saw herself entertaining their friends, the table laden with the centrepiece of a roast boar, an apple shoved in its gaping mouth. If it were up to her, the menu would be braised vegetables, but she had certainly married the wrong man if she ever wanted to become a vegetarian. Ernst's breakfast consisted of salami and eggs, washed down with a cup of strong coffee; *Mittagessen* varied between bratwurst, roast chicken or veal schnitzel; and *Abendbrot* was usually rye bread, sausage, ham and cheese. He disliked vegetables, although if a carrot grew legs and started running away from him, the chase might entice him enough to catch it and eat it raw.

On their way to the exhibition, Ernst had tried hard to explain to her that the pleasure came not from the kill itself. Rather, it was the sport – the skill, and the volume of game bagged in a single day – that made the hunter a professional expert.

'Why can't you just be proud of me, Herta?'

'Proud of what, exactly?' She brushed him off. 'I can't admire the violent deaths of your precious birds.'

Now, her husband stood beside *Reichsjägermeister* Göring, surrounded by a flock of other important-looking men, all wearing their finest dress uniform. The exhibition hall swelled with a sea of rifle salesmen and cocky hunters who strolled past the animal collection: a stuffed brown bear wearing three medallions, a tiny cub at its feet; hundreds of orphaned antlers attached to bleached skulls mounted on poles; and her own husband's Tibetan bird collection. A giant elk head hung on the main wall in a celebratory display of the hunter's triumph. A choir of young boys from a local Hitler Youth group sang the 'Horst-Wessel-Lied' with gusto. To Herta's left, a spiral staircase wound its way up, leading from the balcony to the roof. She felt tempted to climb it and escape from this orgiastic celebration of deliberate death, like a bird in search of open sky.

The hall that held such a huge gathering of men seemed like it was filled with little boys, and her beloved Ernst seemed the most excited one of all. Watching him speak so animatedly to his fellow hunters, she saw a side of her husband she would never be able to reconcile with her childhood image of him. How could a man who held such a deep reverence for nature and all its gifts at the same time be its destroyer?

Ernst had been the shortest in his class. His voice was squeaky, and his mousy hair a wiry explosion that defied the ritual monthly battles against his father's trimmer. Despite being one of the smallest, he could lift heavier weights, lunge further and jump higher than anyone his age.

One morning he threw on khaki shorts and a shirt, tying his shoelaces carelessly as his mother called from downstairs: 'Ernst! *Schnecke!* Hurry up, you little snail. You'll be late for school again.'

He checked the fish tank on his desk. It rested on top of a map of the world, covering over America, which looked huge and blurry under the glass.

'One, two, three, four . . .' he counted out loud, practising his English. The last of the bloated frogs' eggs were promising to hatch, the embryos squirming inside their casing, waiting to burst into their watery surrounds to join their tadpole siblings. He counted them, too, recording various stages of development, some only wiggling the stump of a tail, others already sprouting tiny legs. He fed them with chopped-up boiled lettuce, then opened a jar filled with green aphids picked off the stems of his mother's roses and sprinkled a few in for the older froglets. Several eggs had turned white. He scooped these dead ones out, feeding them to Aldo, who stood beside him slobbering and wagging his tail in anticipation. The water looked murky;

Ernst scribbled a note reminding himself to cut back the amount of food, but not too much or the tadpoles would start going after each other. He measured out fifty millilitres of fresh water in a glass beaker and poured it into the tank. The tadpoles raced around in a feeding frenzy. One that was already almost frog-like, with only a stumpy remnant of a tail, dived off a lily pad that floated on the surface of the tank, landing with a wet plop onto the floor. Aldo raced to scoop it up, but Ernst reached the escapee first, tossing it back into the tank. He continued the rollcall, ticking off a list in his notebook: 'Schatzi, Biene, Hase . . .'

He paused, holding his breath. He peered in from the side of the tank, his eyes frenziedly searching behind rocks and weed. Bratfische was missing. *Scheisse!* Not another one. Full-grown frogness had created a small problem of late in the Schäfer household. The timing of a specimen's momentous leap from the top of the tank onto the wooden floor of Ernst's bedroom was becoming rather hard to predict, often defying the meticulous growth chart he annotated carefully in his neatest *Sütterlinschrift* handwriting. Despite all his attempts to monitor the creatures, urging them to restrict their primordial call-to-land to after-school hours, the excited frogs seemed determined to embark upon their metamorphosal finale by making the perilous journey down the staircase precisely on the mornings Ernst was stuck in class. And, despite his best attempts to force them to take detours, they always seemed to head directly towards the deathtrap of his father's study. A dangerous adventure for Ernst to retrieve them, too, earning him the strap each time one of the slimy creatures hid under the massive mahogany desk, or parked itself like a croaking paperweight on top of an open business ledger, the inky column of figures bleeding into a watery pool.

This was likely to become one of those days, unless Ernst could find that damned Bratfische before it escaped under the door. He enlisted the help of his friend.

'Get him, Aldo!'

The dog obediently started sniffing along the skirting boards and under the bed while Ernst rummaged through his egg collection and checked behind the mouse cage, both well-known frog hide-outs. The rodents scurried away into makeshift burrows, as if the memory of the precocious scientist who had cropped their ancestors' tails – an experiment aimed at exploring inheritable change – was imprinted on their brains. He glanced at the top of a pile of stamp albums and searched in the bottom of a basket of speckled goldcrest eggs collected during the previous week's foray into the woods, an adventure that earnt him a detention from Herr Vogel for not having handed in his history assignment on time. The frog could have been anywhere, camouflaged among bottles of feathery green fronds that held creatures twirling madly in their tiny worlds.

'Ernst!' his mother called again.

Bratfische was nowhere to be found. Ernst's heart pounded and the hunger in his belly slowly turned into nausea, despite the smell of bacon and freshly baked bread wafting up from the kitchen.

'Ernst!' His mother's voice rose an octave with every minute that passed.

He abandoned his search, grabbed his leather satchel and bolted downstairs. His mother was seated in the kitchen, holding a cup of tea. Frau Klein, a walrus of a woman who harboured a weakness for gin, placed a steaming plate of food in front of him. He dived on his bacon and rye, followed by Zwiebelkuchen, her special onion pie, and a cup of hot cocoa.

'This child will be the death of me, Klara.' His mother spoke to the maid as if Ernst wasn't in the room. 'He's always been a defiant little monkey. You know, one evening, when he was only five, he simply disappeared. Poor Albert organised the whole town to search for him. Constable Scharf even sent all of his men into the forest, fearing the worst.'

Frau Klein stopped stirring her pot of soup and turned to look at Ernst, the whiskers on her chin catching the morning sun that was peeking in through the curtains. She caught him licking his oniony fingers clean.

'Do you know where this cheeky son of mine was hiding the whole time?' Frau Schäfer sipped her tea. 'Down in the cellar, behind crates of potatoes. He was busy picking off rats with the slingshot Albert gave him for his birthday. A silly present for a small boy, I must say.'

Ernst grabbed a linen napkin to wipe his mouth.

'May I be excused, Mutti?'

'Yes, yes. On your way. Hurry up, or you'll be late.' His mother shooed him away with the back of her hand, and he buzzed out through the back door.

The children were standing at attention. Ernst snuck into the classroom just as Herr Vogel, standing in front of the blackboard with eyes closed, his face raised to the sky, began crowing. His ruddy jowls wobbled from side to side as the children joined in:

Deutschland, Deutschland über alles,
Über alles in der Welt!

The *Reichspräsident*, Friedrich Ebert, stared down from a picture mounted on the wall, next to the black, red and gold flag. Ernst hurried across the room. He raised the lid of his desk and shoved his satchel inside. Standing to attention, he mouthed random vowels in the bits where he didn't know the new anthem's words, hoping the old rooster hadn't noticed him sneak in late. The children's voices droned on, sending Ernst into a bored reverie, wishing he was outside running around in the woods. A dove swooped down from the rafters and landed on her nest, hidden among the geraniums in the window box. She tilted her head and looked directly at Ernst, as if considering whether he was trustworthy enough to leave her two precious eggs unguarded.

Herr Vogel flapped over to him, squawking in a falsetto, 'Schäfer! Daydreaming again?'

Ernst hadn't realised the song was over. His classmates were now seated, elbows on their desks, hands clasped above open textbooks. A wave of nervous tittering spread across the room, all eyes fixed on him. His cheeks turned red. Gerhard Tierman and Horst Beiner sniggered from the back of the classroom; he knew he would earn a few more bruises on his way home that afternoon. He lifted the lid of his desk again and pulled out his English textbook.

'Ah! Welcome back to earth, Herr Schäfer.' Herr Vogel was standing over him. 'Now, I am sure you would be delighted to read out loud to the class the English essay I asked you to write for homework yesterday. Or did Fräulein Völz forget to do it for you?'

Herta stayed on the balcony throughout the welcoming speeches; no one seemed to notice her absence. There were delegates from around the world, proudly standing beside their country's flag: the Union Jack; the Danish cross; the red, white and green stripes of Hungary. Göring waxed lyrical about virtue and family, and how the beauty of the hunt preserved and replenished nature. As she looked down on the scene below, a feeling of nausea rose within her; now she really did need to find the powder room. She reached it just in time to retch her entire breakfast into the toilet bowl.

CHAPTER 16

7 November 1937

Herta stared out at the rain as she waited for Ernst. The cold wind tugged at leaves that still clung to the trees. A solitary starling fought desperately to stay aloft. The storm hadn't let up for days, and she was growing tired of being cooped up in the apartment. Ernst left early each morning, spending most of the day working in his laboratory. He was so late finishing his thesis, which was now overdue. He would come home when it was dark and spend the rest of the evening either alone in his study or working with Geer, who was organising logistics for the expedition. At thirty-two, with a receding hairline and a solid paunch, Geer looked middle-aged compared to Ernst. Herta thought he was hardly the image of an intrepid explorer. But Geer seemed trustworthy and loyal.

Lately, Geer was more like a wife to Ernst than she was, with all the time the two men spent together. Not exactly the life she imagined as a young bride in the first months of marriage.

Seated in an armchair, she drifted off. In her swirl of dreams, she and Ernst were two birds caught in a trap. An old farmer trudged through snow to release them. They stretched their wings and soared together, high above fields covered with the dead. She tried to warn Ernst it was dangerous to fly with his eyes closed, but all that emerged from her beak was the language of song. Ignoring her doleful cries, Ernst swooped down to fight with wild beasts, returning to her not long after with his heart gouged out. She tried to stop the bleeding with her feathers. Hands sprouted from the tips of her wings as she reached out to him. His was a love so hard to embrace. She lifted him onto her back and carried him away, flying to the top of a distant tree. She would be his eyes.

'I won't let you leave!' Herta shrieked as she jolted from sleep. Her darning fell from her lap.

She rose to fetch a cup and saucer. A huge textbook that Ernst referred to as his bible still lay open on the kitchen table where he had left it after dinner the previous night: *A Natural History of Uncommon Birds*. It was a gift he received from Professor Weigold for being his assistant in Heligoland, while he was still a student at Göttingen. Ernst's books were always strewn across the apartment and usually she ignored them, with their dense exposi- tions on dry subjects such as feathers, bone architecture, egg structure and nest-building. But this one was an elegant leather-bound copy, written in 1743 by an Englishman, with such beautiful, intricate hand-drawn illustrations. She couldn't understand the text, but as she flipped through the pages she came across a slip of paper covered with Ernst's scribble. It was a translation from the preface he had annotated as a possible quote for his thesis:

> *It is indeed my opinion that all those birds which are seen with us only some part of the year pass into other countries when they are out of our sight . . . Many would make sleepers of them, and say they retire to holes underground, and in hollow trees, etc., and that they are so fat that they cannot fly far at the times they disappear.*

A sketch Ernst had drawn of the skeleton of an eagle caught her eye, the delicate spine holding up a large head. Elongated finger bones stretched themselves into wings, like a hand pulling on a glove. If only humans could enjoy the miracle of flight. She had read in one of Ernst's books on Tibet about the *lung-gom-pa*, flying lamas whom Marco Polo reported having seen on his travels. They wore light clothes and could apparently reach up to twenty-five kilometres an hour in the air by swinging their limbs like a pendulum.

Herta cast her eyes away from the book. She wandered around the apartment, which was littered with all sorts of magnificent creatures that once soared above the earth.

*

Ernst stopped in the doorway of his laboratory and looked across at the unlabelled bird carcasses littering his desk, their skins already showing bald patches where the feathers had fallen out. He strolled across the room and sat down in a tattered chair by the bay window that over-looked the enclosure of Bobby the gorilla. He watched the ape as it strolled up and down, shaking the season's early snowflakes from its head.

Ernst's work was not going well, his passion for it dissi-pated. There were other, brighter ornithologists whose ambition burned more intensely, like the men currently filming a couple of South American hummingbird species at the zoo, with full funding from the Reich Office for Educational Film. A military research institute had even given them a camera that was able to record 1500 frames a second, and it was reported they were develop-ing some kind of new flying machine that could hover on the spot.

Even if Ernst was to study with ardent effort, what did all this knowledge amount to anyway? Science only seemed to matter nowadays if it demonstrated some sort of application to the military or big business. His doctor-ate felt as unattainable now as the mystical city of Lhasa, only much less enticing. At least the birds were familiar terrain for him – no bizarre theories of plummeting icy moons, or remnant ancestors of Atlantis. He stared at the bold letters typed on the front page of his thesis: *Avifauna of Tibet: under supervision of Dr Erwin Stresemann.* He was glad to have left his laboratory at the University of

153

Göttingen, and that incompetent fool Kühn, who called himself a professor. Berlin University was truly the epicentre of world academia and it felt good to be in the company of fine colleagues such as Stresemann, who was the author of the popular *Handbook of Zoology*. Even so, Ernst's heart simply wasn't in his studies anymore; he would have loved to be back trekking in Tibet.

He slammed a field guide down on the table, accidentally scratching his hand on the edge of a shrivelled hoopoe. The bird's claws caught the thin skin on his wrist, ripping it open. A searing pain shot up his arm. He pulled out a handkerchief from his pocket, holding it between his teeth as he wrapped it around his wrist to stop the nasty gash from bleeding. His eyes darted around the room, searching for something with which he might clean the wound, resting at last on a bottle of French brandy. He opened the lid and poured some of the brown liquid onto his bloodied handkerchief, swearing as he reapplied it, the alcohol searing his flesh.

'Control yourself,' he said out loud.

The walls seemed to be closing in, the photographs encroaching on him. Here he was in one, kneeling beside the pelts of four brown bears on that first glorious expedition in 1931 with crazy Brooky. Beside it hung a daguerreotype of the Panchen Lama, whom Ernst was fortunate enough to have met in exile near Shanghai in 1934. The revered leader sat cross-legged on his throne, his brush of a moustache obscuring his mouth. Ernst thought he looked like a rare bird on display, feathers preened and oiled, cheeks rouged, eyes ringed with kohl and his thin lips painted red.

Ernst noticed a congealed smear of blood on the hoopoe's foot. Its long, slender beak lay prised open. He could have sworn he heard it laughing.

'Shut up, you ugly beast!' he yelled at the specimen. His breathing quickened. He saw his face in the mirror: eyes bloodshot, cheeks sunken.

He picked up the bird's carcass and flung it across the room. It landed with a thud against a metal bookcase. Ernst stood up. Clasping his wrist, he hurried down the hallway. He struggled with the latch then slammed the door behind him and ran out onto the gravel path.

There had been another hoopoe once. Scratching around in the dirt, it showed off its colourful crest as it pecked at the seeds Ernst's father left out. Ernst stood and watched it feed on what only he knew would be its last supper. The bird leapt into the air and, with a sudden snap, crashed to earth, its cinnamon-coloured body crumpled, striped wings fluttering. It lay on its back, clawing furiously at the sky.

He heard a roar of fury and disgust, and looked up to see his father, face rigid as wax, standing at the study window, the shutter swinging loose in the light breeze. Behind him, Ernst could see piles of papers stacked on the large desk.

'Ernst!' he yelled, stubbing his cigarette out on the wooden frame. 'Come inside immediately!'

As soon as his father called his name, he knew it was all over. Ernst dropped his slingshot and hurried along the path towards the house, feeling the chasm between him and his father deepening with every step. He stood in front of the heavy wooden doors of the study. His father would be seated behind his mahogany desk, one hand holding a pipe, the other stroking his beard that smelled permanently of stale tobacco. As he waited, Ernst could hear him talking on the phone. Although his father's words were muffled, he could make out the urgency in his tone.

He knocked tentatively. After a few moments of silence, he heard his father call out.

'Enter!'

The door creaked as he opened it. The study was lined with shelves groaning with the weight of books of all sizes, their leather spines embossed with gold lettering. Ernst noticed a volume of Goethe's *Faust*. Framed photographs of his father standing in front of an array of his beloved horses covered the walls, alongside a proud display of dour-looking family ancestors, all dressed in their Sunday best. Albert Schäfer had been a looming but absent figure as Ernst was growing up. A celebrated entrepreneur, he ran the successful Harburger Phoenix Rubber factory, travelling the world from Russia to the Americas on company business. Today he wore his usual suit and tie, his hair slicked down with a neat, slightly off-centre part, his moustache covering a mouth set in a crooked line.

'Come forward, boy.'

Ernst walked across the Persian rug and stood in the middle of the room, before his father. Albert Schäfer's lips were pursed, his nose empurpled with rage. He flattened his left palm on a blotter, picked up a fountain pen and began to write. The solemn silence in the room was broken only by the fierce scratching of the nib. His father lowered his pipe and flicked a small yellow booklet across the desk. It landed in front of Ernst. It was his report card, and it wasn't good.

'What do you have to say for yourself?'

'Nothing, sir.'

The hoopoe had been his father's favourite; he fed the flamboyant little show-off every day, enamoured with the splendour of what he called its 'majestic markings'. He frequently bored Ernst with the details of its peregrinations, tales of its annual migration over the hurdle of the Alps, its determined tiny body enduring altitudes of up to 3000 metres in order to arrive back in the Schäfer's front garden at the beginning of each spring. And after breeding inside the old shed, the bird waking Ernst every day at dawn for months on end by hooting its scientific name over and over – *Upupa epops*, *Upupa epops* – he was glad to see it gone each autumn. The old man spoke about how the exultant call mesmerised him, taking him back to the idyllic days of his childhood, growing up on his grandparents' farm. He read somewhere that the hoopoe's numbers had declined since then, and Schäfer Senior thought it was his noble duty to feed the bird and encourage its survival. That day, however, Ernst had seen it as a brilliant opportunity to add a rare specimen to his growing collection.

After several minutes, the clock in the hallway chimed eleven, marking out the time the boy knew he might have left under his father's roof. He could see by the way the man sat up straight, rigid with fury, that his father was finally doing what he thought needed to be done. He had been threatening to send Ernst away for years, so the words he knew were now being etched so forcefully onto a single sheet of his father's best-quality paper came as no surprise. Ernst was almost glad things instantly became so clear, so simple.

His father looked up. Ernst proffered a queasy smile. Their eyes met, but like the same poles of two magnets forced together, they repelled each other's gaze. Ernst stood there, perched between his childhood and the rest of his days, feeling his time in Waltershausen shortening with every swing of the clock's pendulum. He stared at his father, noticing for the first time the grey bristles on his cheeks, skin cracked like that of an antique marionette. Schäfer Senior dipped his pen into the inkwell, accidentally knocking the bottle across the desk. The stain spread across the blotting pad, but he simply moved over a little, ignoring the mess. He returned to the letter, finally signing it with a flourish. Glaring at his young son from over the top of his spectacles, he finally spoke.

'You will leave for Heidelberg this Monday. Herr Direktor was expecting you next year, but I have taken the liberty of calling him to make earlier arrangements.' He opened a drawer and pulled out a leather strap, slowly placing it on the desk. Fingers of smoke reached across the desk, curling around Ernst's throat. 'You have crossed the line with your behaviour this time, and there is no better place than a strict boarding school to drill some good sense into a wayward boy. Discipline is what a young man needs, and I'm afraid your Mutti has spoiled you rotten. This wildness must be tamed.'

In the tainted light of dusk, Ernst headed towards home, taking his usual shortcut through the lawns. He walked briskly. His shadow stopped following him as the sun sank behind the linden trees. The neighbourhood of the zoo precinct was deserted at this hour, the street lamps blinking in the fading light. Children had already been dragged home by their nannies for dinner, bath and bed. A large bird stood on the crossbar of a swing set in the centre of a playground, preening its shiny feathers. *Nebelkrähe*, mist crow. The smell of smoke and fried bacon hung heavily in the air. Ernst's wrist throbbed, and he felt a stabbing pain in his chest. Colour continued to leach from the sky. He spun around, sensing he was being followed, yet saw no one.

Back home, he retreated to his study yet again, a tapes-tried cushion propped up against the small of his back. He surveyed the room, which held almost the sum total of who he was. His achievements were measured in head counts, in the preserved corpses of animals he'd carefully plucked off this earth. Thankfully, he was a crack shot. Almost from the time he could walk, he would secretly tag along on other men's hunting trips. Like a soldier falling in line, in his tiny hiking boots he strode across the most inaccessible places, on account of the birds. He was eager to see their thick rainbow plumage. From behind the trees, he watched as shooters crept silently through the under-brush, stalking a woodpecker or a rare hawkfinch. One old man he followed on many an occasion always took off a bird in flight with one clean shot. He watched the man carefully, trying to learn how it was done. For Ernst, blowing a wing off was not an option; a bird with missing wing bones was useless to a collector. It was either a pellet straight to the breast or it would be left there to die.

A row of tiny bird skulls – a memento mori from many of his hunting expeditions – now lined the top shelf of his desk, tucked between textbooks on taxidermy, zoology, biology. To collect was to control.

Ernst's eyes rested on a dusty brown bottle lodged between a box of cigars and a framed photo of his father. The bottle was a gift from Brooky, when they first met back in 1930, just before they set off on their first expedition together. Although the ink had faded, the elaborate letter-ing on the label was still legible: *Laudanum*, opium from the poppy plant, whose large, delicate blood-red petals flirted with death. The curved bottle on the shelf was a seductress; Ernst had never opened it, although Brooky often urged him to try it, saying it would be life-changing. Even his beloved Goethe had explored the notion *I change my brain, therefore I am*, but Ernst believed that man held the world together only through immersion in nature.

He thought about Brooky's decline into drink, and how fed up everyone became with the American towards the end of their second expedition. The lily-livered adventurer had fled in the middle of the night, leaving Ernst to face an onslaught of Chinese warlords and their marauding tribes. But Ernst, determined to complete the expedition, led the entire entourage through the precarious hills of China by himself. Although they still kept up a correspondence of sorts, Brooky's desertion had tarnished their friendship. Admittedly, there had been some misgivings about the joint project from the start. It felt self-defeating in some way to try to wed German scientists with Americans, their attitudes being so different. But Ernst was an obstinate man, just like his father; once he made a decision, he stuck to it. It was indeed an honour to be part of an American expedition, to be affiliated with an institution as prestigious as the Academy of Natural Sciences of Philadelphia. It gave him the unique opportunity to hunt the elusive panda bear. But he knew that even at the age of twenty-one, he demonstrated more leadership skills than Brooky ever would. Some nights out there in the wilds of Kham, curled up on top of his own bedroll, the mules snorting as they swished at gnats with their shabby tails, Ernst dreamt of his snail-paced progress up the ranks of academia. He imagined himself, funded by some generous philanthropist who recognised the importance of his work, catapulted to the heights of success.

'Why do you have to kill so many of them?' Herta asked him later that evening as they sat in his study, the incident with

Klaus still haunting her. She stroked an eagle that lay on his desk. 'Can't you just observe them while they are alive?'

'Dead birds tell us tales,' he replied, sounding like a father admonishing his delinquent child. 'We can learn all sorts of things from preserved specimens – their diet, for example, or their patterns of migration. And besides, it is important to build a collection for future generations. There's no telling what pressing biological questions will be of concern to our children. This way, future scientists will have material and samples to study. Surely it's better to preserve dead birds for science than simply watch them become dinner for rats.'

'But they would still be alive if you didn't shoot them, Ernst.'

He took the eagle from her and placed it on the desk. 'Don't touch, my dearest,' he said, taking her elbow and leading her to the kitchen, her slippers scraping on the floor in feeble protest. 'It's in the interests of science. You wouldn't understand.'

Oh, that she could take flight from all this, migrate to more hospitable lands. She would climb to the heights of the sky, teasing the wisps of clouds, barely flapping a wing as she cruised over villages, fields and lush forests. Poised somewhere between mankind and heaven, she would travel thousands of miles to see the world. It pained her to see the eagle recruited now as the *Reichsadler*, a symbol of less lofty ideals. If she had those mighty wings, she would set off on her own private exodus, drop the swastika from her talons, swapping it for the olive branch, and

162

perhaps follow the bald eagle across the Atlantic to taste life there. And then, at the end of days, she would fly around the throne of God.

Herta took her precious copy of the Bible from the shelf, opened to Proverbs and read out loud:

'There are three things which are too wonderful for me, yea, four which I know not: the way of an eagle in the air; the way of a serpent upon a rock; the way of a ship in the midst of the sea; and the way of a man with a maid.'

She marked the page and set the book aside. Plunging her hand into a bowl, she kneaded raw minced meat between her fingers, preparing *klops* for dinner, one of Ernst's favourite meals.

Ernst returned to his study and loosened the bandage Herta had wrapped around his wrist. How could his own wife criticise him, see his life's work as barbaric? Herta thought the thrill of the hunt was pitiless, chasing after an animal whose only desire was to survive. It seemed she was incapable of understanding how much it was a spiritual event for him. He, Ernst Schäfer, was not a bloodthirsty man. On the contrary: who else but someone who truly venerated nature would put up with the attention to detail necessary for the preservation of an animal's carcass? Not many were willing to endure the putrid smell of decay in order to bring the world a thing of beauty to behold.

As people gazed through the glass at the dioramas of natural-history museums around the world, they shared in the wonders of nature, and its serenity. They didn't realise it was impossible to be a hunter without loving the animal you chased. Somehow, he needed to make Herta see that he was a dedicated chronicler of the wild, sacrificing his own comfort for future generations, so that through his work all might witness the beauty of this earth.

Himmler must not catch wind of Herta's protests; the man was a bloodhound when it came to sniffing out dissent. Ernst would never forget the time he overheard the Kommandant laughing with another senior SS officer about the Polish intelligentsia: *'We should give them a chance to examine potatoes from under the ground.'* Ernst understood he had to be careful not to end up in a precarious position because of his feisty wife.

He reached up and took the small bottle of laudanum down from the shelf. His fingers left marks in the dust and he wiped them on his trousers. Over in the corner of the room his shiny new leather boots stood tall alongside his worn-out hiking shoes, which lay slumped in the corner. That evening, poring over photos of his trip with Brooky, he tried to slip one of the worn boots on again but, like a jilted lover, it put up a stiff resistance. A pair of Tibetan slippers stood in front of the boots. The Panchen Lama, garbed in robes embroidered with silken threads of crimson and gold, had given them to Ernst as a gift.

Ernst looked up. From his desk he could see Herta reading in the loungeroom, her back towards him. Himmler was right about the benefits of a wife; she gave his restless soul a hearth and a home. He watched the woman he loved as she set the book aside and moved over to a corner of the room. She lifted her precious flute from its case and brought it to her lips. The music was warm and tender, but he could hear the quivering in her breath, like a songbird singing to its friends of its longing to be free. He knew that feeling all too well. Part of him ached to escape from trying to be a perfect husband, a studious scientist, a spotless officer of the Reich. Tibet, like a sultry mistress, waited in the background, beckoning him irrevocably towards her seductive terrain.

CHAPTER 17

Early November 1937

As the new year approached and the departure date loomed closer, Ernst and Herta's apartment became the ersatz headquarters of the expedition. With so many people constantly coming and going, Herta was being driven to despair.

One morning, just before Geer arrived, Herta felt faint as she stood shelling a bowl of peas, clumsily sorting the black ones from the green. She poured herself a glass of water and sat down. Although she ached to ask Ernst if he'd made any enquiries yet about Margarete, she hesitated to say anything, cautiously rehearsing the lines in her head. She tried to phrase her words prudently, so as to not anger him. Lately, it only took a dash of alcohol, or his feeling that he was the butt of a joke, or even a mere drop of sarcasm on her behalf, to unleash the flood of his fury. She felt a fissure between the Ernst she loved – a good man, a decent man, absorbed in the drudgery of repairing the garbage bin – and this beast that emerged. She was finding it harder and harder to predict what might short-circuit his demeanour. It was always small annoyances that triggered his rage. This morning, he was giving her a hand in the kitchen when he came across some mouldy bread. She felt the darkness encroaching as he rummaged around in the back of the breadbox.

'Is this what they taught you in bride school?' He waved the mangled loaf in the air.

She tried to stay calm. Holding the shrivelled pea pods between forefinger and thumb, she pressed until she forced them open with a tiny pop.

'We are in no situation to waste even the tiniest morsel of bread. You don't seem to have the slightest idea how to run a household. Until I finish my doctorate, we simply have to tighten our belts.'

He launched into a speech about family values and the nation's struggle. She knew it would be safer to suffer the indignity of his barrage of complaints silently, but something rose up inside her, like a tiny firefly, penetrating her fear.

'I was simply keeping the stale loaves to grind into breadcrumbs.' She coughed, clearing her throat. 'I asked you to fix the mincer last week. I didn't notice everything had grown mouldy in the meantime.'

'So, you're saying it's my fault you're a sloppy housewife? You seem to have made a habit of blaming me for what are your own shortcomings.'

'Ernst,' she pleaded, immediately feeling regret at having challenged him, 'that's simply not true.'

'It seems I'm a liar, too,' he said, cornering his prey. 'All I ever hear from you is criticism. Never a thank-you. A patriotic German wife would be delighted to take better care of her man. Just look at how Hildegard dotes on Bruno. That man doesn't have to lift a finger at home. I, on the other hand, help you with shopping, tidying, cleaning. If my superiors knew about it, I'd be the laughing stock of the SS. What is it that you want from me, Herta? Am I not a devoted husband? How much more would you like me to do?'

Sleet started falling outside. Herta got up from the table, wiping her wet fingers down the front of her apron, and walked slowly across the kitchen to embrace him. He didn't move when she kissed his cheek. The floor undulated slightly beneath her feet. She kneeled down on the wooden floor, unbuttoned his fly and took him into her mouth as he thrust forcefully in and out. Sticky globules spurted into the back of her throat, making her gag, but she forced herself to swallow his bitter seed and, with it, her fear. They weren't taught this in bride school, but she knew it would calm him down, at least. Her face filled with the musty smell of him.

Geer arrived and sat in an armchair in the study for hours on end, taking calls, drafting letters and drawing up legal documents.

The phone rang. Ernst grabbed the receiver; his nails were bitten to the quick.

'*Allo! Allo!*' a shrill voice called out of the earpiece.

'Shut up!' Ernst boomed, before even checking who it might be. He tore the receiver from its cradle, tossing the phone across the room.

Geer sat still, watching Himmler's charming protégé throwing a full-blown tantrum. Ernst's face turned red with blistering rage, his eyes darting around the room like those of a wild animal, finally settling on the bearskin rug beneath him. He kneeled and patted the bear's furry head, whispering something into its ears.

Geer climbed out of his chair and, taking Ernst's arm, helped him up and led him over to a sofa by the hearth. He sat on a stool opposite, watching as his colleague's breathing slowed, the blood draining from his cheeks.

'I – I'm sorry,' Ernst stammered. 'My humble apologies.'

His outburst ended as quickly as it started, his anger dissolving into the smoke inside the fireplace, carried up through the chimney and out, leaving behind only the hissing of embers. Mounted on the wall, a row of exotic masks stared down at Ernst, like a tragic chorus of ghosts. Geer reached across to a table that stood between them and picked up a carafe. He poured his friend a shot of whisky, the orange flames from the hearth reflected in the sharp crystal edges of the glass.

'It's all too much,' Ernst said, slumped at one end of the sofa. 'I can't see how we are going to manage this without wads of money somehow flying in through the window.'

'We'll do it together, my friend.' Geer patted him on the shoulder.

'The *Ahnenerbe* look like they might pull out, though maybe that's not such a bad thing.'

The expedition's logistics were becoming more complicated by the day. Ernst wanted to trek beyond the forests of Kham to reach the Amnye Machen region, a white space on all his maps. But due to the rising unrest, with rival warlords roaming along the border, he would have to consider crossing into Tibet via India this time. That meant having to sweet-talk the British.

'Leave the money worries to me,' Geer said. 'I've already secured a commitment from the Advertising Council of German Industry for 46,000 Reichsmarks. Between Eher-Verlag, the German Research Foundation and the Foreign Ministry, we should be able to cover the rest of the trip. And you said your rich American friend has promised to make a contribution, too. We'll be fine.'

Ernst sat motionless, dark rings framing his eyes. He lifted a feather from the table and rolled it between the palms of his hands.

'Ah, that Brooky. Despite our differences, he's been a good friend. Sometimes I wonder if I should have stayed in Philadelphia instead of coming back.'

'Don't say that, Ernst,' Geer whispered. 'This is where you belong. You've just got a lot on, with your thesis and all these preparations for our trip.'

Ernst downed his whisky in one gulp. He screwed up his face, as if he'd just taken a draught of poison, then looked around his apartment. Although rather large by Berlin standards, it was antiquated, its creaky pipes groaning like an old man, the oil heaters flatulent and temperamental. His study was usually a sanctuary from the outside world. Today, though, he felt the room closing in on him; the mounted shaggy head of a yak he shot in China seemed to laugh at him, along with its stuffed companion, a crested grebe.

'You're right,' he said, turning to Geer. 'I need to get away.'

'Maybe you should have a check-up first? I know a wonderful physician over on Lindenstrasse. He took over the practice from the old Jew, Ehrlich, who everyone loved so much because he cured their peckers. He probably licked them clean!'

'No, I'm not sick. Just exhausted.'

'Ah!' A smile crept across Geer's face, a glint of camaraderie in his eyes. He lowered his voice. 'A new bride can be very taxing on a man.' He chuckled, taking a handkerchief from his trouser pocket and wiping his brow. 'You'd better look after yourself. Keep your energy levels up, *errhmm*, along with everything else.'

Ernst pondered his friend's words. 'I'm going away,' he announced.

His friend looked at him, puzzled.

'You can all live without me for a few days.'

'Pardon?'

'You heard me. I'm taking my *geliebten Frau*, my beloved wife, on an adventure in the wilderness, right here on our doorstep.' His eyes lit up with excitement, all the life that had been drained out of them now flooding back.

171

'We both need it.' He spoke quickly, words jostling each other to leap out first from his mouth. 'I'll send a telegram immediately to *Reichsjägermeister* Göring. He invited me to join the hunt at Schorfheide this week. I told him I was busy with my thesis, but you know what, my friend, I'm damned if I'm not going to take him up on his invitation to spend some time at his mansion. I'll let him know I'm coming tomorrow. I must tell Herta to start packing. I want us to be on our way by dawn.'

'Tomorrow? Ernst, we're supposed to be setting off for Tibet in a matter of months. You can't just run off with Herta like that. Do you love her more than you love your team?'

'Don't make me choose, my friend.' Ernst laughed.

'Ah, yes, but if it ever came to a choice between Herta and the hunt, I have no doubt as to who would win out.'

CHAPTER 18

8 November 1937

Herta sat beside her husband in the old Opel he'd borrowed from the university as they drove north along the new autobahn. Ernst had surprised her with news of a belated honeymoon at Carinhall. Named after his first wife, Carin, Göring's country mansion was designed by Werner March, the same brilliant architect who had dreamt up the plans for the Olympic Stadium. The hope was that this escape from their apartment, from the city, would return them both to their senses.

They stopped along the way for a break and Ernst took off into the forest to stretch his legs. Herta was standing by a small riverbank when she spotted two greedy carp in the shallows. They made their way towards her, their giant mouths gaping with the prospect of a fleshy snack. As they gazed up at her from their murky *Umwelt*, she wondered how she appeared to them. Did they see her in the same way a human might?

She retreated to a grassy hill and sat in the weak sunshine, waiting for Ernst to return. Being alone in the wild often spooked her, but she would never admit this to her intrepid husband. The quiet out here felt ominous, as if danger lurked in every shadow. Birds interrupted the silence, calling from the canopy of the forest, and insects broke the monotony with their humming *tsk, tsk, tsk*. Surely the wife of a famous zoologist and explorer should be comfortable with the language of nature? The truth was that she preferred to be indoors, playing her flute. After all, wasn't music the profoundest expression of nature? And whenever she had craved the company of an animal, all she needed to say was *puss, puss, puss*, and Klaus used to obligingly jump straight onto her lap, curl up and fall asleep, purring loudly as she stroked his back.

She remembered when she had first found Klaus buried under a pile of rubbish and held the shivering mess of fur in the palm of her hand. His eyes were still closed and one of his hind legs hung limp. His pitiful mewlings were tiny darts that pierced her heart. She brought him back to Frau Lila's, hidden inside her coat. Hildegard crept into the kitchen that night, bringing back cold offerings of fish scraps she had salvaged from the trash. Herta cared for the sickly kitten in the same way she had looked after Margarete. It was good to feel needed again. Over the next few weeks Klaus learnt to totter around, despite his bad leg, growing stronger and more playful each day.

For Ernst, nature was inexhaustible. Herta imagined him at that moment among the wild things, crawling, running and hopping with them across the earth's wrinkles, or simply perched on a rock reading his beloved *Faust*, as if it were the Bible.

When she had again brought up her concerns about Ernst's sponsorship through the *Ahnenerbe* after dinner the previous night, he became so defensive.

'The Devil was the one who came to me, Liebchen. Not I it was who whistled him from hell. A self-willed bird, he flew upon the lime.'

'You can quote your silly Faust as much as you like, but it doesn't make what you are doing right.' Herta was clearing the plates from the table and placing them in the sink. 'Those Ancestral Heritage folk are dangerous, Ernst. I've heard they are up to some strange things and I'm scared of you being involved with them. I've listened to your conversations with Bruno, so I know you share some of my concerns. Having some of them at our wedding was one thing, but the moment you take money from these people you become part of the machine, whether you like it or not.'

'I don't give a damn what hocus pocus they are conjuring in that haunted castle of theirs. If Himmler wants to believe ancient Aryans conquered Asia, who am I to challenge him? As long as he coughs up the money for the trip, I'm happy.'

Herta was silent as she started soaping the dishes and rinsing them. Ernst ran his fingers through his hair.

'You know I joined the party back in thirty-three because I didn't have a choice. My father thought it would be prudent, to help advance my career, and I didn't want to cross him, so I went along with it. It meant nothing to me at the time. Besides, you've seen firsthand how difficult it is to say no to him.'

That doesn't absolve you, she wanted to say.

Ernst was a good man, not rabid in his views like Bruno, yet she could not stifle her unease. Being a part of it all, whether out of a sense of patriotism or sheer opportunism, led one into a moral cul-de-sac.

She stared blankly at the suds in the sink. 'Do you hate Jews?' she asked him, the words erupting out of her.

He sat there in silence, poking at some crumbs left on the tablecloth, forming them into two battlelines. A storm brewed behind his half-smile. He didn't answer her. Somehow, she would have preferred a straight-out snarl, a shout, the slamming of a door.

She abandoned the dishes, dried her hands with a tea towel and left the room, walking down the hallway and into their bedroom. She opened the bottom drawer of the armoire and pulled out a nightgown. Tucked in a corner was an embroidered linen handkerchief. She lifted it from its hiding place and unwrapped a faded photo of three children. A girl and boy stood on either side of a small child, whose blonde braids reached all the way down to the top of her withered legs.

Herta sat at her dressing table. Propping the photo up against the mirror, she pulled pins out from her bun, her long, thick hair unwinding. She picked up a brush and started the tedious work of untangling knots.

Ernst appeared in the doorway, his face still flushed. Without looking across at Herta, he pulled his pyjamas out from underneath his pillow. He sat down on the edge of the bed and started unbuttoning his shirt.

'I was there when it happened,' she said quietly.

'What are you talking about, Herta?'

'That night. When they burned the books.'

'You mean in Waltershausen? I wasn't even in Germany then. You know that.'

'It wasn't just in Waltershausen, Ernst. It was right across the country. It had to do with all of us. And that was just the start. Soon, Jews were locked out of everything. *Dort, wo man Bücher verbrennt, verbrennt man auch am Ende Menschen.* Wherever they burn books, they will also end up burning human beings. Heinrich Heine wrote that, and even his beautiful poetry went up in flames.'

'I was in Western China with Brooky back then. I didn't know about anything that was happening anywhere in the world.'

Herta's eyes bore into the mirror, watching his reflection. 'Brecht, Zweig, Keller, Brod, Dreiser, Remarque, Hemingway. They forced Vati to empty his shelves, calling his library *nichtdeutsch*. A group of students threw his books in a huge pile in the middle of the town square, alongside all the other books they deemed degenerate.'

'Why are you telling me this now, Herta? What do you want from me? You know I had nothing to do with it.'

'They distributed leaflets a day earlier. Fire oaths, they called them. They were to be read before hurling each author's book into the flame. I still remember their eerie chants:

'*Against decadence and moral decay! For discipline and decency in family and state! I surrender to the flames the writings of Heinrich Mann, Ernst Glaeser and Erich Kästner.*

'*Against the democratic-Jewish character of journalism alien to the nation! For responsible collaboration on the work of national construction! I surrender to the flames the writings of Theodor Wolff and Georg Bernhard.*'

Ernst frowned. 'But you know I'm not one of them, Herta. I'm just a scientist.'

'Have you ever thought about the scholars whose place you took? And what might have become of them now? Not only the students, but the professors, writers, artists, musicians, doctors, lawyers. All vanished.'

'What would you have me do, Herta?'

'You promised me there wouldn't be a war, Ernst. But I feel something rotten crawling towards us.'

'I gave you my heart. And my soul.'

'I know you love me.'

'So, you need to trust me. We are in no danger. It's not us they're after.'

'Are you so sure, Ernst?' She stopped brushing her hair and stared at his reflection in the mirror. 'After what happened to Margarete, anything is possible.' She picked up the photo of the three children, blood rushing through her fingers as if she were grasping a hot branding iron. Turning to face her husband of nearly four months, her friend of an entire lifetime, she handed it to him. The windowpanes shuddered. Outside, the gusts of wind rattled at the glass, trying to break in.

'Vati gave this to me on the day of our wedding.'

He took the photo from her.

'I want to know where she is, Ernst.' She placed her hand on his shoulder. 'With all your connections I am sure you will find out something about her soon. It's only a matter of time.'

Ernst looked at her, the blood draining from his face. They undressed in silence and climbed into bed, Herta listening to an owl hooting in the distance.

Herta continued to wait for Ernst by the river. She watched ripples spread across the water, a light breeze tickling the reeds along the banks. The sun disappeared behind the clouds and the air quickly turned crisp, sending a shiver through her body. Herta pulled out a second woollen shawl from her bag. She felt she needed to speak back to the unspeakable, but some things could not be said with words. She would sit quietly and observe, record her muted vision of the world. Herta: her name meant *from the earth*, but sometimes she felt she flew above it, hovering with the birds.

CHAPTER 19

Around mid-afternoon, they arrived at Göring's opulent hunting lodge, built on the banks of Lake Döllnsee, home to a multitude of waterfowl. Driving through the massive entrance, the gates adorned with a shield bearing the coat of arms of a lion and a bear, Ernst wound down the driver's window, inviting a shrieking cacophony of birdsong into the car. The landscape of wild moors, forest and lake, within which the lodge was nestled, was the soothing salve to his wounds. The driveway was long, curving its way under a canopy of trees whose leaves shone red and gold as they clung to overhanging branches. It took almost five minutes to reach the thatch-roofed house. The white stucco walls were punctuated with bronze statues of antelopes and deer. As they pulled in, Göring stood at the entrance waiting to greet them, surrounded by his attendants. He wore a vest over a white shirt with puff sleeves. A bronze dagger was fastened to his belt. Flanked by drooling black Tibetan Mastiffs, his pursed, thin lips showed not even the trace of a smile.

Later that evening, the two men sat in green brocade armchairs in front of a giant fireplace, puffing on their pipes as they regaled each other with their stories of the hunt. A giant globe on a wooden stand rested between them. Göring spoke about the game reserve he had built up.

'I am a friend of animals. The Reich Hunting Law that the Führer and I adopted has given our animals greater protection than any other country in the world. Whoever tortures innocent creatures violates the instincts of the German people. A clean kill is a kind kill.'

'I couldn't agree more,' Ernst said, raising his glass.

Meanwhile, the two wives chatted. The gentle Emmy confided to Herta that she was two months pregnant, although her lack of appetite at dinner had already betrayed her condition to the younger woman. Not long after dessert and coffee had been served, Emmy excused herself and went up to bed. As the men talked, Herta occupied herself playing with Göring's pet lion cubs. The smallest one, Caesar, was as adorable as a kitten, but nothing could ever take the place Klaus held in Herta's heart. Lifting Caesar up, she cradled him like a baby, singing softly as she strolled across to stand before a floor-to-ceiling window. The moon was full in the sky. She stared out at the shining lake, a row of wooden boats moored beside a boathouse, bobbing up and down in the water. In the window's reflection she could see tapestries draping the walls behind her, interrupted only by mounted stags' heads, the scene lit up by magnificent chandeliers.

The lion cub fell asleep in Herta's arms as she stroked his little head, but when he started from his slumber he grabbed her wrist between his teeth. Both Herta and the diminutive king of the jungle squealed as they dropped to the floor, entangled in each other's hold. The feisty cub reared up and lunged at her clumsily with its forepaws, leaving a rent in her chiffon dress. Göring rose quickly, donning a pair of leather gloves that lay on a table beside his chair. He grabbed the animal by the scruff of its neck and motioned to one of his attendants, who procured a rope on cue and lassoed it over the cub's head.

'Take them both back to that damned zookeeper in Berlin immediately,' Göring barked.

'Yes sir.'

'And tell him he's left them here far too long again. The replacement cubs should have arrived over a month ago. These have grown far too big to keep as pets. They don't amuse me anymore.'

'But Herr Göring, the Director himself has written to say the new litter is still in the process of being weaned.'

'Insolence!' Göring spat out the word like a drunkard. 'How dare you? Lutz Heck is a hunting companion of mine. He has always been very cooperative.' His face darkened with anger, all geniality and hospitality draining from his eyes.

He shifted his attention to the butler. 'And you, you imbecile, tend to the young *Frau*'s wounds! Can't you see her blood is soiling the carpet?'

182

The young man scurried off and came back with a silver tray that was laden with bandages and disinfectant. He dabbed at Herta's wound, closing his eyes as she winced. His face was turning pale and he looked like he was about to pass out. Herta took the gauze from his hands and motioned silently for to him leave.

Göring turned to Ernst, purring now. 'My dears, I will let you rest. You have had a long drive and you must be weary. Young love needs time to be alone. Let us meet after lunch tomorrow and I shall show you around the grounds. What's say we go shoot our own dinner, my good man.'

'I would be delighted, Herr *Reichsjägermeister*.'

'Excellent! I'll have my gamewarden make the arrangements. It's not every day I get to entertain Germany's most famous explorer.'

Although Ernst had tasted modest celebrity since the publication of *Mountains, Buddhas and Bears*, about his first Tibet expedition, no one ever stopped him in the streets to ask for his autograph, and, as the state of their apartment attested, he certainly couldn't live off his writing. It was flattering to know his books took pride of place on the shelves of Carinhall's extensive library.

'You must tell me more about your travels in the Orient with that American cowboy. I am so proud that this time you will lead our own heroic team of men into those mystical lands. We share the same passion, my good man,' Göring said, staring at Herta.

Ernst wasn't sure if the man was intoxicated by her beauty or the copious amount of wine he had already drunk during dinner. Göring heaved himself up from his chair, shuffling across the rug to stand in front of the fireplace. A veil of smoke filled the *Jagdhalle*, giving a surreal air to the room. Blasts of wind swept down the chimney, and blackened logs crackled in the giant fireplace as if the Devil himself were trapped in its flames.

'It's sealed then.' Göring swirled brandy around in his glass. 'Tomorrow, as my honoured guest, you shall be treated to an experience beyond compare. Only last week I entertained Ciano, the Italian foreign minister, and the brute was lucky enough to snag a bison. I told him about my plan to host an exhibition of caged Jew-beasts. Their ugly noses remind me so much of elks.'

Herta glanced across at Ernst, who was staring into the fire.

Göring laughed and turned to Herta. 'Frau Schäfer, don't worry your pretty head. I won't keep you away from your husband for too long, I promise. Perhaps you two might enjoy some pleasant boating in the morning, before we meet for the hunt? The ducks are yet to leave the lake. Please find at your disposal all that Carinhall has to offer. You might enjoy a visit to our very own cinema – I believe *Heidi*, with that new child actress who's all the rage, is screening now. We have obtained a copy for a sneak preview. Or you may prefer tenpin bowling? It's the latest fashionable sport, you know. We have our very own bowling alley right here in the west wing.'

'That is very kind of you, Herr Göring.'

'Call me Hermann, my dear,' he said, walking over to where she stood. He took her newly bandaged hand in his.

'Thank you, Hermann,' she said, blushing. 'I would be happiest just browsing through the books in your library, if I may.'

'Of course, my sweet. After all, you are the wife of a famous author. And looking at you in all your radiance, I am sure you are your husband's muse.' He made his way over to the door but spun around at the threshold. 'I do think a young bride would be advised to spend tomorrow morning prettying herself for her husband. Perhaps in the sauna first and then indulging herself in a luxurious massage in one of our tempting new Elizabeth Arden massage chairs?'

Herta looked across at Ernst, hoping he would answer for her, but he was busy examining the hunting trophies that hung on the wall.

'Thank you so much.' She smoothed the creases from her dress with her uninjured hand. 'However, I would very much like to accompany my husband on a boating trip tomorrow morning, if you do not mind, that is. Perhaps I could avail myself of your generous offer during the afternoon, while you men go off hunting?'

'Yes, yes. Excellent idea.'

Herta tried to stifle a yawn. Her head was pounding, and the shadows outside seemed to lunge at her. She was growing tired of the small talk. When Ernst stood up, placing his hand on her shoulder, she almost wished he might carry her upstairs. She still had so much to do

185

before she could place her head on the pillow. There were his boots to polish and rifle to shine. Bride school had not been a waste of time after all. She would have Ernst's rifle gleaming as if it had just been issued and never been fired, his boots so clean no one would imagine he stepped in such murky terrain. Wouldn't Frau Scholtz-Klink be proud of her now, she thought bitterly. And later, in bed, she would perform her womanly duties for the Fatherland.

After finishing her chores, she changed into her night-gown, shivering as she wrapped a shawl around her. She climbed into bed. Herta may be his wife, but she knew that in Ernst's blue dreams, Tibet was his illicit lover. Like one of his migratory birds, Ernst was bewitched, destined to answer the siren call of a distant land; Herta, on the other hand, loved the smell of home. The Thousand-Year Reich needed room to spread its wings, his colleagues said – the more land on which the German people would be able to live, surrounded by the beauty and peace of nature, the better for all. *Lebensraum*, they called it. So much spoken about ancient superstition, and she wondered if one day scholars would write of the monuments that weren't built, or those that would crumble in time like those of ancient cities.

She knew this expedition was the beginning of a new world for her husband. He was about to undertake an adventure in a continent whose skies were lit up by as many stars as there were stones on the ground. So far away from the thunderous arena of civilisation. Meanwhile, she was still learning the geology of the man she loved:

the crevices in his heart and the depths of his moods, changing in a flash like the onset of a bad storm.

And, right on call, he threw her down on the bed, her legs splayed like one of his specimens, doomed to be stabbed alive. She knew if she pretended to writhe and shriek a little, it might heighten his fervour. Instead, she stayed silent, which made him lose control, and his *kleine Mauser*, as he called his manhood, went off half-cocked instead of firing point blank into her.

Herta woke in the middle of the night, Ernst snoring contentedly beside her. She crept out of bed and stood by the window, looking out at the lake, the moon leaving long white trails along the surface. Where did it all cleave, this deep love they shared? Herta had always been certain they would write about Ernst effusively in newspapers, journals and books. He would be regarded as one of the most brilliant naturalists of his day, filling the museums of Philadelphia and Berlin with an extraordinarily rich array of specimens, lauded as one of the first to bring together scientific disciplines. But even though he believed he was looking for unity, his quest for knowledge reduced life to compartments, sections, categories, lists.

On a recent evening at home, Herta had been looking through hundreds of photos, helping Ernst document his previous two expeditions with Dolan. The albums were strewn around the apartment after Ernst had taken them out of the boxes to show off to Geer and Bruno. Snapshots of her husband the hunter, lying on the ground in front of a campfire, cuddling three bearskins, and Brooky wearing a peaked cap and heavy coat, riding a mule across a barren plain. And then she saw the horror. At twenty-four, Ernst had become the first white man in the world to come home with the prize of a baby panda. She burst into tears. Ernst snatched the photo from her hand.

'You don't understand, Herta. It was one of the biggest breaks in my career. President Roosevelt's son Theodore, who happened to be a good friend of Brooky's, was the first to shoot one of these creatures in the wild. When they put it on display at the Field Museum in Chicago, it drew crowds the size of which had never been seen before. So, the museum in Philadelphia wanted one, too, and Brooky told them I was the only man for the job. After camping in those bamboo forests for weeks, we had nearly given up hope. The mission would have been a failure had I not spotted a juvenile hidden in the trees, only four hundred metres away.'

Ernst described how the shot had echoed as he watched the tiny animal fall and become tangled in the branches of bamboo. A badly wounded specimen was a lost specimen, of absolutely no value to a museum, so he carefully fired a few more 'kisses' until the creature dropped to the ground. Running towards his catch, he could feel his heart beating wildly. The baby panda was sure to take pride of place in a diorama in Philadelphia. The carcass would need some tidying up, but it would be the making of his career.

Herta took the photo back from Ernst and looked at it again. The skinned panda was tucked under his arm, his free hand clutching an ornithological find by its scaly legs as he posed for the camera.

Herta threw the photo back on the pile. 'You will never be able to see the real Tibet, Ernst. You are too busy dissecting it.'

'And you know nothing of science, my dearest wife.'

Where was that young child who would frolic in the woods? Some days, she still saw him bathed in sunlight, the boy she knew before, eyes the colour of honey. But duty had blocked his ears to her pleas, while Tibet oozed in through the cracks in the windowpane and floated in through the front door.

As Herta stood by the window, watching the dark lake, Ernst slept fitfully, his thoughts plagued by the photo of them with Margarete that Herta had shown him. He thought his wife was a common starling he had held in his hands all these years, but it had burst into flames before his eyes and some mythical creature emerged to rise up against him. The threat to his career, possibly endangering his very life, had materialised in black and white. His empty promises to Herta to ask about Margarete were no longer a tale spun in the air that he could laugh off as malicious gossip if anyone happened to find out. This photo was proof. It implicated him. He could tear it up, burn it, but somewhere the negative existed. His image had stared back at him, smiling knowingly, as if to say, *you are caught in a trap of your own making*.

One year, when the first day of spring came to Waltershausen, the sodden earth was already filled with ditches and mud from melting snows. Clouds were scattered across the sky like chalky scribbles. Ernst had been itching to race to the forest together with Herta straight after school to visit their secret hide-out, and to search for fox cubs in their carefully concealed dens. But Herta's father forbade her to go out and play, insisting she needed to stay home and catch up on her flute practice. When Ernst turned up at her house that afternoon, she was sobbing.

'Poor Margarete has been stuck inside her room all winter. I really wanted her to come out with us today.'

Ernst stood awkwardly at the door, wanting so badly to share the rush of blossom and hypnotic birdsong with his best friend. He looked down at his feet, shoes worn thin, the brown laces frayed. 'I'll take her.'

'It's too dangerous, Ernst. Vati will hear her wheelchair rattling across the path.'

'Leave it to me. You distract him with your flute and I'll carry her there, then you sneak out and join us when you're finished.'

Herta whistled their secret birdcall to let him know no one was watching. He lifted Margarete from her bed, her legs thin and mottled, dangling limply as he carried her out through the back door. She kept licking her lips, her blonde eyelashes fluttering in the sunlight. Ernst marched with her, climbing over rocks and wading across tiny streams until they reached the clearing in the wood.

Lowering her onto the damp ground, he propped her up against an old pine. She sat surrounded by white cyclamens, her hands knotted in her lap. He would often collect pinecones and place them in a pile before Margarete, cracking them open using a jagged stone and gathering up the *Pinienkerne*, the hidden delicious nuts, as they scattered on the ground. From the pocket of his shorts he would pull out some pieces of chocolate and make sweet pine-nut sandwiches for her.

Today, though, Ernst disappeared for a short while, climbing up the old oak tree to collect newly laid eggs before they had a chance to hatch. He found the nest of a tiny wren, but it was too late. A cuckoo chick had already completed its grisly business of evicting all the other occupants and sat alone in the empty nest, its huge orange throat gaping within its tiny skull. With an insatiable appetite, it waited impatiently for its surrogate mother to return.

Ernst reached in and grabbed the chick, holding its knobbly legs carefully between his fingers. When he laid it down in Margarete's lap, the baby bird squirming and cheeping furiously, her eyes gleamed like faint sparks from the pearly fog of her mind. Even though he knew Margarete couldn't hear him, Ernst sang a song as he stroked the bird.

Kuckuck, Kuckuck ruft aus dem Wald.
Lasset uns singen, tanzen und springen!
Frühling, Frühling wird es nun bald!

Cuckoo, Cuckoo calls from the forest.
He makes us sing, dance and jump!
Spring, spring will soon be here!

He was glad, in a way, that he could be alone there with Margarete to share the delight this bundle of fluff brought her. Herta would never have allowed him to steal it from the nest. Uncurling Margarete's stiffened fingers, he deposited the chick in her palm. What harm would it do if he returned it in a few minutes? Margarete's face contorted into a smile. Snorting, she groaned as the bird's downy feathers tickled her skin. As Ernst looked on, her fingers started spasming violently, closing around the cuckoo like a vice. Before Ernst could do anything, she snapped its spinal column. Then the bird and Margarete went limp.

At break of day the singing of thrushes rose in the distance and the wind roared, as though the air itself was crying out in defiance. Mist cloaked the house. This morning they would go out on the lake; at long last some time alone together. As she lay in bed, waiting for Ernst to wake up, Herta was agonised with indecision – when should she tell him the news? She wanted to choose a time when he was relaxed and in a good mood, away from that clingy Geer, who hovered by his side, morning and night.

This was how she woke of late, the shadows filling the musty corners of the room. They winced in the light when she pulled back the curtains. Some days, she opened her eyes at dawn thinking it was dusk, hoping the long day ahead might already be over. Through the gauze of half-light, she stared at her blank face in the mirror. She recalled how she used to greet each day with bursting excitement at first, dreaming and planning for her future with Ernst, ignoring her father's apprehensive gaze.

The whispering in her head never stopped. When she had returned to bed from the window last night she dreamt she was on a train, holding up an open umbrella, unable to see the other passengers in the carriage. Through the window, she watched blurry green puffs whiz past. The conductor, his face ruddy and pained, handed her a letter. She opened the envelope, and out fell photographs she'd never seen before. She clutched them in her hand and quickly hid them in her bag. People standing in the corridor crowded into the carriage and she felt as though the world was rushing up to crush her.

CHAPTER 20

9 November 1937

Ernst felt relieved as he pulled on his knitted sweater and slipped his legs into dungarees. It was good to be out of uniform, to have peeled off the elegant black cladding of the Führer's special guard. Of course, Ernst always wore it with pride; the prestige and admiration that came with it made him feel like a rare bird himself. And the opportunities that had opened for him were undeniably attractive. Himmler was freeing up Germany's academia, cleaning Jews and communists out of the dusty halls of universities, and the promise of a glittering future seemed within everyone's reach. Himmler's demeanour was a little odd, but to his credit he was shaping a new order. There had been such a narrow focus on specialisation up until now, but finally scientists with a broader vision, whose research had application and relevance to developing the economic might of Germany once again, were receiving the recognition they deserved. You only needed to flip through a copy of *Das Schwarze Korps*, the journal of the SS that at any time was lying open on Ernst's desk, to see the level of expertise Himmler had already attracted to his new intelligentsia. Early membership in the SS had proven to be a wise suggestion on the part of Albert Schäfer, becoming Ernst's ticket to fame and personal glory.

Göring kindly organised for his personal chef to pack them a picnic breakfast – salami, sandwiches, apples, a draught of beer – before Ernst strolled down along a wooden pier to the boatsheds on the Döllnsee lake, checking which dinghy looked the sturdiest and safest for what he had in mind.

The lake was pure crystal, a light breeze tickling its surface. Sunlight crept through the branches of the spruce and oak that lined the shore. The mist was peeling itself off the trees, revealing their canopy of brown, crimson and yellow. Ernst's breath was frosty in the crisp air. Released from the frenzy of the city, it was a relief to escape into the wilderness he missed so much.

A reedy man with a pencil-thin moustache met Ernst at the boathouse. A sudden gust of wind swept the clouds across the sky, setting the wooden boats rolling from side to side like drunken whales, their keels groaning under the effort to balance themselves.

'Schäfer,' he introduced himself. 'Ernst Schäfer.'

They shook hands.

'I have read your books.' The man reached down to untie a rope, his fingers thick, skin weathered. 'Felix Engel, forest warden. I'll be taking you out on the lake this morning, Herr Schäfer.'

'There will be no need for that. I know how to sail one of these little toys.'

'*Reichsjägermeister* Göring's orders, sir. I am to accompany his esteemed guests on a tour.'

Ernst clenched his fists. He was humiliated by his poor performance the previous night, and he planned to right things out on the boat. When they were out in the middle of the lake, he would lay Herta down in the hull and have his way. Playfully, of course. Their cries would be drowned out by the laughter of ducks.

But his fantasy was thwarted by Engel's insistence. Ernst consoled himself with the fact that at least they were going duck-shooting, although that was a far cry from trekking along the Yangtze.

'I envy you your job,' he said, trying to strike up a conversation with the man. 'I abhor the city, feel so restless there pacing its streets like a caged beast. What I wouldn't give to live out here like you, so close to nature, my feet planted firmly on the soil.'

The surly warden didn't answer. He towered over Ernst by a head and refused to put him at his ease, which made his superior even more determined to trump him.

'I couldn't help but notice you are a fan of Goethe,' Ernst said, pointing to a volume that rested on the gunwale of the boat. 'Are you enjoying him?'

Engel flinched and looked away. 'It is a gift to you from my master. He thought you might like to recite some poetry to your bride as I row you both around the lake.'

Ernst laughed. He jumped off the edge of the pier, his coat-tails flying up like wings, and landed in the boat with a thump. He grabbed the book then held it up and grinned broadly.

'My host has excellent taste.' He flicked through the pages as if stroking a lover, every square inch of whose body he could trace, even while blindfolded. His breath quickened. *'What you don't feel, you'll never get by chasing/ Unless it presses from the soul.'*

Engel stood still, watching Ernst scour the pages in search of more lines.

'Ha! Herr Göring is a genius – he thinks of everything.' Ernst felt like a teenager who had found the secret of too much drink. 'I will recite to her from Goethe, a man who wrote for those who love the truth of bird and beast: *Escape! Into a wider land! Nature then your only tutor.'*

He looked at Engel. 'What better way to awaken a lady's passion?' Ernst spoke to him as one spoke into a mirror. Flipping through more pages, he found a final passage he was particularly fond of: *'As we return from dewy fields, dusk falls/ And birds of mischief croak their ominous calls.'*

The conversation didn't falter, because it had never really begun. The warden made no attempt to feign interest in Ernst's enthusiastic recitations. He turned his back and silently went about his business, tying the rope around a bollard. Eventually, he retreated back into the boathouse. Ernst might have leapt out of the dinghy and pounded him for his rudeness if Herta hadn't called to him, her voice filled with light.

'*So kalt!*' she said with a shiver, as she stepped onto the pier. The lace of the plain blue shawl wrapped around her shoulders had woven itself into his dreams the previous night. Overhead, a flock of wild geese sliced their way through the clouds. Deer grazed on the banks of the lake, launching small avalanches of crumbling dirt into the water as they tugged at scattered tufts of grass growing on the shore.

Ernst set the picnic basket down in the boat. He turned to his young bride and held out his hand.

Moments before, having made her way down from the mansion after a restless night, Herta had watched her husband from afar as he busied himself with preparations for their outing. Sometimes she pitied him, as if he were somehow bruised or dented, but there was an intensity in his eyes that she found quite frightening at times. To her shame and dismay, one icy glance from him could freeze her heart in an instant. That morning on the pier she showed restraint and, wrestling with her tears, stood before him smiling. They hadn't spoken about Margarete since she'd shown him the photo. Perhaps after what she had to say he would be in a more generous mood to discuss it again. How manipulative marriage had made her.

She took his hand, climbed into the boat and settled herself onto the wooden bench, tucking wisps of her hair under a scarf. She watched her young husband prop the shiny barrel of his favourite rifle against the gunwale, resting a spare in the bottom of the boat beside the picnic basket. A worn copy of *Faust* lay on top of a pile of old blankets. Ernst chewed his lower lip as he stood looking up, painstakingly studying the sky, the feeble sunlight playing cat and mouse with an assembly of low-hanging clouds. She wanted so much to tell him right then, almost bursting with the news she had first gleaned in the bathroom of the exhibition hall, but she would wait till the right moment when they were out on the lake, away from everyone and everything.

Engel emerged from the boathouse. He walked to the edge of the pier and bowed obsequiously to Herta. 'At your service, Frau Schäfer.'

Ernst stared at him. 'You may go. You are no longer required. I am perfectly capable of rowing a boat myself.' His solid build underlined his determination to do as he pleased, his short, muscular legs rooted in place, like those of an angry bulldog.

A fish leapt out of the water in a streak of silver.

'As you wish, sir.' The warden untied the rope from the bollard with seeming reluctance and pushed the dinghy away from its mooring.

She had heard the warden parrying with Ernst as she made her way down to the lake. A faint grimace seemed to appear on the man's face as his stooped figure faded into the distance. Out on the lake everything was silent, except for small waves lapping at the boat's hull. Now would be the perfect time. Herta hugged her belly with her hands, watching her husband as he rowed.

She wondered what it must feel like to be his prey, unaware of him creeping along the ground, whispering curses as he hides behind fallen logs. He has settled you into a corner and, just as you begin to sing in that throaty, ancient language he will never understand, comes that terrible sound. He has split you open like a ripe pomegranate, no time for ballooning fright. And with your last ounce of strength you stare at him wide-eyed, before rising to heaven.

The bloodstain on the sheet when she woke this morning made her fearful of a small death. Even though it was no more than the size of a pea, its body was already bloated with their future. She felt weary. And sad. Their child would be born into a world that she no longer recognised. For Herta the flowers, the meadows, leaves rustling in the wind, no longer held the promise they once did. Where would her baby live in this new world? She watched a brown wren hop busily from bush to bush. Gentle clouds gathered above, calmly pressing down on them. They formed a halo around the sun, which struggled to escape from their hold. She was safe for now, here in Ernst's hands.

The autumn breeze slowly undressed the trees, leaf by leaf, as they leaned over the water. A flock of ducks rose from the lake, pointed in the direction of the graveyard, where Carin lay buried in her mausoleum. The leader's call carried across the sky. Herta's thoughts flew up with them. Jolted by a sudden lurch of the boat, she clasped her belly. Should she tell Ernst now? She imagined that soon she would begin to feel the baby kicking. And which name to choose? She thought perhaps they should name their first child after a majestic bird.

Dark shapes watched from the shore, their skeleton branches shivering in the dawn. She saw a feather floating on the water, curled upwards, rising and falling in the wake of their little boat. She leaned out to grab it. When she looked up, a solitary reddish-gold eagle stared down at them, its wings cleaved to the lofty ceiling of clouds. Herta saw it as a sign. Their child would be called *Adler*, like the eagle. Ernst would be thrilled to name his son after a bird of prey, although she would have preferred to call the baby *Feder*. Her little feather.

'Ernst,' she said, hesitantly.

Before Herta saw them, she heard the querulous quacking of ducks coming from somewhere behind.

'Ernst. I have something to tell you.'

He grabbed the rifle and bit his lower lip as he aimed. The baby kicked violently as the sound echoed high above the forest – a shot as short and forceful as a single heartbeat.

PART III

PART III

CHAPTER 21

In Photo that He kept on His small desk in Basement, young Shepherd is perched on a wooden beam, legs crossed, as He cradles my head close to his breast, Firestick propped up against us. I don't know where He has hidden the rest of me. In His left hand, He clutches the white neck of a headless vulture, its claws scratching the earth beneath its feet. He sports a beard and moustache, His hair thick and wavy. Against a mountainous backdrop, He is seated in front of a makeshift wooden hut. He gazes lovingly at my face, the way Mother used to. I am staring back, my eyes half-closed, looking peaceful, content to be bathed in His adoration. This intimacy was forced upon me back then, the secrecy of my life invaded by those same eyes that were fascinated by my very existence. I did not choose immortality; it was His yearning for me that brought me here to Glass.

Every day I hear Testing Testing speak in a voice that booms from above. 'Live animal encounter on Level One. Science Live outside auditorium. Enjoy the rest of your day here at the Academy.'

Writer came once and visited me every day for an entire week they called Fellowship. I enjoyed her constant company, although she looked tired and sad, seated on the floor in front of Glass, her book open, whispering secrets to me. She told me she felt guilty, knowing how this looking at me had been made possible. In Life, I did not want to be seen, and Mother always told me to be still if Noise came close to Forest. Writer reads to me sometimes and apologises, calling herself a voyeur. Her heart is heavy because I was torn away and preserved, but her hand pushes Magic Stick furiously across the blank page because I am here. She tells me I am the true Storyteller, says I've written an adventure narrative without moving a muscle. My Visitors are like her Readers, she says, each one claiming ownership over the interpretation of the story I tell.

'This is my favourite diorama of all,' she writes.

I know this because when she has filled the page, she takes a break to drink from Flask, then reads me the words that have appeared. Like this, from the other day:

'The baby panda is a spectacle. Through the sacrifice of his short life, he transcends death. A gruesome artefact, he has been destroyed and removed from his vanished habitat, in an attempt to bring us closer to imagining it. The hunter came in search of exotic landscapes, wild and raw terrain in which to find bigger and rarer beasts. And in the chase, he

made up narratives about the love of nature, his prowess, the heroism of conquering a savage land, having it yield its treasures to a stranger. And the trophies he shipped back home to populate museums and parlours boasted of his skill with a shotgun, his dominion over Nature.'

She takes Magic Stick and scribbles across the page, 'Overwritten, sentimental claptrap!' At times, she thinks I am 'Adorable', writes that down. Then in a flash, changes her mind, crosses out the word and writes in angry, big letters, 'OBSCENE!' What a fickle, grumpy woman Writer can be. Shepherd never harboured such ugly thoughts about me. He worshipped me, proudly showing me off to all His friends.

'Du, Geist der Erde, bist mir näher; schon Fühl' ich mein Kräfte höher,' He would purr as He patted me, calling me His Earth Spirit, a timeless being, the immaterial becoming manifest through me. I must admit, in those days I didn't understand everything He spoke of, but over the years in Glass, I have learnt Wisdom. Now I know that for Shepherd, Nature was the ultimate mystery, and collecting as many of us as He could was His noble attempt to solve it. He was determined to unlock our secrets in the laboratory, then display them to World.

Artist covets me, so grateful Shepherd found me and brought me to her, says my everlasting posture makes me the most perfect model. Writer disagrees. She calls me 'Survivor', but I don't really understand how I can be victimised and saved at the same time. I am laid bare before Viewers, who stop to stare, laugh, smile, some turning pale, tears in their eyes. Some stay for only a moment, others spend months coming back

207

and forth. Scientist tells his students I am Empirical Data, a record of a moment on this earth that will soon vanish. Apparently, my form holds Information that only future generations will discover. Artist uses Stick to copy my likeness. She tells the group seated on folded chairs, their hair the colour of Sky or Bamboo, that 'the visceral pleasure of the backdrop speaks to people in a language in and of its own, the curved walls and foreshortening techniques conveying a vast landscape, painted by Clarence C. Rosenkranz, in a brilliant evocation of habitat.' I don't really understand what this means, but it sounds Important. I guess some of them are in the same clan as Tattoo-ist, because his drawing of me appears on their hides.

What compels them all to have stared at me since Opening on 28 December 1933? I was a part of Him, but now that we are no longer together it is hard to know who I am anymore. In here, I feel safe. Visitors spiral closer and closer, then wander off to see Okapi Glass opposite, which has just been cleaned and renewed, then retrace their steps to me. Some return hours or days later. They never scream, except for Smalls, who often shout and smile at the same time. Do Visitors think of the beauty of my fur, or do they see me as the fragile object of Shepherd's desire?

My face has been endowed with eternal calm, although that is not what I felt at that moment of Noise. Back then, I felt a searing pain and watched the white of my fur turn red. I fell to the ground and cannot remember much, except when He came and cradled my head, staring at me with such love. He was with another, who rolled up his sleeves, following Shepherd's orders to tie my feet together before they carried me out of Forest and away from Mother. I saw the pain in her eyes as we left. I lay helpless in the harness they had made, must have fainted several times as they stumbled through Bamboo, trying to find their way out of Forest. By late afternoon, we arrived at Shepherd's cave. His clan stood around me; I neither moved nor made a sound. They thought I had gone to Death, but it wasn't until Shepherd came up that evening with a blunt knife and drove it into my neck that I drowned in a sea of red.

How lifelike, Artist tells her students: 'Docility crafted into the product, as if the specimen is grateful for its own capture. Now, can you express the essence of the wild in your notebooks? The obsession, the valiant struggle between man and nature.' But she doesn't understand. I am not important just because He brought me from Forest. My crucial role was to help Him understand Himself better in the world.

Activists come in pairs, find me creepy, screw up their faces, cry, say it hurts too much to stay and watch me. They are disgusted, angry, sad, tell each other I should be destroyed instead of being displayed to Public. 'Its very presence glorifies hunting. There is never any excuse or justification for killing an animal.' I trouble them; my Death makes them feel uncomfortable. But how is my Eternal Life any worse than Crocodile whose skin covers President's feet, or Cow whose hide is worn by Small around her middle? I command more respect than the Animal Parts they wear, carry, eat; at least my life has not been anonymously erased.

When He was preparing me for Glass, Shepherd told Curator that He wanted my face to show Placid Acceptance.

'When they look at it, I want them to feel the fulfilment of a deep longing. Satisfaction immortalised.'

I know it was His longwinded way of saying He loves me. I am the Permanent Record of Shepherd's desire. As long as I am here, He lives on, because I hold His story in my very form. While I am here, He is Not-forgotten. He is with me in World.

CHAPTER 22

April 1938

The train from Berlin cut its way through the darkness, rattling past grey skeletons of houses that watched the flickering, dimly lit carriages. The German Tibet Expedition of Ernst Schäfer, under the Auspices of the *Reichsführer*-SS and in Connection with the *Ahnenerbe* Association Berlin, was finally on its way. Ernst had been prudent enough to have two sets of letterhead printed, with and without the SS connection, so they might keep a low profile as they travelled through British India. Seated beside Geer, whose head was nodding sleepily like a doll's, Ernst saw his own reflection in the window as the city disappeared behind them.

By the time they met the others in the seedy port of Genoa the following morning, the *Gneisenau*, a German steamboat, was waiting for them, berthed at the dock. The drizzle that had followed them overnight turned to heavy rain, and they all hurried to get on board. Tonnes of equipment and provisions were already loaded in the cargo hold: pistols, saddles, a shortwave receiver and transmitter, a collapsible boat, Leica cameras, reels of Agfa film, tents, first-aid kits, animal traps, tools for processing zoological specimens, geophysical gear, crates of food, cigarettes and brandy, and boxes of presents for the Tibetans, which included binoculars, old pistols, pocket knives, wrapped biscuits and cheap watches. Gestapo officials had been careful to ensure all companies that supplied goods for the expedition were certified as Aryan-owned. Most important for Ernst was his large one-man tent, a symbolic statement regarding who was going to be boss on this trip.

By afternoon, they set sail on the Mediterranean bound for Ceylon, via the Suez Canal. The men were excited to find themselves in spacious first-class cabins, but this luxury came at a price. Ernst expected them to wear white flannels and play games on deck while socialising with men of influence – businessmen, diplomats, engineers – whose connections might come in handy for the expedition. They gave lectures in English, each one speaking about their unique expertise. And Ernst insisted they meet every evening to examine maps and meticulously plan their forthcoming route. After a brief stopover in Colombo, a freighter was to take them to Calcutta, from where they would board a train to Sikkim, a small region on the border between India and Tibet. The plan was to pitch camp in the capital, Gangtok, if the British allowed, and await permission from Tibetan officials for an entry permit to cross the border. Then they could surge forward into the unexplored lands they were so eager to see, finally reaching Lhasa.

White spaces on a map, unknown terrain in every direction he looked: this was the challenge Ernst loved most, what had driven him since he was a child. As a young student at the University of Göttingen, he had jumped at the opportunity of spending an entire summer on Heligoland, a treeless island in the middle of the North Sea, where he would help Professor Hugo Weigold chart the abundance of birdlife passing through during the annual winter migration. They were working on a new project, to trap and tie bands to birds' feet as a new way of recording their roamings. The island's isolation and wide skies awoke a hunger in Ernst to see all the exotic places he knew existed beyond the narrow horizon of academia.

Ernst remembered vividly how one morning he had stood watching from his small cliffside hut as a tiny bird fought a giant. The swallow's call was urgent. It swooped at the hawk then flew in a steep upward curve, disappearing into a tiny crevice inside the rock face. A whole battalion of swallows arrived all at once, riding the wind as they lifted in a single ascent, moving in as one for another attack. Although the female hawk looked more annoyed than threatened, her hunt had been interrupted by the result of one small bird's tumult.

During his studies, while he was away on field trips, Ernst often thought about how he turned to the wild for peace and relaxation. Yet, for those creatures who were a very part of nature, the playing out of unending drama was life's rule. The hawk had ridden the cliff's updraughts with ease, trying to avoid the pesky swallows by gliding across to a new vantage point. And then it had disappeared like a lightning bolt pointed towards earth with a 160-kilometres-per-hour swoop, a spectacular killing stroke. It rose with a rodent trapped in its talons. The swallows retreated, and the vista turned quiet again.

Ernst wanted to be like the hawk soaring with such mastery above the world, diving with lethal intent. His well-loved shotgun gave him that power and more, for it allowed him to become that little bit godlike over even the birds of prey. He could decide whether to be content watching their dramatic moment as they arrowed in for the kill or, in an instant, fire a wing shot to drop them out of the sky.

The swallow had perched on the balcony rail of his hut, tilting its head as it stared at him, its orange breast beating violently. Ernst wondered what it made of a stranger entering its *Umwelt*. He didn't retreat, yet the bird was defiant. Its species survived because they were able to adapt to adversity and change.

The bird flitted up under the eaves. A loud screeching revealed the reason behind the swallow's fierce tenacity. Ernst looked up at the gaping yellow beaks embedded in tiny heads of fluff: three blind fledglings, totally dependent on their mother. He stood quietly as she swooped back over the balcony and out across the waves, weaving between silver gulls that seemed to be laughing at her fervour. Within half a minute, the male appeared, at first skittish upon seeing Ernst, as if having thoughts of abandoning the nest. Then he, too, ignored the intruder and delivered his package of worms into his offspring's hungry mouths.

The inky blue of water kissed the jagged rocks along the island's edge. A stingray floated past like a black ghost, scouring the shallows. An Arctic tern swooped and turned, diving into the centre of a school of fish. The long summer's day ended with a flurry of birds in a feeding frenzy as dusk began to fall. Ernst whistled, trying to imitate their calls.

A bird's life was a gasp. A swift flew past, grazing the air as it fed. The sky was as full of life as the ocean; beetles, flies, moths and aphids darted about, and birds devoured them like fish eating plankton. The array of birdlife on the island was astonishing – the ferruginous duck, the red-throated loon, the pink-footed goose – and he would shoot them as they glided through the hazy air.

Each day, he returned by lunchtime after hours of trudging through the marshland under a hot sun. He would find Professor Weigold inside the hut, sprawled out on his stretcher, fast asleep, having woken in the early hours to check traps and band the birds he had encountered. The man was a marvel – he had established a modern avian observatory on the island back in 1910, the year Ernst was born. Ernst's afternoons were taken up with preparing and labelling the specimens they had collected that morning.

When dusk settled, blurring the outlines of shapes in the treeless landscape, he heard more exotic creatures whose shadows he followed during long walks along the clifftops. In their short lives, birds braved the elements, journeyed to far-off lands, even if it meant returning with wings torn and ragged. Carving wide circles in the sky above land and sea, the intrepid little travellers went in search of food, shelter and a mate, focused only on ensuring the survival of their kind.

At night, as he fell asleep looking up at the stars, inhaling them into his dreams, Ernst would relive the day's work counting, trapping and preserving birds. With wings that only sleep can bring, he flew alongside them, glimpsing his reflection in the glistening waters below, broken only by ripples from a sudden gust of wind that lifted him soaring even higher into the blue.

CHAPTER 23

It was mid-May by the time they disembarked in Colombo. Ernst wanted to avoid delays and travel across India as soon as possible, well before the onset of the monsoon season. Waiting for them on the dock was a huge flock of local reporters, who besieged the travellers as soon as they stepped off the boat. Snapping photos and hurling questions, they crushed tightly against the men, making it impossible to get through. Ernst swatted at them like flies.

'Dr Schäfer!' A young local reporter pushed himself up front, waving a pencil and notebook in Ernst's face. He spoke in a refined English accent. 'Rumour has it you are here under false pretences.'

'I don't know what you're talking about.' Ernst, exhausted from the trip, tried to keep his composure, gently pushing against the man's chest. 'Please let us pass.'

The reporter persisted. 'But there have been speculations about espionage.'

'Pardon?' Ernst grew agitated.

The team were being jostled by the eager crowd. Shouts came from every direction – *Spies! Nazis! Himmler's men!* – in a blur of accusations.

'We are here on a peaceful, privately sponsored scientific mission,' Ernst retorted.

'Lies!' the young man taunted. 'The papers are reporting that you are all members of the SS. How can this not be a Nazi-led expedition?'

Ernst took the bait. This smear could mean the end of all he had dreamt of for so long and, with it, everything he had sacrificed in order to ensure this expedition went ahead. He wasn't going to let some puny foreign reporter ruin things for them. No longer able to control himself, he flew into a violent rage. Geer tried to hold him back, but it was too late. Ernst lunged at the journalist, pounding him with his bare fists. Within moments the wraith was lying on the ground, a gash across his cheek, blood pouring from his nose. Geer dragged Ernst away in the midst of all the commotion, yelling out to the others to follow. They ran into the relative safety of the customs hall, where two police officers barred entry to the vultures that had swooped across to peck at Ernst's eyes with their flashing cameras.

The team stood in line among businessmen and families. Breathing heavily, flustered by all the unexpected attention, Ernst tried to pull himself together. He opened his bag and took out a leather pouch that held all their documents.

'This could threaten our entire mission,' he whispered to Bruno.

Throughout the lead-up to the trip, Ernst had taken great care to downplay any SS connections, but as soon as they reached their hotel he could see all his efforts had been in vain. On top of the check-in counter lay the Indian *Statesman* newspaper, with a front-page article boasting the headline 'SS Expedition Leaves for Uncharted Regions of Tibet'. After making some urgent enquiries, he learnt that by now both the British and Indian press were running stories in all the major newspapers that screamed a warning: 'NAZI INVASION – Blackguards in India!'

He wired Himmler immediately:

Unheard-of attention in the press in India. Worried re: difficulties to be faced in Calcutta.

It came to light that, just before they had boarded the *Gneisenau* to leave Europe, the *Völkischer Beobachter* had crowed about the SS connections of the expedition all over its front page. This news had caught the attention of the British ambassador in Berlin, who alerted the Foreign Office about the team of so-called scientists.

Nonetheless, the men were soon granted access for the expedition after Himmler had secured clearance through a volley of diplomatic telegrams. They were to be allowed a month in Sikkim. Once they were there, Ernst would figure out his own way to forge ahead into Tibet, with or without permission from the damned British.

He had never been good at waiting; his very being railed against the heavy inertia of time. Telling Ernst Schäfer that he could not have something only made him want it more. Obstacles served as a call to action, in a war against what felt immovable or unattainable.

Once they reached Calcutta, Ernst undertook a six-hour journey north to meet for high tea with the Viceroy, Lord Linlithgow, requesting permission for his team to have their stay extended to six months in Sikkim, ostensibly to observe and film wildlife. This would buy him even more time to apply for permission to enter Tibet.

By mid-June the team reached Gangtok, a busy hub for the wool trade with Tibet. They set up camp at Dilkusha, a lodge near the British residence, while murky sheets of rain clouds threatened to engulf the skies. There they met Sir Basil Gould, the British Consul stationed in Sikkim, a tall and quiet man. Although he received the team politely, checking that all their documentation was in order, Ernst knew Gould was likely concerned about the presence of five German SS officers in the state. Sikkim was a British protectorate, nominally governed by the *chogyal*, or monarch. It was obvious Gould was determined to find out the political motives behind the German expedition; when it came to wiliness, Ernst had met his match in the British statesman. Gould allowed the team to use the grounds of the British residence to organise logistics and hire porters for the next part of their trek. This meant he could keep a careful eye on all their comings and goings.

Ernst chose a dozen strong local men, as well as a cook and an interpreter who spoke Tibetan. They called him *bara-sahib*, or 'great master'; he enjoyed the deference, which was more than his own men ever showed him. He would have preferred to be remembered, though, by the real meaning behind his name – Schäfer, a shepherd. He did, after all, tend to his flock. Instead of a master, this was how he saw his role among men: to guide them through the treachery of the wilderness so they might find peace and sustenance surrounded by nature, in the same way he did. But the natives' minds worked in peculiar ways, and their strong belief in magic and myth turned their *bara-sahib* into a mystical being and symbol. All of his colleagues were endowed with special titles: Bruno was known as *doctor-sahib*; Geer, who was in charge of provisions, became *store-sahib*; and Krause, whose job it was to photograph and film the day-to-day adventures of the expedition, a special kind of magic to the natives, was called *picture-sahib*. Wienert, who was in control of their contact with the outside world by fiddling with the dials on their radio transmitter, earnt the rather obscure title of *tar-sahib*, the meaning of which remained as mysterious to the team as the sounds emitted from the small wooden box were to the natives.

Ernst taught some of the locals how to skin the creatures he shot on his first tentative hunting forays. The authorities would forbid them from hunting once they entered Tibet, but there were certain perks of the expedition he was not willing to forgo. He needed to make sure the men took care not to spoil the pelts and feathers, as these lovely samples were likely to fetch high prices on the international market. Ernst knew he had to rule with an iron fist and be watchful of the natives, who were so sentimental when it came to the killing of animals. The locals were pleasant enough, but they were hopelessly spooked by religion. They baulked at the slightest notion of hunting and had absolutely no understanding of science. Superstition poisoned man's rational will, and Ernst found these peoples' traditions and rituals to be nothing short of barbarism.

There was the vulture, for example, a filthy creature the natives called the *dur bya*. It hovered over mountain funeral pyres, a key partaker in gruesome sky burials the likes of which Ernst had never seen before. The Tibetans did not bury their dead. Corpses, swaddled in sheets, were carted by mules up to a hill outside the village. There, they were unwrapped and hacked into quarters by *ragyapa*, outcasts wearing white aprons who wielded whetted meat cleavers. Their job was considered holy by the Tibetans. With rotting human flesh exposed to the elements, it didn't take very long until the birds, flying gluttons, dived to pick the corpse apart. Holding bones in their beaks, they soared into the sky and dropped them to smash on the rocks below. They would glide back down, circling in spirals with the wind, and peck at the marrow dribbling out. It wasn't the way Ernst would have chosen to be sent from this world, at the mercy of those vermin, especially when he compared the ritual to the beautiful shrine at

Wewelsburg Castle, with the grand funerals held there for respected SS officers.

Early one morning, Ernst rode out into the wilderness accompanied by his new guide, Akeh, with a small bamboo cage strapped to the saddle. Inside, a bird with rose-pink feathers fluttered around, trying to escape. They stopped at a rocky outcrop and the shy Akeh watched his master dismount and carry the cage over to a dusty clearing. Ernst tied the cage to the trunk of a lone gnarled tree, then scattered some seeds on the ground. The bird started to flap excitedly and, as Ernst opened the miniature door, he motioned for Akeh to follow him. They hid behind a large boulder. The bird quickly jumped down from its prison and ran straight to the food, pecking hungrily as it strutted about. Akeh's eyes widened as he watched Ernst cock the trigger of his gun.

'*Schmuckgimpel,*' Ernst whispered. A Himalayan rose-finch.

He threw a small pebble at the bird, which startled and flew towards a branch of the tree. He caught it mid-flight, the shot echoing across the mountainside. Akeh watched as the bird dropped, landing in the dirt.

'Precision.' Ernst lowered his rifle. 'That's what I want to teach you. Catch it while it's in the air.'

'It's wrong to shoot a bird while it flies, *bara-sahib*.' Akeh turned his back on Ernst and walked towards the rose-finch, whose wings were beating feebly, trying to escape from its own demise. He lifted the creature and held it in his hands.

Ernst cocked the barrel, watching his guide through the sight of his gun.

'You must learn how to perfect the technique of shooting a creature on the run. Aim ahead of it. Move the gun along the same arc that the bird is flying in. Only, have your birdshot already waiting there. Let it fly into its own death.'

The rosefinch had stopped struggling, its tiny ribcage now still. Akeh bent down, placing it back onto the dirt. Unflinching, he walked straight towards his master. It wasn't until he stood right in front of him that Ernst lowered his gun. Then, without uttering a word, Ernst handed it over to the guide. In that instant, a duck flew overhead, quacking loudly as it passed. Akeh took aim and fired. It dropped out of the sky and landed stone dead a few metres away from where they stood. He took aim again and shot a pigeon, a pheasant and, spinning around, fired four successive shots at the birdcage Ernst had tied to the tree a few minutes earlier. Ernst had wildly underestimated the man's skill. Within a fortnight, Akeh shot five wild goats, a wild yak, 123 birds and three brown bears, adding to their growing collection. Soon, he would be ready for the ultimate prize – the shapi, a Tibetan sheep no Westerner had ever set eyes on. Ernst's hopes were high.

A few days later, a Tibetan boy appeared at their camp holding a parcel of food. He had been sent from the outpost of a Finnish missionary in Sikkim who had heard news that the German travellers' provisions had started to dwindle. Ernst coveted his hunting specimens so much that he would only allow the men to shoot the occasional yak for meat. The boy also carried some news that Ernst was thrilled to hear. The mythical Tibetan blue sheep had been spotted, alive and roaming in the nearby mountains. Ernst scribbled in his diary that day:

Now I am frantic and ecstatic. I am ablaze – as if a fire were burning inside me. 'Shapi-shapi-shapi,' I bellow like a bull, run up and down obsessively, call all the sahibs into my tent. I jump to my feet. I believe this fellow. Gentlemen, this will be the greatest scientific discovery of the expedition. Devil, devil! This is going to be a success for Germany.

Hunting was like lovemaking for Ernst. His passion for the kill – the crazed arousal as he followed its beckoning call – was a cure for all his restlessness. He would feel insatiable ecstasy as he focused with quivering intensity on an animal he had stalked, the passage of time blurred beyond his rifle sight. He would watch silently as he felt his heart force the blood through his body.

In Sikkim, Ernst shot every animal he came across, not wanting to risk losing an opportunity to bag yet another specimen he could pin down and examine for scientific knowledge. His fervour for collecting animals kept Mandoy, the local taxidermist, busy from dawn to dusk. Working in an open-air zoology laboratory, Mandoy's job was to hide the deaths of these creatures under the point of a needle, stitching their eyes closed so the cruelty of their demise could not be seen.

A fortnight after having already shot his fill of shapi – so many, in fact, that Mandoy couldn't keep up with the skinning – Ernst sat in a cave one morning with Geer, his hunting companion, waiting for yet another sheep to appear. He read out loud from his well-worn copy of *Faust*: '*Not I it was who whistled you from hell;/ A self-willed bird, you flew upon the lime.*'

Ernst yawned, stretching his arms. It had been a late night, fuelled by lewd jokes, and what had been left of their beer. Come morning, he had found himself inside his tent, sprawled out on top of his stretcher, completely naked, the palm of his hand covered with the stickiness of his own vulgar joy. His body had somehow kept its warmth overnight, despite the dip in temperature, but his brain felt frozen.

Geer's night had been rough, too, and the last thing he wanted to hear was dour poetry.

'Can you give it a break, Ernst? I've got such a rotten headache.'

'You heathen! How can you not appreciate the wisdom of Goethe?'

'I prefer to read *Der Stürmer*, myself.' He slapped his hand against his ear, squishing a flying beetle. He flicked it off and wiped his bloodied fingers on his shirt. 'They've run some very interesting articles in the past. Did you read the one where they argued that, no matter how much we want to protect children, every little Jewish baby still grows up to be a Jew? It was fascinating.'

Ignoring his companion, Ernst kept reading out loud:

'Who holds the Devil, let him hold him well,/ He hardly will be caught a second time.'

Geer lay down and rolled over to face the wall. 'Oh, please! Don't patronise me with your literary pretentiousness.' He let out a salvo of loud farts.

Ernst was about to land a punch on his colleague when they heard a rustling outside the cave. The men fell silent. Ernst cautiously crawled to the opening of the cave and peeked out. Unsure if it was out of sheer exhaustion or too much drink the night before, he thought he saw a spectre standing there. It had the body of a shapi, shaggy and sheep-like, with a blond mane and long horns curling around either side of its head. But it was much smaller than the others he had bagged, and almost entirely white. It ran off as soon as it spotted him. He could have brought it down right then and there, but it seemed to be beckoning him to follow, out into the depths of the wilderness.

Leaving Geer and Akeh behind, he set off alone, trailing the animal for miles as it scrambled over rocks and through thorny thickets. In all his years of hunting, Ernst had never encountered an albino creature in the wild. Ernst became Captain Ahab in the chase; the white shapi had presented itself as the *telos* of the day. Catching this ghostly sheep would secure his fame and fortune for life.

Eventually, the chase was not particularly arduous. He cornered the shapi in a copse of stunted bushes and all he had to do was shoot between its eyes. But crouched there, cocking his rifle, ready to pull the trigger, he noticed the ancient gaze in the animal's pink eyes. In the course

227

of any hunt, he engaged intimately and passionately with the beast he chased, testing all his instincts and cunning. So many animals had passed in front of his trusty rifle since he'd arrived in Sikkim, but none as majestic as this white ghost. Ernst crept forward, the breeze blowing in his face. Man and beast's eyes were riveted together for just a moment, but in his hesitation to pull the trigger the animal was off again, kindling an even deeper lust in Ernst to catch it. This one was to be his.

He raced across dry ground, searching for spoor, but it wasn't until late afternoon that he found the shapi again. The hunter had to become the hunted, think the thoughts of prey and predator simultaneously. Ernst's hands rested on his rifle. As though its body were made of stone, the shapi stood motionless, staring directly at him. It looked as if it had been waiting a lifetime for him to arrive, watching the inexorable approach of something beyond its realm. Ernst imagined worms gnawing deep within the carcass. And with one small movement of his finger, the shapi's body reared up and slumped to the ground, clinging to the earth in its last convulsions, eyes filled with surprise. The shot rang out across the infinite sky, concentric rings of the hunter's triumph widening across the plane. Like the coiling of a spring, time expanded and contracted as he waited for the moment his prey might be transfigured into eternal beauty, for all the world to see.

This creature, its fur the colour of fresh snow, was destined to become much more than itself. In death, it would be transmogrified into a splendid temple for others to gaze upon lovingly. Once it was mounted, this superlative pale beast would look entirely worthy of a great hunter's quest, its serene countenance hiding the animal's terror of the chase.

Ernst lifted the sheep with tenderness. His textbooks showed pictures of a wide taxonomy of creatures, but the image on the page, buried among dry descriptive words, never did justice to the reality of the living form. The animal in a book stared out at you, revealing itself boldly, like a model posing for a photographer. In the wild, though, it receded, constantly on the move, hiding deep in the folds of the forest, sinking back into the shadows of the landscape, or falling from the sky to disappear into the horizon.

CHAPTER 24

They marked time in Gangtok while Ernst continued to try to find a way for them to gain permission to enter Tibet and advance towards Lhasa. He arranged a meeting one morning in August with a Sikkimese official and his private secretary, preparing elaborate gifts he had brought with him all the way from Germany.

Whenever Ernst was gone, hunting or on official business, Bruno would use every opportunity to gather his anthropometric data. Dispensing oils and potions from several trunks that were filled with anything from pain-killers to treatment for venereal disease, he soon earnt his title of *doctor-sahib*, becoming a 'medicine man' among the locals and winning their trust. They lined up to see him. It was a craftily calculated move that ended up paying off, as he cajoled his subjects to allow him to take moulds of their faces.

He followed a strict examination routine, no matter how much they giggled or winced. The first thing he needed to determine was their exact eye colour, using charts of many different hues. Bruno's eyes were Himmelfarb, the colour of the sky on a perfect summer's day, according to the official charts of Martin and Schultz. He also carried charts developed by Fischer and Saller to determine the exact shading of the hair, as well as the skin-colour chart of von Luschan.

To Bruno's mind, though, cranial measurements were the most important, and he meticulously listed the length, breadth and circumference of each person's head, the height and width of their forehead and the distance between their eyes. This was followed by careful measurement of the breadth of cheekbones and lower jaw, and the depth of noses. Lastly, he checked the position of their noses, mouths and ears in relation to the rest of their face, looking for traces of Aryan blood left over from the dawn of mankind.

He even bribed his own personal servant, a shy Nepalese Sherpa called Pasang, to allow him to practise mask-making skills on him. Using calipers, Bruno first measured the shape and thickness of Pasang's lips, the length of his feet and hands, and even the length of his penis. He used a wooden protractor to gauge the angle of his nose.

'Please!' Bruno motioned for the Sherpa to sit down on a stool.

Kaiser, the group's interpreter, stood beside them, pouring hot water and acrid disinfectant into a ceramic bowl that rested on a tray. He opened a packet of Negocoll, crumbling up one of the blocks and sprinkling it into the mixture. It formed a gelatinous goo as he stirred.

Bruno was disappointed he hadn't been able to fashion a mask of Akeh instead. Ernst, in his usual obstinate fashion, had insisted on taking Akeh with him to his meeting with the official. He would have made a fine specimen, with his elongated facial features and a narrow, swanlike neck that certainly demonstrated Nordic remnants. Timid Pasang had been a last-minute replacement. As Pasang was Nepalese he was not the ideal subject, but there was no time to lose. Bruno had to make as many masks as he could during their stay in Gangtok.

'Hold still now.' Bruno smeared oil onto Pasang's face before applying the ghastly paste, which would harden into a rubber mask.

As work on the mask started, the Sherpa kept swaying to and fro. Kaiser explained that Bruno's subject still felt unwell after a small avalanche earlier that week had sent a rock hurtling onto his head.

The members of the Tibetan aristocracy who Bruno had seen in photos resembled those in Professor Günther's book on Nordic German races. They were tall, with thin faces, high cheekbones and straight, glossy hair. Bruno had brought all the finest tools of his trade on the journey: spreading calipers, three steel tape measures, sliding compasses of different sizes and a somatometer, a gift from his teacher, the racial expert Theodor Mollison. Bruno's mentor had taught him everything he knew, but the most important thing Bruno had learnt at the insistence of Mollison was to carefully record all his measurements in a notebook.

Without warning, Pasang slumped over, mumbling something to himself. Kaiser eased him back onto the stool.

'Stand him up!'

'But he says he's feeling dizzy, *doctor-sahib*.'

'We are in the middle of an important task and I have no time for these kinds of histrionics. Tell him to control himself.'

Kaiser placed his hand on his friend's shoulder, as if to stop any challenge to Bruno, who had once cured Kaiser's toothache with his 'magic pincers'.

Pasang moaned but Bruno continued with his work, the anthropologist scraping out more plaster from the bowl with his wooden spatula. His breath heavy with the stench of tobacco, he moulded the white paste around the tip of his victim's nose, leaving a small hole for each nostril. Technically, he should have inserted two straws to ensure the man could breathe properly, but there was no time; the material was starting to dry and would soon become unmanageable. Just as he covered the eye sockets, save for two small slits, Pasang sneezed, jettisoning the fragile mask from his face. The mould launched into the air. Bruno and Kaiser reached out madly to try to grab it, but it flew past their hands, landing on the ground with a thud. They stared at their ruined handiwork, which lay sprawled in the dirt like one of Ernst's wounded birds.

Pasang tried to stand, strands of creamy white plaster hanging from his nose and chin. He yelled something and pointed towards the Khangchendzonga mountains. Bruno already knew a variation of what he was saying: that the spirits were angry, and the world was spinning with demons. He'd heard these premonitions a number of times since they'd arrived.

Birds shrieked above them. With his pipe poised between his lips, Bruno pushed Pasang back down onto the stool.

'Calm down, you imbecile!'

Bruno cupped Pasang's fine jaw with his big hand, firmly closing the Sherpa's trembling lips. He started to reapply the plaster, working quickly to cover the small man's high cheekbones and sunken eyes. Bruno blew on it to help it set, and this time Pasang was too frightened to move. Pressing his stopwatch, Bruno sat down to wait, puffing on his pipe through his thin lips. The Negocoll would take thirty minutes to dry completely, after which he would peel it off and pour Hominit into the mask. The result would be a perfect cast, an eerily lifelike portrait of the Sherpa. This moulding technique had become popular back home and was used by professors of anatomy to make models of deformed body organs, or of medical freaks such as two-headed foetuses. Casts were also made of criminals waiting on death row, showing the fine wrinkles of fear that lined their faces as they faced their demise. These human replicas fetched high prices among curators of Europe's finest museums, as popular attractions in otherwise prosaic collections. Universities bought them, too, as teaching tools for students studying racial typology. Depending on how exotic or rare the subject, an individual mask might fetch up to thirty Reichsmark.

Pasang had made strange grunting noises as the mould was reapplied, his hands balled into fists. The ghostly mask covered his entire face, his mouth locked shut so he was unable to talk. Bruno had again left tiny holes around his nostrils. The man's bloodshot eyes were the only window to his fear, squinting through the plaster slits. Kaiser was the first to notice Pasang's head begin to jerk, and Bruno was alerted shortly after by a gurgling noise. They turned to see the stool topple over, Pasang writhing on the dusty ground, his spine twisted into the shape of a question mark. A wet patch spread across his crotch as his body thrashed in rhythmic jerks. The mask began to crack open again and the Sherpa's drooling face emerged like a baby bird breaking through its fragile eggshell.

'Quickly, go and get help!' Bruno shouted, shoving his fingers into Pasang's mouth to stop him choking on the wet clay. 'He's having a seizure.'

Kaiser watched as his friend's eyes rolled back in their sockets, his face turning a dusky grey. He looked possessed by a demon. Kaiser rushed off, while Bruno waited until Pasang's contorting body gradually turned limp.

It was into the midst of this gruesome scene that Ernst returned to camp. Despite his best attempts at diplomacy and bribery, negotiations with the official had not gone as well as he had hoped. Already in a foul mood, Ernst took one look at the scene before him and exploded.

'What the hell is going on here?'

Bruno stood his ground, self-possessed and smiling with sinister cheeriness. 'It's no big deal.'

'What was this pointless exercise for, Bruno? I told you not to start your stupid experiments for a reason, yet you went right ahead and defied my orders.'

'Your orders?' Bruno kicked the dirt. 'My loyalty is not to *sahib* Ernst Schäfer, but to our Führer and Fatherland. In the end, these natives' suffering will lead to our triumph.'

'You are risking the future of this entire expedition with these shenanigans of yours. We need to keep the locals onside if we are to get into Tibet, you idiot.'

'You seem to have gone a little soft lately, my friend. Might this come from years of hobnobbing with the Americans and British?'

Ernst's face turned crimson. Letting out a giant roar, he took a swing at his colleague. Bruno's superior height worked to his advantage as he blocked his enraged friend with an outstretched arm.

'You and I are kindred spirits, Ernst.' Bruno grinned, holding the sturdy hunter at bay. 'You chase animals, while I hunt people.'

A week later, during one of Ernst's brief hunting forays, a local official dressed in finest brocade and silk appeared at the German camp. Bruno tried to take advantage of the surprise visit, luring him into his tent in the hope of measuring the nobleman's features, but Kaiser diplomatically intervened as he knew the official, who lived in Tibet, was a dignitary of the Sikkimese royal family.

When Ernst rode back into camp, he hastily arranged an impressive impromptu reception for their honoured guest, strategically placing all their scientific equipment – cameras, binoculars, altimeters – at the entrance to his tent. Inside, he seated himself atop an inflated air mattress, in an attempt to look more imposing. He called for the servants to prepare fine delicacies, including German biscuits and hot tea. Ernst assembled elaborate gifts he had brought with him for occasions such as this: an HMV gramophone, some records, a set of fine china. He wanted to win the favour of this dignitary, so he might persuade him into influencing Tibetan officials to allow the expedition across the border into Tibet. It was fortunate that Bruno's first impulse to measure the man had been stymied at the outset.

Ernst's honoured guest left camp with his mules groaning under the abundance of gifts, including bags of potatoes, rubber boots, woollen socks, chocolates and tinned vegetables. Ernst penned a diplomatic letter in which he expressed his deepest wishes to visit Tibetan monasteries and learn more about the beautiful culture. He even gave away all their soap, glad to be rid of the final smell of civilisation.

CHAPTER 25

November 1938

The old peasant woman smiled, her eyes squinting like two deep wounds. She was so frail she might have flown away with the slightest snowdrift blowing across from the surrounding mountains. Yak fat smeared on her cheeks to protect her skin from the wind and sun, she squatted barefoot in front of Ernst, holding out a makeshift tray. On it she had arranged a line of dead mice of various colours and sizes, the larger ones' tails hanging stiffly over the edge. Ernst sat at a spindly table, sipping tea from a metal cup. He was rugged up against the cold, wearing a woollen sweater and leather pants.

Word had spread far and wide that the Germans, as well as acquiring all sorts of artefacts such as weaving looms or decorated wooden tables, were also collecting dead animals. When it came to wildlife, Ernst had developed a reputation among the locals as the man who bought everything that once had a pulse. Each day people would arrive on foot, travelling long distances from remote villages to trade their meagre wares for a handful of rice or sugar. Bartering with the natives had become a form of entertainment for Ernst and his men; they took it in turns to see who could cut the best deal. Krause, the team's entomologist, had so far claimed victory, having collected thousands of dried bumblebees brought to him by natives. He allowed Ernst to use his Leica camera, capturing him proudly displaying the insects laid out on a blanket.

'You and your annoying bugs,' Ernst said; he loved to tease Krause.

'If the world's insects stopped buzzing, life on this earth would collapse. They comprise the vast majority of all forms of life on earth, more important than all your mammals and birds combined.'

It was not only insects Krause was collecting. He had also accumulated 1600 varieties of barley, 700 varieties of wheat and 700 varieties of oats. Himmler was particularly interested in these seeds, hoping to develop hardy new crops for the colonies he planned to establish across Eastern Europe. He believed that, in the future, German scientists might plant them to control the weather in Tibet. The reclamation by Aryan settlers of ancestral lands would increase dew, create clouds and force rain to make a more economically viable climate.

While Ernst haggled with the woman, he looked at the corpse of a yak, laid with its feet up, just outside his tent. Flies crawled out of its nostrils. Kneeling on the ground, Mandoy picked up his knife and carved along the length of its bulging abdomen, disembowelling the huge creature. Black blood was congealed inside its veins. A rigid sparrow lay on the ground beside the yak, its death so tiny and neat by comparison.

Ernst hadn't been feeling well. His attempts to find a way for them to enter Tibet were still not bearing fruit. The British were doing their best not to cooperate, since political tensions had heightened between the two countries. He started to think they might have to resort to the plan his sympathetic British friend Francis Younghusband had furtively suggested: 'Just sneak over the border.' Meanwhile, Karl Wienert was trying to ward off a different enemy – rust. Generated by the onslaught of petulant storms, it became a constant threat to his precious equipment. He complained the others didn't understand how vital the instruments were to his mission as a geophysicist. If Ernst lost a rifle he could always buy a new one from the natives, but try replacing an expensive Hildebrandt theodolite or chronometer in this wretched nowhere-land.

When Wienert had raised his concerns one night at their campfire, Bruno drew on his pipe, scoffing at the man's reliance on equipment: 'Even if it were all to fail, you still have your notebooks, as well as your memory of this majestic landscape. How hard can it be to draw a simple map?'

Ernst tried to keep the peace among his men. He knew Wienert regarded anthropology as a soft science, and Bruno as a fool. Unlocking the earth's mysteries was the Holy Grail for German geologists and geographers; a person's heritage was intimately connected to the ground upon which he trod. Wienert was frustrated that Bruno couldn't acknowledge that; it took a deep scientific understanding of the importance of geographical space to see how it held the very future of the German race, the *Volk*. It was something felt in one's bones. Wienert had expressed to Ernst the irony that Bruno, the expert among them whose job it was to examine and collect exotic skeletons, had not an inkling of the connection between *Blut und Boden*. Blood and soil.

This trip was the culmination of all that Karl Wienert had learnt. He had been preparing for it throughout his studies, and now all those hours spent in lecture halls and classrooms at university were starting to pay off. He had completed his doctorate eighteen months before, and now phrases like *Lebensraum* and *Drang nach Osten* – the push to populate Slavic lands with hard-working German folk – made sense here in this vast land even further to the east. His teacher Wilhelm Filchner, himself an ardent explorer who had trekked solo right across Northern Tibet at the turn of the century, had tried to instil the idea in his students that not only was it a geographical imperative, it was also a sacred right. Wienert's task was to establish a series of geomagnetic stations across the Himalayas. The bizarre power held by the earth's mysterious magnetic field could turn explorers' compasses into crazed harpies, setting entire expeditions blindly off course. Too often, teams of men and their animals were snatched from the face of the earth, vanishing into the ice and wind. His work would enable men who followed in his own footsteps to leap with certainty across the white space on their maps.

Wienert's research required a variety of intricate instruments, all heavy and cumbersome to lug across such hostile terrain. The porters had to carefully load and unload the mules at the beginning and end of each day, ensuring theodolites were strapped snugly back into their wooden cases, and magnometers rested inside their specially crafted brass boxes. The measuring tent not only protected both the geologist and his equipment from the vagaries of inclement weather, it also allowed covert measurements to be taken, away from the prying eyes of the natives.

Ernst thought about all of these logistical challenges, thrown his way by man and nature alike, as he appraised the dead mice on the tray. He patted them and picked up the largest one by the tail. The shopkeeper smiled broadly, revealing a row of blackened, rotting teeth. Through Kaiser, Ernst struck a deal with the woman, after much bargaining and laughter among his men, to purchase her wares for a mere 100 grams of sugar.

After picking off bloated leeches from their ankles and thighs at the end of the day's explorations through sodden, muddy valleys, the men bathed and prepared for dinner. At night, gathered round the campfire, they recounted their day's adventures. Each man read from his field diary, in which both scientific and personal observations were noted. Ernst had insisted on this daily ritual from the start, to remind them of the true purpose of their expedition.

By the following afternoon, heavy rain had set in, sending them all to hide inside their tents and huddle under blankets. Ernst preferred to be alone with his thoughts after everyone retired. At first, he had tried to soothe his nerves by playing simple tunes on the harmonica Herta had given him on their wedding day, but instead of the music calming him, it only made him feel lonelier. More and more, his diary became his trusted companion. He often grew weary of his colleagues; the blank page was where he could pour out his frustration as well as his joy without fear of anyone's mockery, especially that of Bruno. Perhaps, one day, when he was famous or long dead, or both, these pages would become precious artefacts of a glorious bygone era.

He looked at the date: 9 November. A year had passed since that day hunting ducks on the lake at Carinhall, with Herta seated at the opposite end of the boat, smiling at him with such hope in her eyes. He pressed his pencil firmly on the page:

Sometimes, when the haste becomes too much, when the problems become too unfamiliar, too incomprehensible, too involved, when it is difficult to come to conclusions because of constantly changing opinions, I grab my shotgun and flee into nature.

The gun was his consolation. He kept it beside his mattress. On cold, lonely nights, in the throes of guilty heat, he fondled its shaft, sinking back into dark rapture, an escape from the conspiracies of men. The British had always done birds well, grooming the wild countryside to accommodate the sport of the shooter, but there was a greater thrill hunting game in the true wilderness. A sudden shriek, a blur of feathers above the trees, a flash of red wings flailing, and Ernst would be off in pursuit.

Herta hadn't always called Ernst's love of the hunt a bloodlust, nor had she always looked upon his curated collection of specimens – those alive and those breathless – as a kind of freak show. When they were children she had held him in awe, as he shared with her the treasures he had collected. His prized possession was a feather that came from an eagle-owl, *Bubo bubo*. On one occasion, while Herta stroked it with her finger, Ernst had taken out his notebook and, with the concentration and dedication of a biblical scribe, traced the details of the rachis, its spine, from which the barbs, barbules and barbicels radiated out, woven together in communion. The feather was waterproof, oiled and made airtight by a layer of down.

'It has branches like a leaf,' she said, lifting it onto her palm. 'And it's almost weightless.'

He reached over and pulled at the white bow on her head. 'Feathers are dead. Just like your hair.'

She held the feather aloft and let it go, watching it gently spiral down. Ernst caught it in his palms before it reached the ground.

Ernst read everything he could find about the natural world, sneaking into his father's study whenever he was away on business. Young Ernst would devour the exciting travel adventures of a Karl May or Jules Verne novel. But his favourite book was the one that sat permanently on his father's desk. It was an antique copy of the *Egyptian Book of the Dead*, a collection of magic spells that guided the dying through the mysteries of the afterlife. Ernst would hunch over it, engrossed in tales such as that of the god Anubis, half-jackal, half-man, and the goddess Ma'at, who would measure the weight of human hearts against the feather of truth, plucked from an ostrich. Those with heavier hearts were devoured instantly. Only those with buoyant hearts were permitted entry into the realm of the dead.

While Ernst was writing, immersed in memories of Herta, Bruno walked into his tent unannounced. 'Why are you sitting here all alone?'

'I enjoy my own company.'

He sat down on a rickety stool. 'Listen, I need your help, Ernst.'

'What's up?'

'I'm not making enough progress with my research.' Bruno opened up his field diary, throwing it down in front of Ernst. 'See here,' he said, pointing to some squiggles. 'The lower class of Tibetans that most of my measurements have come from are a mongrel race, with strong mongoloid tendencies. We need to get closer to Lhasa, where I can focus my work on the aristocracy. That's where I'll find traces of true Aryan blood.'

The tent was lit by a kerosene lamp that sat hissing on a camp table.

'I'm doing all I can to get us to Lhasa. You know that. And as I've said to you countless times, I'm afraid you are abandoning real science for a skein of flimsy lies, my friend,' Ernst said. 'The research of the *Ahnenerbe* is constructed on treacherous ground.' Ernst pulled a tattered book from his pocket and threw it across the table. 'You need to read this.'

Bruno picked it up and flipped through the pages. '*Ach!* I have no time for this fantasy rubbish of yours, Ernst. I, for one, have important work to do.'

'That's just the point I'm trying to make, you imbecile!' Ernst thumped his fist on the table, upsetting an empty teacup. 'Don't you see? Faust is an academic who has reached the limits of his learning. He seeks a more meaningful life, wants to gain knowledge about nature and the universe.'

Akeh interrupted their parrying, placing yak-butter tea and snacks on the table.

'I don't follow your point. What has this got to do with my research?' Bruno was unflinching. 'Science is the natural order of things and, as such, it must follow the swastika.'

Ernst bit into a stale biscuit. Bruno's field diary lay open in his lap, collecting the crumbs.

The lamplight flickered in Bruno's eyes. 'We have no choice but to answer *das Gefühl*, the pride of being German, the call of our race.'

A strong wind whistled outside. The sound of someone splitting wood, the edge of the axe crashing down, echoed around them. In the shadows of the tent some trunks were huddled one on top of the other, filled with telescopes, binoculars, rifles and film equipment. Ernst shifted slightly in his chair. He did not like to be challenged by his men, and somehow Bruno always managed to get right under his skin.

'Has your sermon finished now? It's making me sleepy.'

'Don't play naïve with me, Ernst. Our work is not just about our own selfish interests. Science must take into consideration the important things happening in our time; there are such huge opportunities we cannot ignore.'

'Science is pure and elegant in itself, not a pony to be ridden around a circus ring. We must be left to our own devices, to follow Truth, free as birds to fly to dizzying heights.'

Bruno smirked. 'You are the one who shoots birds down from the sky.'

Ernst inhaled sharply, his pulse soaring. 'Enough of your insolence.'

'You won't shut me up so easily, you hypocrite. You have been courting powerful benefactors your entire career and are finally tasting the rewards. You're not the only one who can quote from your beloved Goethe: *"Tell me with whom you associate, and I will tell you who you are."* The only reason we are here now is because you sought the patronage of the Reich.'

'We are men of science, not followers of fairytale and superstition. This notion of a lost civilisation of Atlantis

247

rising up somewhere in the desolate foothills of these mountains is a fatuous lie, and you know it. It corrupts our expedition and the reputation of German science. Himmler is *verrückt*, twisting it for his own gains.'

'Now you think he's crazy? You don't seem to have been too reluctant to cosy up to Uncle Heini. I'm sure your dear patron and his colleagues at the *Ahnenerbe* will be interested to hear his *Wunderkind's* real views. We are dealing with far more than your bottled frogs and ragged bird carcasses here.' Bruno stood up and puffed on his pipe.

Ernst lunged at him, landing a blow to his cheek. His friend toppled over with a crash, landing on the lamp. Tongues of flame leapt up in an instant, licking at the canvas walls.

'Akeh, quickly! Hand me that jug!' Ernst's loyal servant, clasping the tray he had been holding, didn't move. Ernst reached across and doused the fire with the freshly brewed tea.

Bruno rushed out of the tent, swearing at Ernst under his breath.

They needed to get to Tibet soon. This state of limbo was taking its toll on them all.

The dog found it first; they heard the loud crunching before turning to see the skull clamped firmly in its mouth. The place was deserted, the moon low on the horizon as light seeped out of the evening sky. A pile of prayer stones and tattered flags signalled they had stumbled upon a Tibetan grave, rather unusual to find in such a remote village. Ernst and Akeh worked quietly to unearth the body.

A scrawny dog had followed them along the path from the village, circling around them, scratching and sniffing at the growing pile of dirt they had dug up. Ernst felt unnerved as the creature fixed him with a bloody eye. It looked uncannily like a stray that had shadowed him on the way home from the laboratory one evening in Berlin. He had wondered if a wild cat had escaped from its cage at the zoo. It had moved closer and closer, until Ernst could smell its foul breath and see its black eyes. A curtain of fog had parted and the scrawny creature limped forward, as though strolling onstage to deliver a soliloquy. The animal panted loudly, stopping every now and then to scratch its fleas. Ernst had encountered a multitude of fascinating creatures in his short but illustrious career – beasts that any circus master would give his right hand to lead around the ring – but this dog didn't seem to fit any category or breed Ernst had ever seen. Could it have magically reappeared now in Tibet? He must be losing his mind.

The dog had gone back to digging and found the prize they were all searching for in a matter of minutes. Ernst tried to lure it away but the mongrel growled, eyeballs rolling wildly, its snout covered in dirt. He was not going to watch such a fine specimen become a mangy mutt's dinner. A Tibetan skull would fetch an excellent price back home. Ernst pulled a dry biscuit from his pocket and held it up as an offering in exchange for the skull. The dog glanced at it slyly for a moment but went straight back to its bony banquet. Ernst, flushed with rage, reached out to grab the skull but the dog sank its jaw into his forearm, shaking its head. He wrestled the dog for the bones, playing an ugly tug-of-war. With his free hand Ernst reached for the pistol strapped to his belt, drew it and swiftly shot the animal in the head. The dog jerked in protest, before the last quiver of life left its body. Ernst lifted the skull from the dirt where the dog had dropped it. He stood holding it in his hand and stared, like Hamlet, into the disconcerting blankness of the eye sockets.

'Get me some more of these skulls,' he said, pressing a few rupees into Akeh's palm.

Ernst tore a strip off the bottom of his shirt and wrapped it tightly around his arm. The rewards of finding this specimen would be worth suffering the injury. Berlin University had one of the most impressive anatomical collections in the world, and he knew how much faculty professors wanted to make their mark in the scientific world. Bruno would tend to the wound when they returned to camp. They had both decided it was best to set aside their ugly disagreement. Things had got out of hand, tempers fuelled by the frustration of waiting. Tibet and Lhasa lay before them.

Before they left the cemetery, Ernst surveyed the scene. In his nearly three decades on this earth he had seen more dead creatures than living ones. The cold anatomy of death was so harshly distant from life's flappings, crawlings and wanderings. The joyful miracle of life ended here, with these bones. Bodies provided only temporary shelter from the inevitable pall of death. The ancients dissected corpses to search for the secrets of life. Medical students in Berlin hid behind fumes of formaldehyde, draping sheets over cadavers they stripped to the bone to learn how to preserve the body's tenure. Artists, comatose with turpentine, addicted to their own creative juices, studied the geometry of cadavers with their eyes. And all the while, the Tibetans simply gave up their dead to the birds.

CHAPTER 26

December 1938

Twenty-five kilometres from the border of Tibet, they stumbled into thick rhododendron forests. Tantalisingly close to their hallowed destination, yet prohibited from entering, they snaked their way along narrow paths, crossing treacherous bridges woven out of vines. They would take advantage of their prolonged stay in Sikkim to pursue their research, as best they could. As they moved upwards, into the thinning air, the mules slipping in the mud, they were forced to cut new trails into the suffocating bush. The clouds were shreds of white across the blue sky.

Ernst decided to pitch their base camp on a plateau beside a small monastery near Thangu, not far from the Zemu Glacier of Kangchenjunga. That evening, the group of young Germans sat around a huge bonfire celebrating the winter solstice, all their conflicts suspended for now as the prospect of adventure in Tibet loomed. In unison they sang an SS marching song, celebrating the message they received from Himmler, in which he had written that he was promoting the entire team:

SS marches in enemy's land
And sings a devil's song
We care about nothing around us
The whole world can praise or curse us
Wherever we are, we move forwards
And the Devil will merely laugh.

They took turns reading from their field diaries, their conversation fuelled by local beer. Ernst flicked through his, looking for something that would fascinate his men. He started reading his entry for that day:

We are at the frontier! It is the realm of our most powerful yearning. Up there, not far away at all, is the border pass. The entire sight reminds one of the enchanted forests of our children's stories, where underneath wickerwork and roots only cunning goblins and malicious gnomes pursue their furtive, secret agendas.

He squinted as he struggled to read his own handwriting, but eventually gave up. Instead, he launched into recounting the story of when he found himself stranded in the wild for the very first time. In the telling, he felt transported back to boarding school in Heidelberg. In Ernst's first week away from home, he had been summoned by the headmaster early one morning. He remembered staring at the back of an older boy's blond shaven head as he led him down the corridor.

'Bathe in dragon's blood. It makes you invincible,' he said to Ernst.

'What do you mean?'

'Just kidding.' Turning to look at Ernst, he smiled, his eyes sharp and blue. 'How long are you in for?'

'Two years.'

'Well, this is just the beginning for you then, my friend. The old boy likes to give all his new students a private induction ceremony.' He smirked and turned to keep walking.

'So, what's with the dragon's blood?'

'You'll see. He's planning to take you on a little excursion into the Odenwald. That's all I can say.'

When they arrived outside a green door, his guide knocked twice.

A voice boomed from the other side. 'Enter!'

The older boy looked at Ernst, who was gnawing at his cuticles. 'Just keep calm. We all went through this and got out alive.' The door squeaked loudly as it opened. Ernst was escorted inside, standing to attention before the headmaster's desk.

'That will be all, Ludwig.' The man rose from his leather chair and walked over to the window, turning his back on the boys. His hair was thinning on top, wisps of grey licking at his large ears.

'Yes, Herr Direktor.'

This seemed to be the only name by which people addressed the surly headmaster. Ludwig turned, closing the door slowly behind him as he left.

Ernst waited for the man to speak, panic slowly building as he puzzled over Ludwig's cryptic suggestion about dragon's blood. After what felt like an eternity, the headmaster finally spoke again.

'Are you familiar with Wagner's music, Schäfer?'

'Yes, Herr Direktor,' he croaked quietly, his throat feeling dry.

'Good. Go get your things. We are going on an outing.'

'An outing?'

He turned to face Ernst, his eyes ablaze with sardonic joy. 'You will speak only when spoken to. We do not tolerate troublemakers here. You must learn to show respect.'

Ernst stood silently, his stomach roiling. He couldn't help staring at the man's hairy ears.

'Did you hear me?'

'Yes, Herr Direktor.'

'Good. Now go and change into casual clothes and meet me at the front gate at eight o'clock sharp.'

Running back down the corridor towards his dormitory, Ernst fought back tears, biting his lip till it bled. He was determined to prove himself, to not surrender totally by showing this man any weakness. He could not allow this sense of dread to swamp him.

He was waiting for Herr Direktor at the designated spot on time, his rucksack packed neatly with clean clothes, a canister filled with fresh water and the brand-new notebook his mother had given him just before he left, inscribed with the words *fur Meine tauere Schnecke*. He saw the man stride across the lawn from the main building, carrying nothing but a bunch of keys and a paper bag. He pointed to the car park, and made his way over towards a black Mercedes. Ernst followed him.

'Get in.'

He started the car and reversed, winding the window down. A warm breeze caressed them as they followed the road out past the township, continuing in silence for several miles through the countryside. They soon reached the entrance to a dense forest. A small wooden sign announced they were in the Odenwald. They continued along a dirt track that led deep into the woods, before the headmaster brought the car to a halt in the middle of nowhere. It was late morning by this point, and Ernst had hardly eaten any breakfast.

Herr Direktor opened the boot of the car and grabbed a duffel bag, from which he produced a rifle.

'You stay here and don't touch anything,' he said. Leaving the car door wide open, he disappeared into the green canopy.

The day wore on and Ernst, surrounded by tall pine trees, listened to the call of a cuckoo and a woodpecker's persistent hammering. How he wished he could speak to them. He had taught himself to mimic crows and blackbirds perfectly, and sometimes they even answered him, but to understand what birds were saying would have been so wonderful.

Although he was no stranger to being alone in a forest and wasn't scared, he grew hungry, used to stuffing his pockets full of Frau Klein's freshly baked cookies before venturing out into the woods back home. He looked around for some wild mushrooms, but it was far too early in the year to find any. Herr Direktor still wasn't back by the time evening fell. Ernst grabbed some handfuls of clover to fill his belly. He crawled into the back seat of the car and fell asleep, to be greeted the next morning with the smell of bacon and Apfelwein.

Herr Direktor was seated on a log.

'Come join me, Schäfer.'

'Were you frightened last night?'

'No, sir.'

'Good. Good.' He pulled a piece of rye bread from the paper bag and handed it to Ernst, who smelled rifle shot on the man's hands.

'Your father tells me you are crazy about animals.'

'Yes, sir.'

'Well, we have something in common then.'

'Yes, sir.' He ate eagerly.

'He is quite worried about you. I believe you are handy with a slingshot, and that's what got you in trouble.'

'Yes, sir.'

'Well, a young man's passions need to be tamed, his skills honed. From now on, you will join me every week to learn the magic of surviving in the bush. I will teach you the honourable sport of hunting, using a gun.' He took a swig from a hipflask that smelled more pungent than the

Apfelwein he offered Ernst. 'But you mustn't breathe a word to your father. It will be our special secret. Okay?'

Ernst nodded. His heart beat rapidly, but he risked no questions.

'This is the very spot where Wagner's Siegfried killed the evil dragon Fafner, who began his life as a giant, stealing the magic ring of power. After Siegfried slayed him, he drank the dragon's blood, which gave him the power to understand the language of birds.' The man handed him the flask.

That's what the older boy had been referring to yesterday. Did Herr Direktor bring all the boys out here, or only those he felt were special in some way? Ernst took a swig and felt his throat catch fire. He stared at his new headmaster. The sun broke through the branches and lit up his face with a golden glow. He didn't seem so formidable after all.

Ernst finished relating the whole story to his colleagues at base camp, expecting them to be riveted by the bravery he had shown, even as a youth. Instead he looked up from the campfire and saw that Geer and Krause had nodded off. Bruno cupped a hand over his mouth, trying to stifle his laughter, while Wienert spluttered and coughed, pretending to sip his tea. Ernst's knuckles turned white as he clutched his field diary tightly.

'Poor little Ernsti Wernsti,' Bruno sneered. 'Herr Direktor drank one too many beers and couldn't hide what a pathetic sycophant he thought his pupil really was. Such a terrible trauma for a young man. He must have thought you were so extraordinary. I guess that's why he performed the same ritual with all the other boys as well.' He kicked his sleeping colleagues in the ribs. 'Wake up! Our brave leader needs everybody's sympathy.'

The men slowly stretched their arms out, opening their eyes to see Ernst and Bruno standing jowl to jowl.

'You can laugh at me all you want, Bruno, but you live in a box. Some of us have our sights set further afield. *A narrow life will not suit me!*' Ernst fired a quote from his beloved *Faust* as though it were a round of ammunition.

It only made Bruno laugh even harder. 'Don't worry, little man. Goethe will come to your rescue with his terrifying book. Our enemies will take one look at the cover and surrender on the spot. Such an easy kill!'

The men couldn't contain themselves; the hilarity at their fiery leader's expense was contagious. Ernst stormed off in a foul mood, retreating to his tent, where he spent the rest of the evening alone. He longed to be in Herta's arms again. She was the only one who had ever understood him. Ernst lay on a stretcher, reading from his well-worn copy: *Live as a beast with the beasts*. He was wilderness made flesh.

Heavy rain fell that night, but dawn greeted them with a vista of mountains blanketed in white, rising out of the earth like a huge backbone. It was the first snowfall of the season. Ernst heard the frenzied shouting of the natives from inside his tent, which reached a crescendo by the time he emerged. The porters were already up, talking among themselves, huddled around some fresh tracks that led up to the edge of what they called the Green Lake. In this desolate, frozen world, with their trembling silhouettes framed against the cerulean sky, they looked like a band of tiny insects. Unlike their *sahibs*, they weren't scared of rumbling avalanches or the thundering collapse of a glacial surge; these calamities they simply attributed to punishment from the gods for aberrant or evil thoughts. It was things they could not explain that terrified them most: those dark shadows that penetrated a man's soul.

Fear of ghosts was so widespread in Tibet that over generations it had become the preoccupation of many a Tibetan priest. Lamas classified phantoms into almost 400 varieties, representing millions of evil spirits that haunted the masses of simple folk. This cataloguing of ghostly nomenclature, together with intricate outlining of each one's unique characteristics, was a matter of the most serious study. It reminded Ernst of Linnaeus's *Animalia Paradoxa*, a bestiary populated by mythical creatures such as the manticore and the hydra. Yet the lamas used their so-called knowledge of all things phantasmagorical to concoct ways of combatting the creatures' unnatural influence, as Tibetans saw ghosts everywhere. Ernst found this belief in spectres preposterous, but that didn't prevent him from leveraging this fear of shadows on occasion, to keep his own men in line.

Bells tied around the yaks' necks were tinkling in the crisp air, and the sound of gongs carried across the plain from a distant monastery, as Akeh came running over.

'*Bara-sahib*, come quickly! The men have found something very concerning.'

Ernst yawned, stretching his arms out like a bird preparing for flight.

'This better be important. You know not to disturb me before my morning coffee.'

Akeh bowed. 'Yes, *bara-sahib*. But you will see for yourself.' He led his master over to the circle of men who stood shivering several hundred metres away from the camp. They were staring down at giant tracks in the snow.

'*Migyud* has been here,' Akeh whispered. 'They all want to leave.'

One of the greatest legends about the mountainous regions in which they were camped was of the *Migyud*, a prowling, furry giant that thundered through the shadows of the Green Lake. Some called it the yeti. Whatever its name, the natives were petrified of the creature. They wove the most fantastic hair-raising tales that reminded Ernst of accounts of far-flung early travellers he had read as a young boy; even the pelican was once a mystery, believed to draw blood from its legs to feed its chicks. These mythical creatures were all nonsense of course, the warped joke of some crazy taxidermist conjuring implausible fakeries and fables. He heard some of his own porters were even spreading rumours that Ernst, like Siegfried, was prone to drinking the blood of animals he hunted.

The group turned to Ernst, waiting for his response.

'It's just a bear,' he said, unpacking his rifle. He knew this wouldn't reassure them at all. They dreaded these creatures, believing them to be an incarnation of evil spirits.

'With deepest respect, *bara-sahib*, about something unseen it is wise not to judge, rather than boldly pronounce what it is,' Akeh said.

Ernst raised his voice. The louder you spoke in these regions, the richer and more powerful you were seen to be. 'With all respect to you, Akeh,' he mimicked his servant, 'even if it is the *Migyud* doing his rounds, or just a haunted bear, you have me to protect you.' He lifted his rifle, took aim and fired into the mist.

A murmur passed through the men. Heated debate started between Akeh and one of the porters, who pointed repeatedly at the footprints and then up towards the mountains. Finally, the men started walking slowly back towards camp, and began their business of tending to the animals, unpacking equipment and preparing for breakfast. Ernst stayed behind as if to examine the tracks, stifling his laughter behind a woollen scarf. After the humiliating row with Bruno last night he had been unable to fall asleep. He needed a distraction, and his restless exploits in the snow during the early hours had definitely paid off. He had instilled terror in his servants and hoped they would now respect him more as their protector. The yeti was a myth perpetuated not only by the natives, but also by British explorers to the region who kept its true identity secret in order to hold the upper hand with the locals. The mythical creature was simply a Tibetan bear.

*

The next day, Ernst was woken early again, this time by distant birdsong. The morning was almost windless, and the sun a wash of pallor, glowing weakly in the misty horizon. Ribbed clouds formed a flimsy veil across the sky. He had dreamt that the creatures from every hunt he'd ever been on came crawling back to life – hooved, feathered, clawed and tusked – migrating from the shores of death to encircle him. Vines climbed up, entwining his body, trussing his limbs with thick stalks. Insects leapt up from soggy soil, gnawing at his skin. He saw himself ooze out from himself, the birds and beasts he had taken from the world feeding hungrily on him. They feasted on the heaviness of his flesh until he merged with grass and dirt. A guttural cry came from his throat as vultures soared above him, crouching on the clifftops as they dropped his solid bones, which plummeted to earth, smashing on the rocks below. A chorus of birds circled, in an exhilaration of wings – curlews, nightingales, Arctic terns, plovers, snipes, swifts – as flies feasted on his innards. He saw the fragile membrane that separated him from the animal kingdom. Man was a mirage, a small shadow of a figure walking across a vast desert. Screaming in terror, Ernst was answered by a crested lark that imitated his cries, accompanied by songs of disgust from a wood warbler. One of the vultures stretched its wings, gliding above the scene before swooping down. Ernst felt its talons sink into him as he closed what was left of his eyes, his heart, his brain. He forced himself to grow a beak, defied the smoothness of his skin to sprout feathers. Raising himself skywards, he escaped towards the south, in a migration from man to bird.

The day melted into evening as Ernst's world became shrouded by a wild fever. He shivered and sweated by turns, imagining he was close to paradise, or hell; it didn't matter which. His aching body betrayed him, his heart pounding, mind half-crazed with thirst. He felt pale maggots feeding on his flesh. Maybe he was already dead; perhaps he had died without noticing? What a curse a body was, a bundle of bones simply waiting for time to undress the fleshy coat.

A half-circle of his colleagues stood vigil around his cot, their faces floating above him in a haze. Animals fled, with hunters locked in their jaws. Starfish merged into the sand, spawning stars in their millions that rose to take up their place in the night sky. And the medicine man stood shimmering alongside them, his mastiff jaw hidden behind a moustache as wiry as a cat's whiskers, the stale smell of human remains on his breath. He examined his patient's frail knees, the deep hollows under his eyes, prodded his abdomen with a cool hand. Ernst watched the hand morph into a killer's paw.

In the cold mists of the following morning, he lay on his stretcher, shivering. The cook entered hesitantly, carrying a mug of steaming tea on a tray. As Ernst looked about his tent, the tarpaulin walls swelled like the sails of some giant ship soon to be swallowed by treacherous waves. When he was a child, he had believed in an afterlife, dreaming he would return to earth as a majestic bird. If he died here, would the *ragyapa* collect the dregs of his life and offer them up to the vultures?

After a few torrid nights, he was released from the teeth of the feverish beast. Those murky days lying alone in the darkness of his tent were soon forgotten when he was greeted by a letter delivered by a representative of the far-reaching British postal service. It had taken three months to get to them, but the document – a complete, yet triumphant surprise – was in Ernst's hands at last, adorned with no less than five official seals.

To the German Doctor Sahib Sha-par, Master of 100 Sciences,

A heartfelt thank-you for your letter of the twelfth day of the ninth English month, together with two boxes containing a gramophone, records and two pairs of binoculars.

Concerning you and the other Germans, Doctor Wienert, Mr Geer, Mr Krause and Mr Beger (altogether no more than five people) requesting to visit Lhasa and the holy Tibetan monasteries, please understand that, in general, entry into Tibet is forbidden to foreigners.

Although we know if we allow you to enter, others might come the next time, it nevertheless appears from your letter that you intend only friendship and to see the

holy land and its religious institutions. Acknowledging
this, we grant you permission to enter Lhasa for a stay of
two weeks, on condition that you promise not to harm
the Tibetan people and consent to not hunt or kill any
birds or mammals, which would deeply hurt the religious
feelings of the Tibetan people, both clergy and lay.
Please take this to heart.

Sent from the Kashag, the Tibetan council of ministers,
on the third day of the tenth month of the Fire-tiger Year

Ernst, breathless with delight, howled to the others
to come quickly – he could finally bring them some good
news, after weeks of tempers flaring to breaking point.
They gathered around as he read the letter out loud.
A huge cheer rose from the group. The men embraced,
patting Ernst on the back. Bruno chuckled at the idea that
anyone might try to stop Ernst from hunting. The weak
sun was trying to peer out from behind the clouds.

Opening the last bottle of beer, Ernst raised two fingers
in a victory sign and said, *'Einer für alle und alle für einen,*
my Musketeers! *Nach Lhasa!'*

CHAPTER 27

January 1939

The gem embedded in the 'roof of the world' lay before them. Ernst stood gazing down upon the Forbidden City of his dreams, flanked by his four colleagues and a large caravan of servants and muleteers. They were about to become the first official German expedition in history allowed to enter the holy capital.

Even though Ernst had visited Tibet twice before with the Dolan expeditions, he had never entered the desert-like plateaus around the foothills of the Himalayas they had just crossed through. Eastern Tibet boasted such a dramatically different landscape, with its lush bamboo forests and tempestuous rivers. He wasn't alone in his dreams to reach Lhasa and beyond; for hundreds of years, explorers, missionaries, esotericists and spies had drawn on legends and fictions of the city as an earthly paradise. While they viewed the country as a caricature of itself, Ernst would now see it clearer than anyone.

Their entourage made their way towards the ancient city, crossing the vast plane below the Tanggu La Pass. Lhasa embraced the icy Kyi Chu, the 'River of Happiness', which meandered through the valley and formed wetlands teeming with the rarest species of migratory fowl. The snow-covered peaks they had traversed several days before now seemed to be floating on the horizon. At the tiny village of Chu-gya, they stopped to watch the entourage of a respected spiritual Buddhist teacher, a grand *rimpoche*, pass by. His gilt helmet reminded Ernst of a character in the comics he used to read as a child, where medieval knights duelled each other on horseback.

Nothing could have prepared them for the vision of the Potala, the grand white-walled palace of the Dalai Lama poised graciously on Morburi, the famous red hill. Ernst called it the Vatican of Tibet. Its golden roof shone in the sun. The Potala was awaiting the arrival of the fourteenth Dalai Lama, a boy who had been found a year earlier in the remote village of Kumbum in Eastern Tibet. He was believed to be a reincarnation of the previous spiritual leader, though he was still too young to be brought to Lhasa to take up residence in the palace.

As the German expedition rode through the Bargo Kaling Gate, their arrival was announced by the tinkling of bells tied to their mules. All of Ernst's rifles, as well as the team's geomagnetic equipment, were carefully concealed inside their luggage. Two flags strapped to poles, which were fastened to the saddle of one of their yaks, fluttered in the breeze. One bore the insignia of the double *Sieg* runes of the SS, and the other proudly boasted a swastika: itself a common sight in Tibet, as an ancient symbol of good fortune.

Much to Ernst's indignation, and contrary to the Tibetan tradition of lavish welcomes, there was no grand party or fanfare to greet the caravan. Instead, some lowly officials were sent to present them with *khata*, ceremonial white scarves. This greeting party soon beat a hasty retreat, leaving the team surrounded by a circle of beggars. Ernst guessed this humiliating reception had been orchestrated by Hugh Richardson, the reedy leader of the British mission, who seemed to have a strong dislike for Ernst, perhaps taken in by the newspapers' claims that the true purpose of the German expedition was espionage. As they advanced through the group of bedraggled wretches, Richardson rode past them on horseback, straight-backed and stiff, his nose in the air. Ernst's instincts had been right. The haughty Englishman didn't give the German Tibet Expedition so much as a nod.

Their first week in Lhasa passed quietly, with Ernst busily trying to organise meetings with various dignitaries, seeking permission to extend their stay. They would need longer than a fortnight if they were to have the great privilege of watching the Tibetan New Year celebrations. Meanwhile, Bruno set himself up again as the ersatz doctor in town.

As the day that marked their halfway point in the city dawned, a line of people were already waiting outside Tredilinka. The expedition's humble and not-altogether-hygienic lodging, provided courtesy of the British mission, soon became a makeshift clinic and dispensary of sorts, as Bruno's reputation for pulling rotten teeth, curing headaches and bandaging sore fingers spread. He never charged for his services, and the lowliest of peasants, right up to the cream of Tibetan aristocracy, all sought his counsel, bringing him gifts that ranged from fresh eggs to a suit of armour and a horse. Even the wife of the regent, a striking woman with a lithe neck and long, dark hair, called for Bruno often, feigning various ailments.

'Can you make me live for a thousand years?' she whispered on her first visit, in perfect English she had learnt from her British tutors.

'Pardon?'

'You Germans have invented the greatest war machines, so surely a man of your many talents has already discovered the elixir of life. I will repay you handsomely.'

'All I can do, your Highness, is narrow the gap between life and death.'

'Then at least spend some time with me, easing my itch.'

Behind drawn curtains, Bruno examined her intimately and found a festering syphilitic chancre sore, courtesy of her British tutors.

Over the next few days, the regent's wife summoned the 'medicine man' to visit her twice a day, asking him to examine a swollen foot or a painful breast. She would pour him yak tea from a china teapot. He became besotted with her beauty, and what started as a placid scientific interest soon turned to fervour, as he revelled in the lurid ministrations he was allowed to perform.

At first, Ernst deigned to ignore it, but within days his colleague's obsession with the woman became ugly and urgent. The 'home visits' could potentially become more than just an embarrassment, posing a real threat to their welcome in Lhasa. When he confronted Bruno in their quarters, he started out with the intention of speaking to him calmly. But Ernst's pent-up frustration over his thwarted diplomatic appeals to extend their stay rose to the surface.

'The role you have taken on as physician has won you widespread adulation among the locals. Your position is to be used for the expedition to gain a stronger foothold in Tibet, not a humiliating excuse to throw us all out.' Ernst began to shout. 'It could cost us dearly if you keep seeing this woman. You are making a mockery of us all! If the British get hold of this, we are finished.'

A venomous smile appeared on Bruno's face. 'It's her choice, my friend. I am only extending the hand of German goodwill.'

'That's not all you're extending.' Ernst stood up, grabbed his copy of *Faust* from the end of the bed and whacked his friend on the side of his face. 'I don't need you catching her disease. As leader of this team, I forbid you to examine any of these women unless they are appropriately attired and chaperoned.'

Bruno's eyes turned icy. He tapped a long fingernail on the table, his tongue flicking in and out as he licked his chafed lips. 'Himmler asked me personally to research the anthropological rumours that Tibetan women hide gemstones in their pinkest recesses. I was simply following orders.'

'That may well be the case, but have you forgotten about Hildegard and your little daughter?'

Bruno was silent for a moment. 'No more than you are missing your dear Herta.'

Ernst began to wring his hands, as if preparing to jump on his friend and choke the life out from him. Instead he turned to leave, firing one last feeble round: 'You are a foul monster.'

Ernst couldn't fall asleep that night. Despite the chilly weather, the air inside Tredilinka was fetid and hot. He lay sprawled across a thin mattress, pushing a pencil across a page of his field diary, the smoke from his pipe curling upwards. He wrote in the dark, not wanting to wake the others, his untidy script like the muddy footsteps of a drunk insect. In Ernst's half-dreams the night before, sweetened by too much beer, the regent's wife stood at the foot of his stretcher, hovering like a phantom. She appeared even more beautiful than in real life. He reached over and caught her wrist, lifting her up to throw her onto the bed like a pile of linen. Heaving himself on top of her, he grasped at the stickiness between her thighs, straining against her body until it split straight down the middle. He nuzzled her belly, his feverish tongue licking up the blood that oozed from the trough of her ribcage. She tasted of salt and *yerma*, the dried peppercorns used by the Tibetan aristocracy in preparing sumptuous banquets. He gazed down at her and, as she stretched out both hands in embrace, her skin began to melt away. She fixed her mouth on his shoulder and he felt her devour his flesh, her appetite insatiable.

Her image evaporated into a wisp of smoke. Ernst, his hand trembling, folded the pouch of tobacco in two as he drew on the pipe again. The night, black and glossy, brought with it the eerie feeling of someone breathing on his face. Herta appeared before him, her small breasts and nipples pointing at him through her thin cotton dress. Her presence was a thin, shimmering shape, reaching out.

'Come with me,' she said.

She was there for only an instant before he exhaled. With the force of his breath, flesh fell from her bones and she disappeared.

The following morning, Ernst stood on the rickety wooden balcony of Tredilinka, watching the square below thronging with merchants and customers haggling over merchandise. He spent a couple of hours wandering around the marketplace, with its array of pungent teas, nutmeg and chilli peppers, fine silks and colourful trinkets. Wanting to escape from the crowded alleyways, he decided to take a stroll out along the sun-kissed river. He needed to be in the proper frame of mind to face the flurry of meetings he had organised with important Tibetan leaders. As he walked, he noticed a young woman following closely behind. She was looking at him shyly and giggling. Flattery was temptation enough. Should he allow himself to indulge in a little harmless indiscretion? No one would find out. Surely Herta would have taken his measure as a good man and forgiven him his natural urges. She would never judge a little 'distraction' for a fellow out here in the heathen wilderness, so far away from all that he loved. He missed Herta and felt homesick for the Fatherland. If the rumours they were hearing were true, and Germany was heading into war, he felt it his duty to be back home soon. But he also needed to spend enough time in Tibet to make sure his return would be a triumphant one. He wanted to shine in his patron's eyes. He waved the small temptress away and sat down by the riverbank, alone.

He would have loved to share his innermost thoughts with Herta; what he wouldn't give to be back in her arms. No one would ever be able to know him as well as she did. The men thought him a trifle unhinged – he could feel their eyes upon him all the time – but it was because his heart ached so much for her. Some days all he dreamt of was to be reunited again with his darling wife. He imagined her, his *Liebling*, seated beside him on the riverbank. They would talk about the beauty of the birds here, and how they seemed to hold a majestic wisdom. Herta knew that as soon as Ernst began to learn a place, he understood the winged creatures that lived there. He could close his eyes anywhere he went on earth and tell exactly where he was, just from local birdcalls. Their plaintive, wailing cries spoke the language of his heart.

The call of a Tibetan lark woke him early the next morning. He looked out across the city towards the west. The Jokhang Temple was nestled among ramshackle buildings of the Old Town, its golden roofs reflecting the pink hues of sunrise. He had heard about the strange religious rituals performed inside the Jokhang and wanted to see for himself what mysteries lay within its ancient walls.

Ernst set off along the winding paths of the city, a pack of mongrels following him through narrow alleyways, down towards what was considered the most sacred place of worship in Tibet. When he crept inside the temple, he was mesmerised by a sea of burning candles. The space reminded him of his childhood, seated beside Herta and her family during Sunday worship, enchanted by the votive candles' dancing flames.

The air was thick with the acrid smell of oily yak-butter lamps mixed with incense. He watched pilgrims prostrating themselves, while others turned large wooden prayer wheels. A monk noticed Ernst standing beside the narrow entrance to the temple and offered to take him on a tour. Holy shrines, with their many variations of incarnations of the Buddha, lay hidden behind the cloisters. The strangest one, crouched behind a door made of chains, was the shrine of the goddess Palden Lhamo. Ernst had heard some Tibetans believed she had been reincarnated as Queen Victoria. He wondered what the haughty Hugh Richardson would think of that.

In the end, despite all of Ernst's extravagant banquets, obsequious entreaties and the showering of expensive gifts on all manner of dignitaries, it was Bruno who helped get their permit extended. In Ernst's frantic efforts to please the aristocracy, he had neglected to include an important Tibetan member of the Kashag on any of his invitation lists. The government official had taken deep offence, so Ernst visited him immediately to try to apologise for the oversight. The man's wife lay on a mattress, coughing and groaning, her clothes drenched in sweat. Ernst decided to take advantage of the opportunity to make amends, and called for Bruno to come straightaway. The self-appointed medicine man arrived and opened his bag of tricks. The woman felt better within fifteen minutes, after having swallowed the magic potion of two aspirins. Two days later, their permit was extended until March.

The colourful week of celebrations approached. As thousands descended upon Lhasa for New Year festivities and the Great Prayer of Mönlam, incense filled the air, alongside the stench of unwashed pilgrims and shaven-headed monks wrapped in their crimson robes. Ernst and Krause spent days filming vibrant parades, archery competitions and dances, against the backdrop of freshly painted buildings and rooftops adorned with colourful prayer flags. On their donated cameras, they captured these rituals for a newsreel Himmler had encouraged them to film during their trip. They planned to call it *Geheimnis Tibet*. Secret Tibet.

At night, after a butter-puppet performance, fireworks lit up the dark streets. The regent invited them to attend the devil dance; they arrived to find the eastern courtyard of the Potala decorated with curtains embroidered with fierce dragons. Ernst and Krause filmed warriors who wore rusty helmets and medieval costumes as they moved to the sound of trumpets blasting and drums beating all around them. The performers, dressed up as demons with animal masks, twirled in time with skeleton dancers.

The feeding of the poor was an arresting spectacle in which staples of tea, butter, flour and cake were piled up in front of the Dalai Lama's throne, and the food was surrounded by dried-out yaks for them to feast on. When the doors opened, beggars leapt over one another in the struggle to devour whatever they could, as quickly as possible, a frenzied event that ended with everything gone within twenty minutes.

The meeting with the regent himself was the climax of their stay in Lhasa. After exchanging *katas*, a ritual of the strictest etiquette they had practised carefully beforehand, the men sat around a table that was laden with a traditional Tibetan banquet. Seated high up on his throne, the regent was flanked by surly bodyguards, the wall behind him covered with exquisitely embroidered *thankas*, elaborate wall hangings. The regent's entourage were all dressed in their finest silken robes, and the German scientists had trimmed their beards and washed their clothes for the occasion. Ernst made sure to bring many gifts: a set of German china, several types of medicine, Zeiss binoculars and a prized Philips radio set. He strategically asked for their gift of Nazi flags to be hung right next to the *thankas*.

Ernst spoke passionately, hoping to forge a link between the two nations: 'As the swastika represents for us Germans, too, the highest and most holy of symbols, so may our visit be a meeting of the Western and Eastern swastikas in friendship and peace.'

The meeting was a triumph for the team. Ernst even convinced the rimpoche to write a letter to Hitler, though the Tibetan regent likely possessed no in-depth knowledge of who the man he addressed as the Führer actually was.

To his Majesty Führer Adolf Hitler, Berlin, Germany
From the Regent of Tibet,

Your Majesty,

I trust your Highness is in the best of health and is
progressing well in all your affairs. Here I am well

and doing my best with regards to our religious and government affairs. I have the pleasure of letting your Majesty know that Dr Schäfer and his party, who are the first Germans to visit Tibet, have been permitted to enter Lhasa without any objection, and every necessary assistance was rendered upon their arrival. Furthermore, I desire to do anything that will help foster the friendly ties and relationship between our two nations, and I trust your Majesty will also consider this essential.

Please take care of your good self and let me know if your Majesty desires anything.

I am sending a separate parcel that contains a Tibetan silver saucer and lid with a decorative red teacup. Please also accept a native Tibetan dog as a small remembrance.

Sincerely yours,
Reting Ho-Thok-Thu

On the fifth day of the New Year, the Great Prayer of Mönlam began, and Ernst filmed the chaos of thousands of monks taking over the city. He was horrified to see holy men overindulging in smoking, drinking and other illicit acts. The peak moment of the centuries-old New Year celebration was the prophecy of the *Nechung,* the state oracle. Listening keenly to the pronouncements of this spiritual medium, via a translator, Ernst was bemused by its prediction: *'Be wary of the mountains which lie on the* border – *flying people will approach the land of snow, from the sky . . . A dragon rules their world.'*

The oracle also uttered a special prophecy about Ernst and his team: *'The strangers who came from far away across the sea . . . love our teachings, but they also carry something else with them.'*

CHAPTER 28

In spite of the hospitality of their Tibetan hosts, the political tensions with the British were becoming almost unbearable for the team. With the postal connection interrupted, they were left entirely dependent upon the sparse, often contradictory news from their rickety shortwave radio. On the afternoon of 15 March, they gathered together after lunch to listen to a crackly broadcast. They huddled close, straining to hear the news, but the transmission kept breaking up, much to Ernst's annoyance. There was a hum of frustrated murmuring in the room as they struggled to make sense of the broadcast, piecing together words like 'invaded' and 'occupied'. They knew something of enormous consequence was happening in Europe, but the staccato announcement left them all confused and nervous.

'Shut up, everyone!' Ernst said. 'Krause, can't you fix the damn thing?'

Krause fiddled with the wires and dials, but all his efforts proved useless.

'*Scheisse!*' Ernst's hands were shaking. Pushing his way past the others, he ran straight out the door. In his frustration, Ernst panicked, deciding to rush across to the British mission ensconced in their own ramshackle residence. Despite his deep antipathy towards Hugh Richardson, he knew he would at least learn the truth from him.

When Ernst marched in unannounced, the Englishman was seated in an armchair, drinking tea from a rose-patterned china cup. Ernst, whose beard had grown long and unkempt again, was met with a look of disdain.

'Well, well, well! Hello, my dear Dr Schäfer. To what do I owe this surprise visit?'

Ernst smiled. He cleared his throat, preparing to use the mannered, obsequious English he had put to such good use in Philadelphia. 'I do beg your pardon, barging in on you like this, but our radio seems to be on the blink. We heard there are some unusual goings-on back home. I wonder if you might clarify what is happening over there.'

Richardson took a sip of tea, crossing his long legs. 'Well, let's just say it's nothing I didn't expect. I always knew this appeasement nonsense was a ruse of your beloved Führer.'

Ernst waited for him to continue.

'Would you like to join me for afternoon tea?' Richardson asked, in the manner of a guard offering a prisoner his last meal.

'No, thank you. I've already eaten.'

'Ah. Good, then. I won't hold you up. You must have a lot to do today.'

'Tell me what has happened.'

'Of course, with absolute pleasure.' He placed his cup back on its saucer. 'Your friend Hitler has invaded and occupied Czechoslovakia. German troops rolled in during the early hours of the morning and took over without any sign of a fight.'

Ernst felt a wave of nausea rise up. This was a potential disaster for his expedition. Appeasement allowed them to stay in Tibet far longer than they had ever expected, and this abrupt turn in world events was likely to endanger not only the future of his entire expedition, but also his career.

Ernst tried not to show his distress. 'Your government will be fine with that, won't they?'

Richardson stood abruptly, his manner cold and officious. 'I certainly hope that they will not. It seems your Führer has his eyes set on mopping up the world. I wouldn't want to be one of those so-called lesser breeds you folk seem to have such hatred towards.'

It was clear from the man's stance that the meeting was over. Ushering Ernst towards the door, Richardson spoke to him with quiet enmity. 'I do not wish to see you ever again, Mr Schäfer.'

Sure enough, despite Ernst's elation at everything they had managed to achieve in such a short time in Tibet, heavy clouds started gathering over the fate of their expedition. In the days after news of the annexation, malevolent rumours, which at first only approached like a fine mist, finally arrived as a downpour of curses, slander and vulgar intrigues against the team of Germans. It was with deep regret that Ernst decided the time had come for them to make their withdrawal. He was certain now that if they stayed and the situation grew worse in Europe, Richardson would be the first to have them all interned in a British prisoner-of-war camp.

Ernst was devastated. As he told the team, he had hoped they might have been able to stay on a little longer, but his men's safety was his first priority. They would travel the shortest route towards the south, to reach India again. This would take at least two to three months, so they needed to leave immediately.

Privately, Ernst was far more concerned with the fate of their precious cargo of specimens, which needed to be sent home box by box. Every step of the way, from muleteers to cargo-ship handlers, would require delicate diplomatic negotiation, something Ernst usually navigated like a fish darting through water. But the situation was rapidly changing, and the British would try to complicate their way at every opportunity. He could not dare to risk losing their hard-won treasures, so he made it his mission to personally ensure there would be careful handling at every part of the journey home. Ernst knew better than most that when it came to the authorities, diplomacy and discretion were always of paramount importance, as were manipulation and bribery. After ensuring their yield was securely loaded onto a waiting cargo ship, the plan would be for the five explorers to fly from Calcutta over Karachi, Basra, Baghdad, Athens and back home once again to their beloved Fatherland. He had come so close to achieving all he desired, but now his wings had been clipped. Like Icarus, Ernst feared he would fall back into a sea of anonymity.

Amid the flurry of preparations for their departure from Lhasa, Ernst found his thoughts drifting back to his father's study in Waltershausen. He recalled the day, distant in time but still festering in his mind, that his father sent him off to boarding school. How would he say goodbye to his secret woods, leave everything he had worked so hard to collect, all his extraordinary specimens, behind?

'I don't want to end up working in an office, Papa,' he pleaded. 'My place is in the wilderness, living as close to the birds as I can.' What he'd meant to say was, as far away from human civilisation as possible.

Before Albert Schäfer had a chance to take out the strap and thrash it over the flesh of his rebellious son, there was a clacking of footsteps down the corridor, followed by a loud, insistent knocking at the door. The clock had just chimed eleven.

'Herr Schäfer!' a small voice called from the other side. '*Bitte schön*, come quick!'

The door creaked open and Herta popped her head around the edge. Ernst, who stood silent now before his father, turned to look at her.

'Please forgive the interruption, Herr Schäfer, but Vati has sent me to ask for your help. Urgently!' There was a trace of panic on her face.

'What's wrong, my child?' He lowered the strap to his desk.

Herta looked across at Ernst, tears suddenly rolling down her cheek. 'It's Margarete. She's been hurt.'

Albert Schäfer hauled his jacket on and rushed outside. Ernst recovered from a moment's shock that his father seemed to know about Margarete and grabbed Herta's hand. Following close behind, they ran together down the empty street.

'What happened?' Ernst asked.

Herta breathed hard, trying to hold back her tears. She told him how she had dragged Margarete upstairs to her room, wanting to show her the beautiful feather collection he had given her. Herta built a tower of blankets on her bed and, climbing to the top, showed Margarete how she was teaching herself to fly. Her sister giggled, clapping her hands, her eyes lighting up as Herta leapt from her perch onto a pile of pillows thrown on the bedroom floor. Herta loved the rush of air on her face as she dived. Wanting to share that feeling with poor Margarete, she heaved her little sister up onto the cliff of bedding.

Mutti, finding Margarete's room empty, called out to them, the sound of heavy footsteps approaching as she climbed the flight of stairs to Herta's room. Herta tried to pull Margarete back down onto the bed before Mutti found her up there, but it was too late. Their mother burst into the room.

'What on earth are you doing?' Mutti yelled, as if by sheer volume she could make her youngest daughter hear again. 'Get down from there!'

In a flash, Margarete's fingers fluttered like feathers at the tips of her wings, and she jumped.

When Herr Schäfer arrived with Ernst and Herta in tow, Frau Völz was waiting for him at the front door. She ushered them down to the back room where Vati was bent over his youngest daughter, who lay slumped and still on the floor, her arm bent like a broken wing.

'Her head was almost touching the ceiling,' Mutti told them, her breath raspy. 'She sat up there with her arms stretched out, feet together.'

The adults busied themselves with finding some bandages and a piece of wood to fashion a makeshift splint. There was no question of the doctor being called. Herta sat down on the floor and lifted her sister's limp hand, stroking it gently. Ernst kneeled beside them. Margarete's eyes darted back and forth, finally landing on Ernst's face. Whimpering, she looked at him, her brow furrowed, as though searching for an answer.

What might her question be, Ernst wondered. While the adults were arguing over what to do, he leaned down and whispered in Margarete's ear, as if she could hear him: 'The grown-ups are too weighed down with the troubles of the world. You are so small, with feathers and bones as light as a baby cuckoo's. Patience, my little bird, you still have plenty of time to learn. First you need to grow your wings.'

Just before the adults shooed him and Herta away, Ernst was sure he saw a smile flash across Margarete's tiny bird-like face.

Five days after the ominous news broadcast, Ernst and his colleagues vanished from Lhasa. They set out just before sunrise. Ernst led his caravan south, taking several days to cross through the treacherous snow-capped mountains. By mid-April they reached Shigatse, where each of them hurried to complete their research. Time was running out. Events back in Europe saw a flurry of telegrams and letters arriving from friends and family, begging them to come home.

How would it be to return after so long? It was hard to believe only eighteen months earlier he had been enjoying the luxuries of Carinhall with his dear Herta.

Bruno hastily gathered anthropometric data from up to ten people a day; Weinert completed his measurements at fifteen geomagnetic stations; and Ernst went out on forays with his slingshot and rifle to bag a slew of specimens, ten rare blue pheasants among them, to add to his already enormous collection.

A month later they trekked back across the Tibetan plateau, with not a tree in sight to shade them. On 24 June, Basil Gould summoned Ernst to meet with him at his camp on the banks of the Dochen Lake. His manner was unusually hospitable.

'I am delighted to extend an invitation for the group to stay an extra two months in Sikkim.' Gould smiled, raising his glass in a gesture of friendship.

Despite the delicious roast he was served, Ernst became wary of this sudden about-turn in attitude, surely a plot to stall their departure. He decided to continue their journey home, knowing full well that if war was to break out in Europe, Gould would, like Richardson, immediately intern his team as enemy aliens.

One night, Ernst and his men fled to Calcutta, abandoning their loyal guides without so much as a goodbye. Once they arrived in the bustling city, the five Germans hastily made preparations, packing up and organising transport of the spoils of their expedition at the docks. They needed to ensure safe handling of over 40,000 photographs, 18,000 metres of film footage, thousands of animal specimens and bird skins, wasps, bees and other insects, as well as all the seeds Krause had collected for Himmler. The bird skins were tightly stacked together top to tail, their shimmering feathers folded delicately. Ernst and his team had also acquired thousands of priceless ethnographic artefacts: nomad tents, *tsampa* bowls, rugs, *lama* trumpets. They ensured heavy locks were placed on their German-built boxes to protect their contents from theft. The most difficult task by far was building crates for live Tibetan animals – native dogs, wolves and cats among them – to be shipped back to Germany, where they would fetch a handsome price from various zoos.

On the evening they were to catch their flight back home, just before he joined the men who were waiting for him in two cars near the docks, Ernst couldn't resist taking a moment to examine his prize specimen once more: a bearded vulture, the *dur bya*, luminary of the Tibetans' sky burials. This bird alone made the whole trip worthwhile.

Ernst reached into the box and fingered the orange feathers on its neck. The bird preferred to live in desolate regions. Although it waddled clumsily when it was on the ground, with a wingspan of over nine feet it could gracefully soar to heights of over 6000 metres. It was not very vocal, except for when it engaged in courtship displays, letting out shrill whistles to attract a mate. Its diet was unique, consisting almost exclusively of bone marrow. Immature birds took up to seven years of practice to learn the skill of dropping bones from a height of 100 metres, smashing them onto the rocks below before swooping down to hollow them out.

The bird had once been known as the Lammergeier, the 'lamb-vulture', because its kind was believed to attack the unsuspecting offspring of mountain sheep. Ernst had heard stories of them swooping human babies up in their sharp talons and carrying them away. Yet, for Tibetans, the bearded vulture was a sacred bird, revered as a protector of the land. Disguised as *dakinis*, or angels, the birds fed on a corpse, taking the soul of the dead person up to the heavens to await rebirth.

If, as the Tibetans believed, Ernst could live his next life as a bird, he wanted to return as a majestic Lammergeier.

CHAPTER 29

4 August 1939
Templehof Airport, Berlin

Steel birds circled over *Welthauptstadt Germania*, the world's capital. Here was their own city right below them, looking more beautiful than ever, the Spree in the distance gently winding its way alongside Unter den Linden and the Tiergarten. It was a glorious sunny day and to the east Ernst could see the Zoological Gardens, where he had proposed to Herta. It seemed like a lifetime ago now.

Reichsführer Himmler, who was seated right beside him, pointed out the window. 'You see over there, just near the airport?'

Ernst looked down at the remains of a large concrete building.

'That used to be the Columbia-Haus camp.' Himmler laughed. 'We used it for prisoners when Gestapo headquarters was overflowing. But they demolished it last year to make room for extensions to the air terminals.' He scratched his chin. 'Never mind. Not to worry, my son. There are plenty more camps on the planning board.'

The team's retreat from Tibet had been organised by Himmler himself. As the British Indian Airways flying boat took off from the Hoogli River in Calcutta, Ernst gazed out of the window, knowing he might never return to this exciting part of the world in which he had spent the bulk of his early twenties. With each gust of wind that buffeted the aircraft, he felt as though he were falling back to earth, dragged down by thoughts of regret.

Somewhere between Calcutta and Baghdad they developed engine trouble and had to make an emergency landing in Karachi, where they took the opportunity to transform themselves into clean-shaven, well-dressed German citizens. They boarded a Junkers U90 waiting to fly them to Vienna and, from there, the *Otto Killenbeth*, Himmler's personal aircraft, brought them to Munich. There, Himmler joined the five young adventurers, and they all entered a private room where Himmler and his chief of staff debriefed them over a cup of coffee. Ernst was presented with a *Totenkopfring*, an SS death's-head ring inscribed with Himmler's signature, a cherished item awarded only to unblemished SS officers: men with clean reputations and clean family lines.

They made the last leg of their journey to Templehof, built shortly before the Olympics. As they closed in on the airport, Ernst saw that its design suggested an eagle in flight, with semicircular hangars resembling a giant bird's wings spread out.

They stepped off the plane into a warm summer breeze, accompanied by the enthusiastic *Reichsführer*. He and Ernst walked happily side by side towards the terminal, Ernst's men remaining respectfully a few steps behind. They were paraded past the façade's imposing limestone columns and made their way through the lofty entrance hall, where they were greeted by a large crowd cheering *'Willkommen!'*

Ernst Schäfer was feted as a national hero. His dreams had all come true.

In spite of all the celebrations, Ernst was haunted by the question of what he might have achieved had he been able to stay longer in Tibet. Given the leisure of a few more months, he would have relaxed more and camped alone in the wilderness. Herta had always implored him to simply enjoy nature, to sit quietly and just observe a bird's behaviour. She was right. He would have taken his time, jotting down notes and sketching new species in his journal, before shooting them to add to his collection.

As Ernst was ushered out of the terminal, he noticed the stars glimmering in the slowly darkening sky. According to World Ice Theory, the earth, along with the entire universe, was spiralling towards the only star that had ever existed, our very own sun. The twinkling lights Ernst saw were merely reflections from distant glaciers and ancient moons of ice plummeting towards earth. The giant implosion of everything that had ever been would be the final conflagration that would swallow all existence, in the same way science and love and Tibet had devoured Ernst. The season was changing, and he had followed the call to fly home.

CHAPTER 30

Mother taught me that the extra moment it takes to say goodbye is never a waste of time. A mother's love can never let go, she said. I am beckoning Sleep to come to me, so I might close my eyes and dream. It is blustery outside; the clouds gather and are whisked away before they have a chance to rain down. It's the same with Sleep; the more I wrestle for it, the more it runs away from me. I remember Sleep from my days in Wild, can still feel how it would drape itself over me after Play, when I rolled around on the ground or climbed up and down Bamboo as fast as I could. And the croaking and hooting all around would make my eyelids heavy. I try so hard to remember Wild, to remember the Then, when we were all together.

For more than eighty years, says Curator, I have been joined to my Adult Female and Adult Male, held together by Concept and Glass. Each of us travelled great distances to stand next to each other Forever. Shepherd told me I would still be here telling His story in a thousand years. I wanted so badly for that truth to be my only cage. He said my flesh has become His spirit and I am proof of Science, not God. But how then to understand today's visit by Curator, and Assistant who held Panda File in her paw, writing briskly with Stick as he spoke? I see Guard's face as he turns away and Girl, whose eyes rain as she packs up World Wildlife Fund Bag. My eyes stay dry. Even when Jerkoff tells me I would make a nice Panda-covered chair, with matching coffee table.

I see a ragged flock of geese fly past Window, like a moving scar in Sky. 'Migrating,' Scientist told Students once, 'from one side of Wild to the other.' Perhaps that's what Shepherd meant for me, to give me freedom beyond the night that used to swarm with shining eyes and flying shadows. I plummeted into the limbo of continuous present behind Glass. I always wondered whether I would instantly grow old if I ever left Glass. Curator says we must make way for the New. He wants to have Workers haul me back to Basement, at least until my type are able to qualify as Extinct, in which case I can be dusted off again and brought back. I will soon be closed away and forgotten, like a nameless tombstone, standing outside of Time, simply watching it pass before me. Long ago, inside one of the thousands of long metal drawers down in Basement, I saw a faded label attached to some tiny bones that were as yellow as old teeth. Scrawled in black ink were the words

'Phalanges (Ailuropoda melanoleuca) the toes of a Panda Bear'. It was signed 'E. Schäfer 5/13/1931'.

They came in the sleepless, small hours of Sunday 18th to remove Glass, bearded men with exhausted eyes holding coffee cups decorated with Bamboo. They also carried a sign: 'Endlings – A Room of Extinct Species'. Stars watched all night outside Window, until darkness lifted. Curator has brought all manner of bird and beast together for the new exhibition. A button-eyed giant Haast's Eagle faces a Honshu Wolf, a Great Auk stands beside a Tasmanian Tiger. It takes me some time, but finally I recognise Thyla from those days down in Basement spent with Shepherd. How I wish I could smile and say hello to her. I'm so glad she will finally make it into Glasslands after all those years of waiting. Having once been shipped safely from afar in Crate, they have all come to a standstill here. I am honoured to make way for them even though Curator will abandon me to the darkness, where I will vanish on the other side of Permanent Storage, sinking into Time. It is important for Visitors to see what can no longer be seen. Scientist told Smalls that the way my type is destined anyway, it may not be long before I will be brought back to appear in New Glass with all these strangers.

But what will become of my Glass Mother? She will be 'rehoused', they say. Taken to the Big Museum to join the Fake Panda there, whom Curator says was fashioned from dyed bearskins. Apparently, we are Illegal; our sole purpose now is Preservation. Assistant says it is sad to be losing me;

297

she is used to saying hello every day as she walks past on her way to Administration, or back to Café. Curator tells her that all I am is a fibreglass dust-collector with a fur coat, and that she should Get a Life. I would be very interested to know where one might go to Get a Life.

CHAPTER 31

9 November 1937
Carinhall

Autumn undressed the trees as sunlight squinted between their branches. Waves tickled the small boat, which rocked gently. Ernst looked over towards Herta. She smiled at him and wrapped her shawl around her shoulders. When she closed her eyes, she saw colourful patterns swirling around the imprint of his face.

Last night, she dreamt he finally found Margarete and brought her home. Despite his gruff exterior, Herta knew the heart of the boy had not changed after all. He loved her, had always loved her. She felt his lips on her forehead, his hand stroking her hair as she breathed in his scent, his animal smell. They were each so different and yet the same. He had carved out who he was in nature, whereas she preferred to disappear in its folds, melting into its beauty. This was the perfect time to let him know he would become a father soon. While he was away, she would stay with Mutti and Vati, and have the baby in the town where they had both grown up. She hoped it would be a boy. By the time Ernst returned from his adventures in Tibet, their little son would be old enough to run and greet him. Two years from now, perhaps things would be different and Margarete would be allowed to live freely. They could all begin anew.

Her shawl fell from her shoulders. She opened her eyes and reached down to grab it.

'Ernst,' she said softly.

The oars creaked in their locks. He hadn't heard her.

'Ernst.' The life inside her insisted on making itself known. She spoke a little louder this time. 'I have something to tell you.'

A flock of ducks emerged from the shelter of the forest without warning. Ernst thought about how he had worked so hard to reach a position in his career where he was poised to become the top in his field. He couldn't risk losing that now. Surely he had provided Herta with everything she needed. What more did she want from him? Any other woman would have been content with the comfort and security that simply came from being Ernst Schäfer's wife. He heard the ducks' garish laughter. There was always some convenience in the death of a bird whose wayward flappings had threatened the entire flock.

As soon as the first duck's panicky quack pierced the air, Ernst lifted his rifle and aimed. Moments before he fired, he registered Herta calling him.

The shot exploded, and Ernst saw Herta look up at him and gasp.

He felt the swish of her skirt against his leg as she fell back. He reached out, trying to catch her, but she landed in a pool of water at the bottom of the boat. Leaning across, he held his hand over her chest. A sudden gust of wind slapped him as he kneeled to lift her in his arms. Her eyes met his, but there was no flicker of light or recognition. He knew that look from thousands of kills: the vacant stare of the nearly dead.

Her shawl began to look like a world map, bloody continents divided by blue pashmina oceans. Holding her pallid hand, his thumb stroked the gold wedding ring he had slipped onto her finger months earlier. He leaned in close and kissed her lips, tasting her salty blood as it trickled down her chin. The colour was rapidly draining from her face as she left for uncharted terrain. The flock of ducks, his only witnesses, had already escaped to the far side of the lake, shrieking in the wake of gunshot that still seemed to echo through the whispering trees.

Silence swallowed the air.

'Help!' he cried into the canopy of rainclouds slowly gathering above the lake.

Looking over to the shore, he saw the silhouette of the warden, Engel, emerge from the cabin.

'Hurry!' he cried across the water. 'There's been an accident!'

The warden ran along the pier and jumped into a dinghy. He rowed briskly towards them, but by the time he arrived, Herta's face was already porcelain.

EPILOGUE

You held me in your arms, watching my blood mix with the rusty water pooling in the bottom of our boat. My last wish was to speak the language of bird and bear, panda and elk, my voice holding the chorus of their cries, so that you might hear their pain. All those you have stoned, shot, dissected and stuffed. All those whose marrow you have sucked and whose blood you have drunk. I wish I could see that young panda standing patiently in its glass case, staring out into the impervious face of time. I would tell the beautiful bear that I am the only one you didn't succeed in pinning down. Let the thousands of specimens you have pillaged from the safety of the wild and brought to display in domestic parlours and museums around the world be shown for what they are. Their enforced immortality could never take away the beauty of their fragile, fleeting lives.

I fly away from you now, no need for final words. The most powerful language belongs to them. It's the animals who make us human.

AFTERWORD

Ernst Schäfer

After his return to Germany from Tibet, Schäfer remarried in December 1939. During World War II, he led the Sven Hedin Research Institute for German Genealogical Inheritance and was a member of Himmler's elite Circle of Friends, the *Freundeskreis RFSS*. In 1942, Himmler put him in charge of the planning of a huge expedition of twenty German scientists under strong military guard into the Caucasus to incite a Tibetan rebellion against the Raj, which never came to fruition due to the ongoing war campaign. That same year, Himmler sent him to film medical experiments on inmates at Dachau concentration camp.

Schäfer was imprisoned by the Allied military government at Camp Moosburg in 1945. In 1947, when he was transferred to Cell 264 at Nuremberg in preparation for his trial, he wrote that he felt as if he had metamorphosed into one of his specimens, trapped in a cage. But Schäfer knew how to wriggle his way out of a tight spot. He asked for a typewriter and tried to manipulate his way to freedom, pleading his innocence in English to the US Army's judge advocate general, Telford Taylor, one of the prosecutors of Nazi criminals:

During the longer time of the Hitler regime, the aims of which were not known to me, I therefore was abroad working for the benefit of an American scientific institution and risking my life for it . . . After my life had been promulgated in the European press I was out of obvious reasons called back to Germany and simultaneously appointed an honorary leader in the SS. This constituted one of those notorious machinations of the Nazi leaders to bind young and able scientists to their system and it was effected without my own free will. I am a completely unpolitical man who waged a never-ending struggle directed against the Nazi system, in the course of which I protected Jews, Poles, Russians and German persecutes, within the realm of my institute. I faced a choice between emigration and devoting my exertions to the common cause of humanity . . . I chose the last, or rather there was no other choice without seriously endangering the lives of my co-workers, the lives of my wife and my children, and last but not least my work. There are scores of Nazis, many of my colleagues with a shadowy past, who were quickly given back the bliss of freedom after the war and are now happily teaching in universities, both here and in the United States.

Schäfer also volunteered that Himmler held strange views about the occult and berated his colleagues at the *Ahnenerbe* for their pseudoscientific beliefs. In 1949, Schäfer was exonerated. His interrogators in the trial came to the conclusion that, on balance, he had done more good than harm, and handed him a Category V certificate, which deemed him denazified. They demanded he pay a fine of twenty-five Deutschmark, after which he walked free.

Upon his release he took up a position as a professor in Venezuela, establishing the Caracas Botanical Garden. He returned to Europe in 1954 to become an advisor to King Leopold III of Belgium. He served as curator of the Department of Natural History at the Lower Saxony State Museum from 1960 to 1970. He died aged eighty-two in Bad Bevensen, Germany. He was survived by his wife, Ursula, and their three daughters.

Nazi Party membership #4690995
Summer 1933: Joined the SS
1936: *Untersturmführer*
1937: *Obersturmführer*
1938: *Hauptsturmführer*

Herta Völz

Outside of Schafer's diaries, I have not been able to find any official record of Herta, besides her death certificate and a photo of her father, Lothar, standing outside the Heidelberg Pädagogium. Ernst Schäfer is reported to have been remorseful that he killed her, but the incident, in what has been suggested was a cover-up, was ultimately blamed on the warden, who was charged with manslaughter.

Bruno Beger

In 1948, Beger was exonerated by a denazification tribunal. In 1960, he was arrested for his part in a Jewish skeleton collection acquired by murdering inmates of the Auschwitz concentration camp. He was released four months later, but when the case came to trial in 1970, he was found guilty of being an accomplice to the murder of eighty-six Jews. Although he was sentenced to three years' imprisonment, on appeal this was reduced to three years' probation. He died in Königstein, Germany, in 2009, aged ninety-eight.

Edmund Geer

Geer, who had been a member of the Nazi Party since the 1920s, was exonerated at the Nuremberg trials, assigned Category IV ('Follower').

Ernst Krause

In 1942, Krause and Schäfer were sent to visit Dachau to record and film medical experiments performed by the notorious Nazi doctor Sigmund Rascher. Prisoners were locked in simulated-altitude chambers and their vital signs recorded until they died of excruciating pain and convulsions from a lack of oxygen. He was completely exonerated in the Nuremberg Trials, assigned Category V, and went on to become an academic.

Karl Wienert

In 1942, Wienert worked on a project sponsored by Himmler to search for gold in Bavarian riverbeds. He was completely exonerated in the Nuremberg Trials, assigned Category V, and later had a successful academic career, working as a geophysicist in Pakistan, where he built a geomagnetic observatory. From 1958, he was the head of the Earth Magnetic Observatory in Munich. He died aged seventy-nine.

Gertrud Scholtz-Klink

The head of the Nazi Women's League, by 1940 Scholtz-Klink was married to her third husband, SS-*Obergruppenführer* August Heissmeyer, and made frequent trips to visit women at political concentration camps. At the end of World War II, Scholtz-Klink and Heissmeyer were briefly detained in a Soviet prisoner-of-war camp but escaped shortly after. With the assistance of Princess Pauline of Württemberg, they went into hiding in Bebenhausen. They spent the subsequent three years under the aliases of Heinrich and Maria Stuckebrock. In 1948, they were identified and arrested. Scholtz-Klink was sentenced to eighteen months in prison on the charge of forging documents, but in a 1950 review she was classified as the 'main culprit' and was sentenced to an additional thirty months. After her release in 1953, Scholtz-Klink settled back in Bebenhausen. In her 1978 book, *Die Frau im Dritten Reich* ('The Woman in the Third Reich'), Scholtz-Klink espoused her continuing support for Nazi ideology. She died aged ninety-seven.

ACKNOWLEDGEMENTS

Help came from so many generous people in the writing of *The Hollow Bones*. My deepest gratitude to Meredith Curnow and Tom Langshaw for their extraordinary encouragement, brilliance and support. Jacinta Di Mase and Natasha Solomun are a strong and fabulous team, whose unwavering faith in my writing goes beyond the call of duty. A special thanks to Alice Nelson for believing in Panda and friends from the start. Carol Ann Major, Emma Viskic, Brenda Walker, Lee Kofman, Peter Bishop, Catherine Therese, Ashley Hay, David Carlin, Hayley Katzen, Amanda Webster and Andrea Rothman are my crew of gifted writer friends who have held my hand along the way. Barbara Ellermeier, David Templeman, Isrun Engelhardt, Gidi Ifergan, Ned Gilmore, Jennifer Vess and Dani Measday provided me with extraordinary help in many (often bizarre) matters of research and fact-checking. Louise Ryan, Bella Arnott-Hoare and the team at PRH are a cheerleading force beyond belief. Alex Ross designed the book cover of my dreams, and I thank Jo Butler for her proofreading. I am indebted to Julianne Schultz and Varuna the Writers House for a *Griffith Review*–Varuna writer's fellowship. A Bundanon artist-in-residence fellowship afforded me peace and quiet to write, in the delightful company of a burrowing resident wombat under my studio. An early draft of the manuscript was a finalist in both the Disquiet-SLS-Dzanc Prize and the Churchill Trust fellowship award, which gave me a huge boost in confidence to proceed with the work. My dear friends Sandra Levin, Deborah Leiser-Moore, Diana Hanaor, Julie Lustig, Daryl Karp, Brendan Higgins and Donna-Lee Frieze kept me sane during the process. There would be no book without my wonderful family, Yohanan, Alon, Ella and Maia Loeffler, who are my greatest support, and were the first to encourage me to write this story. They also cooked meals for me, workshopped ideas for the narrative and provided astute editorial advice. I could not write a book about sentient beings without acknowledging my constant, faithful non-human companions, Kotzy, Pup, Ruby and the Fish.

A NOTE ON SOURCES

I referred to many texts in researching *The Hollow Bones*. Particularly helpful were *The Master Plan: Himmler's Scholars and the Holocaust* by Heather Pringle (Hyperion, 2006) and *Hitler's Monsters: A Supernatural History of the Third Reich* by Eric Kurlander (Yale University Press, 2017). *Nazis in Tibet* by Peter Meier-Husing (Theiss, 2017); *Himmler's Crusade* by Christopher Hale (Bantam, 2003); and *Tibet in 1938–1939: Photographs from the Ernst Schäfer Expedition to Tibet*, edited by Isrun Engelhardt (Serindia Publications, 2007), have been invaluable resources. Also useful were: *The Private Heinrich Himmler*, edited by Katrin Himmler and Michael Wildt (St. Martin's Press, 2014); *From Racism to Genocide: Anthropology in the Third Reich* by Gretchen E. Schafft (University of Illinois Press, 2004); *The Nazi Doctors: A Study in the Psychology of Evil* by Robert Jay

Lifton (MacMillan, 1986); *I Shall Bear Witness: The Diaries of Victor Klemperer 1933–1941* (Weidenfeld & Nicholson, 1998); *Letters from Berlin* by Margarete Dos and Kerstin Lieff (Vintage, 2012); *Tournament of the Shadows: The Great Game and the Race for Empire in Asia* by Karl Meyer and Shareen Brysac (Counterpoint, 1999); *Biologists under Hitler* by Ute Deichmann, translated by Thomas Dunlap (Harvard University Press, 1996); *Berlin 1936: Sixteen Days in August* by Oliver Hilmes (The Bodley Head, 2018); *Lhasa: The Holy City* by Spencer Chapman (Chatto & Windus, 1940); and *The Yangtze and the Yak: Adventurous Trails In and Out of Tibet* by Marion H. Duncan (Edwards Bros, 1952). Surrounded by books about such dark times, it was a joy to turn to a range of books about nature, including *The Genius of Birds* by Jennifer Ackerman (Scribe, 2016); *The Meaning of Birds* by Simon Barnes (Head of Zeus, 2016); *The Life of Birds* by David Attenborough (BBC Books, 1998); *Being a Beast: Adventures Across the Species Divide* by Charles Foster (Metropolitan Books, 2016); and *The Breathless Zoo: Taxidermy and the Cultures of Longing* by Rachel Poliquin (Pennsylvania State University Press, 2012).

Brooke Dolan's field diaries, along with many photographs and documents from the Dolan–Schäfer expeditions provided by Jennifer Vess at the Academy of Natural Sciences at Drexel University, Philadelphia, were an invaluable source of information, as was the assistance with specimen-viewing thanks to Ned Gilmore, Collections Manager. Barbara Ellermeier provided me with an abundance of research material related to not only the German Tibet Expedition, but also to 1930s Germany. I also drew on Ernst Schäfer's numerous books and diaries, as well as photos and film footage of his various travels.

ABOUT THE AUTHOR

Leah Kaminsky won the Voss Literary Prize for her debut novel, *The Waiting Room*, which was also shortlisted for the Helen Asher Award. The author of nine books, she holds an MFA from Vermont College of Fine Arts.